Wet Work

By Scott Harrington

Robert + Dawn,

Thank You!

Many thanks to the people who helped with review and revision of this book. A special thank you to Michael Pearce for his subject expertise and editing help. A grateful thank you to Catana Harrington for help in editing and cover design.

Chapter 1

Marc Ferand stepped from the large stone building in downtown San Jose and began walking south.

"I'll never get used to this damned weather," he thought as he watched the fog move in. *"Who would ever want to live in California?"*

A native of southern Arizona he had rarely seen fog growing up, now it was a constant reminder of how much he missed the hot sun and scorching desert that so many people complained about.

Ahead of him, a cat leapt from a garbage can, making Marc jump three feet backward.

"Damn! Stupid cat!" He growled at the running feline.

Fighting to get his heartbeat back under control, six years working on computers had done nothing to control his health or girth, Marc leaned against a rail and panted for breath.

"I hate this town, I hate it," Marc muttered to himself for the thousandth time.

Finally arriving at his car, a Mustang convertible, Marc reached for the door handle, glad that the new cars didn't need to use a key. Marc barely noticed that a piece of the fog seemed to solidify until there was a man near him moving quickly toward the mustang. Marc turned to acknowledge the man and felt rather than saw the sudden blows to his heart and left lung.

"O, God! He stabbed me!" Marc thought feverishly, *"I'm gonna die!"*

Dropping the briefcase, Marc reached to feel the two wounds. Sweating and shivering, he began to cough blood. Much to his dismay, there was no blood on his clothes, no holes in his brown vest.

"Why..." he stammered, his heart had already stopped beating and blood was flooding his right lung.

The stranger leaned down and grasped the briefcase. Without a second look at Marc Ferand, he was gone, secure in the knowledge that the two strikes had killed Marc before they had been felt.

1

"How..." was the last word Marc Ferand spoke as his large body crumpled against his new sports car.

Albert Dewal considered himself a great success. At 42 years old, he was one of the wealthiest men in America. Founder of the enormously successful MIGIsoft software giant, he had never married. Until now he had not had much time for women. Romance and women had been the one thing he could not work out a program for. At only five feet five inches tall, with a face pockmarked by youthful acne and a paunch brought on by sitting at a console writing programs, Albert was less than desirable to the opposite sex.

"I think I'll let her stay a few days." He mused looking down at the voluptuous brunette lying naked on his bed. "Once this DOD deal closes, I might even hire her roommates for a week on the yacht."

Security at the Dewal mansion had been designed by Albert himself with the help of a retired Army Green Beret. Albert had handled the motion, infrared, and thermal sensing aspect of the security himself. Colonel Thomas had been recruited by Dewal to handle the manpower and guard dog side of the operation. If Albert Dewal was not the expert on a given subject, he would find and hire the person who was.

Given the extensive electronic security, the roving two-man patrols at random intervals, and the four attack-trained Rottweilers spread about the grounds, Albert Dewal felt completely secure and invulnerable in his fortress-home.

He couldn't have been more wrong.

Retired Col. Lloyd Thomas had a fantastic job. As head of security for MIGIsoft International since 2001, Thomas had presided over the firing and prosecution of three employees engaged in selling company technology, had captured and arrested two Koreans, one Japanese, and one Russian who had attempted to steal secrets from the company....his company.

Yes, Col. Thomas loved his job, at least he did until yesterday. Loved the five-figure salary, the bimonthly bonuses, and the company paid vacations, ...until a Defense Department programmer/designer had been murdered less than two hundred yards from *his* company and a briefcase full of *his* company's secrets had been stolen.

Marc Ferand had arrived at MIGIsoft headquarters at 9:00 am, 0904 hours by the security log. Clearing security had taken a little over half an hour, the process normally took no more than five minutes, but the necessity to verify identity through the Department of Defense meant a hookup with the DOD's painfully slow computers. Truth be told, the DOD's computers were some of the best in the world, but then they did not have an R&D department in the building constantly upgrading the systems. Ferand had spent the rest of the day with the techs and programmers. Col. Thomas had personally escorted Marc out at 1912 hours. The Colonel had to be the one to see Ferand out because there was only one exit from MIGIsoft headquarters that did not need to clear security, a 2" thick solid steel door with twin deadbolts and a separate alarm system. Only the Colonel and Albert Dewal had keys and knew the combination. Employees were forbidden to take any work home and all packages were inspected before coming or going. Every door exit was set up with an electromagnet to scramble anything magnetically recorded, every door but the one Marc Ferand left by.

Col. Thomas was busy enjoying a new Monte Cristo cigar when the intercom had buzzed.

"Thomas here."

"Colonel, I believe we have a problem," Stewart said.

Thomas felt his stomach drop. "What happened?" he growled.

"There's a cop here asking about some dead guy in a suit. Sir, it's Ferand."

"Shit, shit, shit!" Thomas barked, "Tell the cop I'll be right down, don't tell him anything else. Get out there and make sure nothing leaves, especially that briefcase!"

"Sir, I already asked about that. There was no briefcase with the body."

"Damn!" The Colonel shouted as he slammed the phone down. It took him less than five minutes to call the DOD and fill them in. Response from the feds was immediate, Thomas had been answering San Jose Police questions for no more than ten minutes when the F.B.I. rolled up and claimed jurisdiction.

In less than an hour, the Feds had cordoned off a three-block radius and had every agent within forty miles called in to help with the investigation. Every pedestrian, motorist, businessperson, and apartment dweller was stopped and questioned. The investigation inside the three-block radius took the seventy-two agents most of the night. As each agent reported in, "nobody saw anything", the Colonel's mood got worse, if that was possible. The F.B.I. forensic team, considered the best in the world, was still scraping and bagging at 0400. If there was any evidence at the scene, it was up to the lab boys to find it now.

"Find anything yet?" Colonel Thomas growled at agent Jares.

"No sir Colonel. I'm sorry to report that the only hope we have for a lead will have to come from the crime lab."

Jares was the senior agent on the scene and as such was in charge until further notice. Jares did not think that it was a good idea to allow a civilian inside an investigation, but his orders had been explicit, "Give the Colonel anything he wants and if he doesn't want to answer a question, skip it!"

"Well, let's hope they get lucky." The Colonel thought. *"I have to call Albert in a few hours and tell him what happened. By the time the dust settles on this one we may both be working in the Antarctic."*

"The briefcase was that important?" Jares queried.

"More than you know, or I can tell you." Thomas sighed.

"Sir, may I ask, if this was so important why wasn't Mr. Ferand escorted to his car?"

"I don't see any problem with answering that." Thomas pointed to a steel door in the side of the MIGIsoft building. "Nobody knew that Mr. Ferand was coming today or when he was leaving, not even me. I let him out through that door there and watched him walk to his car. I chuckled when I

4

saw him jump from a cat but thought nothing of it. When he reached his car and began to unlock the door I went back inside. Marc Ferand had a courier clearance and experience with 'sensitive' packages. Since nobody knew he was coming or going, there wasn't supposed to be any risk."

"Sir, what was in the briefcase?" Agent Jares ventured, "what could be so important?"

"Sorry Agent, I really am, I know what it's like to work in the dark, but I can't tell you."

As Thomas turned to leave, Jares's cellular phone rang. "Jares here. Yes...I see. Do you have a cause yet? I know it killed him, I want to know what 'it' is! Well keep looking...yes I'm at this number all the time."

"Sir, that was the forensic team assigned to the body. All they can tell me so far is that a pointed object of some kind ruptured the heart and right lung. What they can't figure out is what could do that kind of damage and not rip the clothing or leave any residue on the body."

"A blunt-ended stick perhaps?" Thomas ventured.
"No sir, that would leave traces of wood or paint if it was painted."

"Steel or plastic?"

"That's the best guess so far, and it's only a guess at this stage."

"Understood. Let me know if you hear anything else, I'll be in my office assessing the potential damage. I need to call Washington and let them know how bad it is."

With that the Colonel headed back to his office, to write down his notes and prepare himself to call his boss, Albert Dewal.

"Yes sir." Agent Jares said, happy he wasn't in the Colonel's place.

While Jares and the Colonel were discussing the problem at hand, twenty miles away a man crouched in a tree overlooking the opulent estate of Albert Dewal.

Neko sat and waited as he had for the last four hours. He was used to long waits in uncomfortable positions, and four hours was nothing compared to the 36-hour training lockups in that little black box.

Waiting was a necessity in his line of work. Yesterday he had waited seven hours for Ferand to leave the MIGIsoft building, but he had finally been rewarded. After leaving the briefcase at a drop, Neko had come to Dewal's estate to finish the second part of his assignment. Now after four hours he was ready to move, although the patrols were supposed to be random and these guards were exceptionally good, it was human nature to fall into patterns. Neko was going to exploit this common mistake.

Neko had been provided with exact schematics of the house and its grounds. He had memorized every detail. There was an outer fence twenty feet high, thirty feet of clear 'killing' ground, and another twenty-foot fence. The section between the inner and outer fence was patrolled by the dogs, this was divided into a north and south section so that there were always two dogs on either side of the house. Beyond the inner fence were the roving patrols that moved in and out of the trees and foliage but never closer than ten yards from the house. From the inner fence to the house was approximately fifty yards.

Neko was on the south side of the estate, this meant he only had to deal with two dogs and one roving patrol. Silently, Neko withdrew a small cloth bag with a piece of blue-black rope protruding from the opening. To the end, he tied a small, rubber-coated grappling hook with spring-loaded hooks. Carefully drawing his arm back, he threw it at the top of the inner fence. With a dull 'thunk', the hook hit the top of the fence and bounced off. Cursing inwardly, Neko began to draw the rope back, but the nearest Rottweiler had heard the noise and was coming to investigate.

Without hesitation, Neko reached into his shoulder pocket and pulled out a small tube. Flicking the plastic plugs out, he put it to his lips. With a small "thpt", he let loose a dart to strike the guard dog in the neck, just below the ear. Noiselessly the dog crumpled to the ground. Neko threw his hook again, this time it caught. Cinching it to his observation perch, Neko slithered across the rope and dropped inside the inner fence.

Neko glanced quickly at his watch, the time was 0427 hours.

"How bad is it really?" Thought the Colonel.

He was busy trying to figure how to explain such a gross lapse in security, his security. The Colonel did not believe that Ferand's death and the missing briefcase were just a violent statistic. Someone had leaked information, somehow the meeting and the contents of the briefcase had gotten out. The big questions were 'who?' and 'how?', the little questions were endless.

"How bad is it really, though?" Key sequences in the programming code were kept separate and had not been shown to anyone but the man who designed it and Albert Dewal, even the Colonel hadn't seen those sequences. Without the key sequences, the program in the briefcase would look like a hundred other 'tracking' programs. The schematics in the briefcase were also incomplete. Everything in Marc Ferand's briefcase was to be evaluated for plausibility. Ferand was to test the basic 'frame-up' and see if what Dewal told the DOD was possible. Without the missing schematics and the key sequences of the programming code, all of which were locked in Dewal's house/fortress, whoever had initiated the theft and murder had nothing of real value.

"How can life change so fast?" Colonel Thomas mused, "yesterday, I loved this job. Now, I have to tell Albert we lost millions in research. The only consolation is that we didn't lose it all."

Chapter 2

"What's the status of our little operation?"

"The first part of the prize has already been received. Neko is working on the second part as we speak." Kelsi answered.

"Any problems?" God, his voice grated like nails on a chalkboard.

"None yet. Neko was not pleased with the short notice of this mission, but I think he secretly liked the challenge it presented."

"Not to mention his exorbitant fee."

"Yes, but he will not fail us." Kelsi responded, "as far as we know his only failure was very long ago and I blame hormones for that one."

"Let's hope that's true. At one million dollars a job he had better not make any mistakes."

"He is very proud and serious about his skill, he would not divulge anything."

"One million to him, 1.3 million to our little stooge and ten million to our spy, make this a very expensive undertaking."

"Yes Sir, but if we get the actual prize the reward could number in the billions."

"I'm well aware of the rewards Kelsi, but I would be a fool not to worry about the risks. Keep me informed of any new developments"

"Yes, Mr. Cross." Kelsi turned and strode from the CEO's office.

The 'E-mail' and the phone message Icons were flashing when Albert Dewal sat down at his computer. A glance at the digital clock on his desk told him the time was 5:06 a.m.

"*I haven't been up this early since...hell if I wasn't up all night, until now, I've never been up this early.*" He thought. "*Must be this DOD deal. Has me spooked. I'll check messages then call the Colonel at home and wake him up for breakfast.*"

"Go away bogeyman!" Albert said out loud to calm himself and as if on cue a man stepped from the shadows of the large bookcases and moved toward Dewal.

Before Albert could shout the man had reached him, standing in front of his glass desk Albert had no idea what to do. Should he yell? Would the patrols hear him? Could they get to him in time if they did hear? There was a gun in the armoire to his left, but could he get to it? All this flashed through his mind in a split-second, and all of it was irrelevant.

Neko had already gotten the thumb drive and the schematics from the wall safe. He had found and emptied the Glock, being careful to return it to the exact position. He was getting ready to go kill Dewal when the geek came shambling down the stairs. Neko simply stepped back into the shadows of the office to wait for his prey.

Now as Dewal's mouth opened to scream, Neko's hand shot up through the soft underside of the jaw, rupturing the upper trachea along the way, and stopping all sound. With an easy graceful turn, Neko slammed the back of Dewal's head into the metal edge of the glass desk.

Albert's eyes bulged in terror at the sight of this man. He tried to scream but there was sudden, terrible pain and now he was falling, no, forced backward. As his head hit the table, his spinal cord separated between C1 and C2. All pain stopped and Albert Dewal the Billionaire was gone.

It was now 0527 hours. Still, too early for Albert Dewal to be up, But the Colonel couldn't wait any longer. Although he had tried several times to call his boss during the night and the investigation, there had been no answer, other than the computer. It was not unusual for Dewal to ignore the phone, the house computer would take messages which would be checked later. If there was still no answer, he would have one of the men on the grounds go and wake the boss up. Dewal had to know, plans had to be made, and Thomas had to tell his boss that he had failed.

"...leave a message at the tone or push one to send a fax." Colonel Thomas hung up the phone, not bothering to leave another message. If Albert was checking his messages, he would have already called back. The Colonel quickly dialed another number.

"Gate, this is Syms."

"Syms, it's Thomas."

9

"Yes Colonel, what can I do for you?"

"Syms, I need to talk to Mr. Dewal, but he's not answering the phone. I need you to go wake him and have him call in. This is an emergency."

"Yes sir, Colonel. He'll be calling you shortly."

"Thank you." Thomas hung up the phone and waited for his boss to call. Syms was a good man, he had been with the Colonel for about 12 years and Thomas knew that he was competent and thorough.

As the phone rang and the Colonel reached for it, he felt a sudden chill.

"Thomas here." He answered

"Colonel, this is Syms. There was no answer at the door." Thomas felt his stomach drop. "I walked around the side of his office. Mr. Dewal was laying on the floor in a pool of blood."

The Colonel's heart pounded painfully in his chest.

"Have you told anyone else yet?" Thomas responded quickly, the professional taking over.

"No sir, I'm waiting for your orders."

"Lock it down tight! Nobody in or out without my authorization. I'll call in the Feds. You call in every man not already on duty. Don't touch anything, anywhere. Form a perimeter outside the fence. Nothing goes in, nothing goes out!" Thomas wondered what else could go wrong. Twice in one night, his much-vaunted security had failed, and now his boss, his friend was dead.

"What about the girl that was in Mr. Dewal's bedroom?"

"Put some clothes on her, handcuffed her to the bed, locked her in the room, and put a man outside the door to keep her there."

Hitting the speed-dialer on his phone, Thomas spoke rapidly. "Stewart, lock the HQ building down. All work stops, no calls in or out. Everyone is to be searched. Anything that is MIGIsoft's is to be seized and that employee held for questioning. I need phone logs for........" Thomas went on with his instructions, even as Stewart barked orders at the other end of the line.

When he had finished with Stewart, Thomas dialed a number he had committed to memory the night before and spoke into the receiver. "Agent Jares, we have another problem. A big problem.

Chapter 3

This was not the first time Colonel Thomas had been to Flagstaff, Arizona. As a young army lieutenant headed to Fort Ord, California, he had taken route 66 cross-country. Much had changed since then, the San Francisco Peaks rising beyond the ever-growing town were still as impressive as the first time, but this time he didn't have the luxury of stopping to go hiking with the Elk and Deer. Colonel Thomas was here on business.

"Augh.....unh." The sounds of a man in pain were mixed with the thud of a body and the 'whap, whap' of a person 'tapping out'. Colonel Thomas approached the front door of a small warehouse type building. The only markings on the exterior of the building were the address in bold black letters and the word 'NINJUTSU' in foot tall red paint. As he entered the Dojo a few heads turned to see him. One of these motioned to a bench on the side for the Colonel to sit on. Thomas settled in to observe the class.

"YAME! (stop) A lot of you are trying too hard to make this work. It's not speed or strength, but rather the 'Taijutsu' or body movement........." The man who had stopped the group moved to the center of the students and began to explain anew the principles involved. He was approximately six feet tall, medium build, not skinny, and certainly not fat. He had his hair cut shorter than military requirements and piercing blue eyes. Not excessively handsome, neither was he ugly. There was more of the rugged outdoor look and confidence the Colonel could feel from across the room. "Jim, come here. Strike me."

"Hai, Master."

"Not master, I am your Sensei." The man admonished. "I have not mastered this art and may not ever."

"Hai, Sensei."

"Now, strike me."

The student, Jim, assumed a posture with his knees bent and balance low. The strike, it looked like a punch to the Colonel, came at a slow enough speed that the Colonel didn't understand how it couldn't be avoided. The

"Sensei" pivoted on his right foot, allowed the strike to pass him, then dropped his right hand just behind Jim's thumb joint on the striking hand. Continuing the pivot, the Sensei dropped to his left knee. Jim flew past him, legs airborne and going over his head. As he struck, the Sensei came up off his knee and pinned the attacking fist in an outward reversal lock. With a look of pain on his face and a gritted "uhhh", Jim began hitting the floor, tapping out. The movement of the Sensei had been so smooth and slow, the Colonel wasn't sure how he had made Jim go airborne and then into a joint lock.

"Did you all see how I took the energy Jim came with and simply moved that energy on past me? I didn't put him into omote gyaku until he hit the ground. I simply laid my hand on his and pushed the energy he had already given me."

"That looks easy when he comes slow, Sensei," a short, young woman said, "but doing that when he is coming fast is a lot harder."

"No, Leslie. It's easier when he comes fast. The problem is that, if we went full speed with this technique, it would completely tear the rotator joint in Jim's Shoulder." The Sensei responded. "If you can do it slowly, doing it fast is easy. Jim isn't at the level where he could protect his shoulder from the technique. Most of you aren't, so I want everybody doing this even slower than Jim and I did it. Remember, it's about continuing the energy that the attacker gives you."

Thirty-five minutes later after the class had bowed out, one of the students was telling Colonel Thomas about the art when the Sensei walked over.

"Is there anything I can answer for you?" The Sensei's voice was soft yet as clear as if he were shouting.

"Yes, are you Trace Conner?" Thomas queried.

"Yes, I am. What can I do for you?"

"Can we talk in private? This is a sensitive subject."

"Hai! Yes, come this way."

Trace stopped to change out of the simple black Gi and into street clothes while the Colonel waited. As Trace reentered the Dojo proper,

13

Thomas' eyes widened somewhat. Looking at the left breast pocket of Trace's T-shirt and the 'Budweiser' logo printed there in gold.

"You were in the teams?"

"Oh...no. A friend of mine works with the SEALs in San Diego. He gave me this shirt. I would have loved to be a SEAL, but there's just too much exercise involved!"

"I thought the physical side of that would be simple for a Sensei. Especially for the rather mysterious Ninja."

"While it's true there is a lot of exercise in the art itself, there is not the necessity for the kind of 'superhuman' endurance that SEALs need. While a SEAL needs that kind of physical and mental power, I have the Ninjutsu to fall back on. In other words, I cheat." A smirk appeared on Trace's face and the blue eyes twinkled.

"I see, for a minute there I thought someone had missed something very important." Glancing at his watch, Thomas said, "Have you eaten yet? It's almost nine-thirty. I'll buy you dinner while we talk."

"Sounds good. I'll drive, there's a great little place down the road." Again, with the smirk.

Ten minutes later they were seated at a Sushi bar, which proudly proclaimed its location on Historic Route 66. Colonel Thomas had never cared much for Chinese food, let alone Japanese food, and what he thought was just raw fish. Now looking at the prices, he couldn't see how anyone could come here often without a six-figure salary. The Dojo didn't look like it could produce that kind of income.

"Do you eat here a lot?" Thomas began.

"God no. Look at the prices. We only came here cause you're buying."

"Why not a steakhouse, I thought Arizona had cattle," Thomas muttered under his breath.

"Arizona does have cattle, and great steakhouses." Trace answered. "It also has Ninjutsu and Sushi bars. As long as you came for the one you might as well try the other."

Introductions had been made during the short drive from the Dojo to the restaurant.

14

"So, tell me, Colonel," Trace began. As he did so, he watched two men enter through the front door. "What exactly do you want from me?"

One of the men was blonde, about six feet, two hundred pounds, and well built. The other man was about five foot ten, more muscular, probably two twenty with the olive skin and dark curly hair associated with Italians. Both men were armed. The blonde carried what looked to be a Beretta in a right-hand cross-draw holster on his belt. The 'Italian' wore a bulge beneath his jacket that looked to be a larger pistol.

"They were or are military." Trace thought to himself. In the reflection of the mirror behind the bar, he studied the men. The blonde pointed towards the Colonel and almost as if on cue, Thomas started talking.

"Understand that nothing I tell you can be repeated."

"I understand, and you have my word that it won't. But, how do you know I can be trusted?"

"I had a background search run on you. You came up clean."

"Won't my mommy be happy." The sarcasm went by the Colonel unanswered.

"Two days ago, a man was killed as he left the MIGIsoft research facility......." The Colonel went on to explain about the death of Marc Ferand and Albert Dewal. All the while Trace watched the two men come closer. Though they had split up and were coming through the patrons from different sides, Trace had no trouble watching them.

"So, we want you to test our security. We need to know if it was possible to do these things without inside help. If not, we need to know who's bad." The Colonel concluded.

"Why me? There are other Ninjutsu Sensei in the U.S., some have been in it longer than I have. Some are just plain better and a few even live in your neck of the woods."

"That's not what I hear. I was already going to contact you to test our security for a project in the works. I heard from Muro Corporation that you found some gaping holes and helped fix their security. Most important, you are an unknown to my company, the military, and the spooks"

15

The blonde man was less than ten feet behind the Colonel and had seemingly been missed by Thomas. The Italian had moved up to the end of the bar closest to the exit and was slowly moving closer.

"No security is ever perfect, you should know that. I just helped them fix holes a truck could drive through. Somehow I don't think you'd make those kinds of mistakes Colonel."

"I sure hope not, but the fact remains that two people are dead. My company is in trouble and I need some answers. Starting with 'HOW?'"

At that point, the last two people sitting at the bar stood up and left. With their departure, the blonde man approached the Colonel. "Mr. Thomas, come with me."

Thomas pushed the blonde's hand away from him. The Italian's right hand disappeared into his coat as he reached for the Colonel. In a blur Trace moved, Thomas never saw what hit the blonde, only saw him go down with a scream and grab his right leg. Thomas did see Trace strike the Italian in the center of the chest with the flat of his hand and watched as the assailant fell clutching his chest. In the space of a heartbeat, both would-be attackers were down, writhing on the ground in pain.

"Colonel..." Trace spoke clearly, his blue eyes having strangely turned a steel gray. "If you felt a need to test me, you need only have said so. If I had thought the threat to your life was real, I may very well have killed both of your men."

"We took the precaution of unloading their weapons in case you did take them away and tried to shoot them. But, how did you know they were fake?" Thomas was not sure he wanted the answer, those eyes were utterly disturbing to look at now.

"Colonel, it would have taken no longer to kill these men than to disable them. I would never have wasted time trying to use their weapons. As far as the fakes, you didn't seem to notice them. That, I found unlikely, given that you should be paranoid as hell right now. Of course, if a professional wanted you dead, you would be, but they wouldn't do it in a restaurant. The clincher though, was that neither you nor blondie down there should try acting for a career. You'd starve."

"If you knew it was a test, then why didn't you say something?"

"And miss a chance to show off? Please. So, did I pass your test?"

"With ease, I'm afraid. What did you do to them? I never saw you hit Will, blondie as you call him. Russell over there" Thomas gestured toward the Italian "is one of the toughest fighters I've ever met, and you dropped him like he was nothing."

"Hardly, Russell's pretty solid. I counted on that when I hit him, so I hit him hard. Essentially, I made his heart spasm and skip a few beats. The result is like a mild heart attack, scary as all hell, but no lasting effect. The reason you didn't see blondie go down was that I struck the neural plex on the outside of his leg with my boot. Again, no lasting damage, but a lot of immediate pain. As well as the all-important loss of that limb and his balance for a few minutes. "

Thoroughly impressed now, Colonel Thomas reached into his jacket and pulled out the faxed autopsy reports on Ferand and Dewal.

"Not exactly pleasant dinner reading, but tell me if anything jumps out at you."

For the next forty minutes, Colonel Thomas watched as Trace read and ate. Thomas also got a chance to learn more about sushi. Much to his surprise, the things that sounded the most disgusting were the ones he liked the most. Eel sounded less than appealing, yet unagi, as it is called, was broiled and delicious. Thomas even liked the urchin, something a small number of sushi lovers ever develop a taste for. Trace set the last report down.

"The man must have a lot of medical knowledge," Thomas thought, *"he read all that and didn't ask any questions. I kept having to look up stuff in the medical dictionary."*

"Was Ferand armed?" Trace asked, "What about Dewal?"

"Ferand carried a snub-nose .38, but it was still in the holster."

"Hip or shoulder? Same side or cross-draw?"

"Hip on the same side," Thomas answered, unsure of where the questions were leading.

"And Dewal?"

"There was a Glock in the armoire three feet from where he was found. Of course, Albert wouldn't have been able to use it even if he had reached it. He never wanted to take the time to get proficient with it. He always assumed that the security we had put in place was airtight. We were both wrong." Thomas looked down at his hands, thinking again about his recent failures.

"Do you, and the FBI, realize that the same person, or people trained by the same person, killed both men?"

Thomas looked at Trace skeptically. "One man, both murders? How?"

"Let's start with Ferand. The lab report says that the heart, the spleen, and the left lung were all ruptured. The report says that there were two blows. As for the weapon, wood was ruled out. A tessen, or war fan as some call it is a possibility, but unlikely because they are iron and would have left either rust or an oily residue, and neither one of those were found. Plastic is still a possibility, but also unlikely. If someone had walked toward Ferand with a weapon in hand he would have at least made a grab for his gun."

"Well, after all that's ruled out, what did he use?" Thomas was getting impatient and feeling more than a little spooked that this man seemed to know more than he did after reading two autopsy reports.

"First off, I didn't say man, I said person."

"Christ, now it's a woman?"

"I didn't say that either. Slow down, thinking that only a man could do this would be arrogant and stupid. Whoever it is, they are thorough. They could have left Ferand with the single strike to the heart. Symptoms would have been the same as a 'sudden death' heart attack. Only an autopsy would have revealed the strike. That means our killer wasn't worried about getting caught. Two blows were delivered to insure death. Either one would have been fatal, but the killer wanted no way to save the victim. The same situation applies to Dewal's murder. After crushing the trachea, Dewal was going to die, but the killer made sure by breaking the neck so far up that there was no chance of survival." Trace paused to let the information sink in.

"Great, we've got a thorough, calculated killer. What you didn't answer is how?"

"You don't want to tangle with this person. I believe that both men were killed with 'hand spears'."

"Hand what?"

18

"Different arts have different names, but the effect is the same. The hand is held rigid and used to 'spear' body parts."

Thomas was incredulous, "Is that really possible?"

"Some martial arts schools specialize in it. Others simply introduce it and move on because it's very difficult to learn, but our killer has had a great deal of practice with it."

"What makes you so sure?"

"On Ferand's clothing, they found skin oils outside his shirt over the strike points, but deeply pressed into the fibers. They attributed it to Ferand, but he couldn't have pushed the oils deep into the center of the strike points. He would have clutched at his chest, digging oils all around the center, and he did. On Dewal's throat, they found what appeared to be very faint scratches, but again they ruled that out because it didn't fit. Both reports fit with my theory." Trace finished.

"So.....where are these schools? The ones that teach this stuff?" Colonel Thomas was finally beginning to feel like he had a chance in this game.

"One of them is mine, although that is unlikely. Few students have been taught the skill, and fewer still are anywhere near mastering it."

"Could you inflict these wounds?" Thomas studied Trace's face closely as he asked.

"Yes," Trace looked at him levelly. "I could."

Chapter 4

Trace glanced down at his waterproof Citizen watch. The luminous hands read 3:32 a.m. He had arrived at the Dewal compound at 11:30. Trace had told the Colonel to warn his men that he was coming and to be extra alert. The Colonel had argued that the killer had not forewarned the guards, but Trace insisted. During the time Trace had studied the roving patrols, he had moved around to the south side of the estate. Climbing high into a tree near the fence he settled in to watch the guards and to find the team that was surely hidden in the shrubbery somewhere inside the second fence. Studying the trees in the half-moon light, Trace noticed a horizontal stripe on a tree about fifteen feet away.

"Wouldn't have noticed that if I hadn't gotten so stiff sitting here and had to move." He thought, *"I've got to do more classes outside. Get more used to fieldwork."*

Climbing down and moving to the striped tree, Trace was careful to avoid the patrols. As he climbed up and began to examine the stripe, he quickly understood how the killer had passed the fences undetected. Trace had a good idea now of the patrol sweeps. Two patrols were assigned to the north and two to the south, with one random patrol that would move around the entire grounds at will. Although the patrols were random there was never less than a seven-minute delay between sweeps, and usually more than that. The random patrol had settled into the shrubbery on the East Side of the house. Although Trace could still see them, he knew that as soon as he dropped down the brush would block their view. As the nearest patrol moved away, Trace crawled along the limb over the outer fence. Dropping fifteen feet to the ground, he took a deep breath and watched the dogs rush at him.

"We shouldn't have told the men. It will be impossible to get in, and I need the answers."

"Colonel, I watched him, and I don't think we should underestimate him," Russell said.

"I saw him drop you and Will, something I didn't think anyone could do. I'm not underestimating him, but I am worried he wanted to play a game when I need answers." The Colonel rounded the corner and entered the office of the late Albert Dewal. "Look, it's almost four a.m.. Will didn't see him get off the plane and there's been no contact."

The Colonel felt Russell bump into his back and turned to look at him. "Not so close, we....."

The Colonel's voice trailed off, Russell was standing with saucer-shaped eyes, staring at the apparition between himself and the Colonel. As Thomas' eyes focused, he recognized the shape of a black, non-reflective Tanto blade less than an inch from his own throat. Looking over to Russell, the Colonel was shocked to see his personal Sig Sauer shoved into Russell's mouth.

"You're both dead." It was a simple statement, and the Colonel felt sweat run down his spine even as the chills ran up. "I told you I'd be here. I am, and I have some of your answers." Trace put away the razor-sharp blade and handed the Colonel's pistol back to him. As the gun was pulled away from Russell, the man staggered visibly and leaned against the wall.

"Sorry about the dramatics, but I had to prove it could be done, or you might not believe what I tell you."

Glancing over at the alarm display panel, the Colonel saw that the system was still armed. "How the fuck did you do that?!" He stammered out.

"Relax. Have a drink, Russell looks like he could use one." Trace moved around the desk and sat down on the leather-backed chair. Studying the cracked glass where Dewal's head had struck, he began to explain. "First, let me say, your people are good. Some of the best I've ever seen."

"Obviously not that good." The Colonel spat.

"Actually, yes they are. The patrols moved at random and were hard to predict. The roving patrol did very little to give away their position and always moved at odd intervals."

"Yet you got past them."

"Yes, but I studied them for more than three hours. The only thing I could count on was a seven-minute window to get from the outside fence into the house. That would be nearly impossible for anybody to do, given the distance and other security measures involved."

"Well then, the first thing I need to know is if there was inside help." The Colonel looked at his guest.

"Hard to tell. Whoever the killer was, they are very, very good. Better than me."

Thomas found that hard to believe. "Start at the beginning. Tell me how he...she did it."

"On the south side of the estate, a little to the west is a large oak tree. The killer threw a rope over the inner fence, tied it to the oak, and shinnied across to drop inside the inner fence."

"The dogs would have seen him."

"Not necessarily, the dogs have to cover a lot of ground and the wind makes it hard to hear everything. Even for a dog. After that, the killer followed a patrol up near to the house so that if another patrol looked in his direction they would only see the first patrol. When he got fifteen yards out, the killer broke away from the patrol and climbed the wall to the guest balcony. That's where they entered. The same as me." Trace paused.

"But the alarm system is still on, the motion detectors cover the last ten yards and there was no evidence of tampering on that door." Thomas countered.

"When the killer got ten yards out, he dropped to the ground. At this time of the morning, the ground is wet and cold, by slowing his breathing and 'wetting' down he was able to fool the motion detector which looks for fast, warm-bodied motion."

"That's impossible." The Colonel was aghast. " These are the best detectors made."

"Nonetheless, I did it." Trace continued, " Once on the guest balcony, the killer blew iron dust onto the door to locate the magnet inside. Placing a small electromagnet on the frame with superglue, he overrode the sensor, picked the lock, and went in. Dewal had turned off the internal system, just as you did, so the killer was free to move around inside. After killing Dewal, he

22

left the reverse way. The door was closed and then re-locked. Your killer was not at all worried about getting caught."

"So, did he/she have inside help?" Thomas returned to his most pressing concern.

"If he...she did, it wasn't much. The abrasions on the tree limb came from at least an hour or more of sitting, crouching, and adjustments. The killer spent time studying the patrols, just like I did. If he...she had help, that wouldn't have been a necessity, or at least it wouldn't have taken as long."

"So, the killer didn't have help." Thomas was relieved.

"I didn't say that. I said they didn't have much help. Were there any oddities, surprises, or unusual guests that night?"

"No, everything was normal until we found Dewal's body."The Colonel deliberately left out any mention of the call girl.

"Then if the killer had help, it wasn't from your people here." Trace smiled at the relieved look on the Colonel's face.

"Back to the dogs." The Colonel resumed his questioning. "Did they hear you?"

"Oh yes. They saw me too. That's why I said the killer is better than I am."

"Well, if they saw you, how did you get by them?"

"First, remember that like all real attack dogs, they don't bark. They just attack."

"Exactly!" The Colonel interrupted. "How come you're not bleeding to death?" Thomas's eyes opened wide. "Oh, God! You killed my dogs?!"

Trace looked at the Colonel maliciously. Ever so slowly the smirk spread across his face and finally into a smile. While the smile helped to relax Thomas and Russell, the Colonel did not think it was funny.

"Do you know how long ...." The Colonel stopped when Trace held up his hand.

"I didn't kill the dogs, fortunately, I didn't have to."

"Then how?" Thomas was dumbfounded.

"I cheated."

The bewildered looks on the two men's faces told Trace it was time for another demonstration. After the Colonel turned off the alarm system, the three men went out to the inner fence. The two patrols on the south side saw them and came over to watch. Neither patrol came too close, they knew that the third man meant they had failed again. Walking to the nearest gate, Trace flipped the latch and opened it. All but the Colonel, Russell, and Trace backed away from the dogs. To everybody's dismay, Trace held out his hands and the two dogs took treats from him.

"They aren't supposed to take food from anyone but their handlers." The Colonel growled.

"Or from you." Trace answered. "Or from the pack leader."

"What?" Now they were really confused.

"That doesn't explain anything," Russell responded. "They should have torn you up before you had time to get friendly."

"True, there's a trick I used." Trace paused, he had been scratching one of the dogs and found something there. "Now this," Trace pulled a small dart from the dogs' neck, "is how your killer stopped this dog." Handing it to the Colonel, "Probably had a sedative that would calm the dog without making it look dead. After a while, the effect would begin to wear off and only the dog would know."

The Colonel pulled a tissue from his pocket, wrapped the dart, and gave it to one of his men, with orders to get it to the Feds yesterday.

"So, what's this trick?" Russell asked.

"Come on." Trace responded. "I'll show you."

With that, the group of men moved to the north side of the estate and the front gate. As Trace neared the two dogs unfamiliar with him, they both began attacking the fence in an attempt to get at the stranger.

"Russell, call them away long enough for me to get inside." Trace said, then added. "You can tell they don't like me....yet."

Russell did as he was told. As soon as the dogs got to where Russell was standing, about fifty yards away, Trace flipped up the latch and entered the dog run. Immediately, both dogs turned and ran full-on to attack the intruder. Without a sound Trace held out his hands, palm up, treats in both hands. Impossibly, later all the watchers would swear it was a trick of the fog and light, Trace seemed to grow and expand to nearly twice his original size. Both dogs stopped a few feet from him, eyes wide, after a moment, they dropped their heads in submission. After that, both dogs were happy to take the treats and affection from this new leader.

"Damn!" Russell exclaimed. "I would never have believed that if I hadn't seen it. How did you do that?"

"Trade secret. If I told you, I'd have to kill you." Trace said sarcastically. "Besides, at this point, you wouldn't believe or understand the 'pushing energy' aspect of what I do. Hell, I don't even understand how it works. I just know I can do it."

Russell wasn't sure if Trace was joking or not, but he decided it wasn't that important to know after all.

"What if the dogs didn't stop for your 'trick' as you called it?"

Turning to answer, his blue eyes cold and hard. "Then Colonel, I would have killed one or both." This was said so matter-of-factly that Thomas did not doubt for an instant that is exactly what would have happened.

"Well Kelsi, is it worth all the money we spent?"

"The information is being evaluated by our whiz kids now Mr. Cross," Kelsi responded, irritated that Cross's nasally voice was bothering him so soon. "First we have to beat the passwords, then the encryption before we can even begin the actual construction phase."

"I am aware of that. The question is whether we can build it before MIGIsoft can build theirs."

"Our source says that there was only one disk. We now have more than MIGIsoft does. They may never recover from the loss. For certain they will never beat us to a prototype, or international sales."

"NOTHING is for certain, Kelsi" Cross whined loudly. "and never say 'never'."

"Thank you for your help, Trace. Enjoy a night at the hotel, we'll get the tab. Here are your check and your ticket. You're scheduled to leave for Phoenix tomorrow at 7:45 am." Thomas concluded.

"Thank you, Colonel. What are you going to do now?"

"Right now, I'm waiting for Albert's sister to show up. She was the sole heir and we had to track her down in Argentina. Until she gets here nothing happens. We took a bad hit on this. Not just Albert's death, but the loss of some pretty important information."

"Anything else I can help you with?"

"If I find out who's responsible, will you terminate them? For a fee of course."

"I don't terminate people for other people. It's too hard to tell who's right." The hard eyes glared at the Colonel.

"Understood, just needed to know."

Chapter 5

The chirping of the cell phone brought Thomas out of uneasy sleep. After Trace had left for the hotel, Thomas had spent the day meeting, organizing, and trying to stem the inevitable crash that would come, sometime after 11 PM he had fallen asleep. Lying on the couch in his office, he glanced at his watch. The time was 2:17 a.m.

"This is Thomas."

"Lloyd, it's Catherine. What the hell is going on? What happened to Albert?" Despite the gravity of the situation, the Colonel couldn't help but marvel at the sensuality of Catherine's voice.

"Catherine, where are you? No, don't answer that, this phone isn't secure! Look, we need to bring you in safely, and we need to do it as soon as possible."

"Loyd, are you at the office?"

"Yes, let me set up a meet so that we can bring you in safely."

"Loyd, I will be pulling up to the office in about two minutes. Meet me out front." Catherine hung up without waiting for a reply.

"Jesus, she's coming in without protection." Thomas breathed a silent curse about civilians and security. Picking up the phone he began to issue orders in preparation for the arrival of the new head of MIGIsoft.

"What have you got?" Kelsi demanded. Standing behind the 'whiz kids' as he referred to them, he watched as screens full of data flashed by. All of it meaningless to him, nothing but gibberish.

"Mr. Kelsi, what we got is naught. This encryption is pretty tough stuff, we're still on the first level. No telling how many levels they have. We just do 'em one at a time." Answered the leader of the group, Jeff. A charismatic, good-looking kid with a dark side. He loved to tweak noses and change things just to irritate people he didn't know. Most of the 'whiz kids' looked, talked, and acted like your typical computer geek. Not Jeff, he ran them like a talent agent but always seemed to know more than any of them.

"You guys are supposed to be the best. Was I wrong to hire you? Should I go elsewhere?" Kelsi threatened.

"You could go to someone else," Jeff answered, "but if you want into this, we're the only ones who can do it for you. At least the only ones this year."

Colonel Thomas stood nervously in front of the building, five men stood with him. All had their weapons drawn, all were tense. Suddenly a cab came around the corner and rushed towards them. Screeching to a halt, the back door swung open and Catherine Dewal emerged, headed straight for the front door of MIGIsoft. As the security team covered her into the building, the last man paid the cabby and tipped him generously.

"Tell me what happened, Loyd. All of it" Catherine ordered. For most of the men there, this was the first time they had seen the elusive Ms. Dewal. For nearly all of them it was love at first sight. She was almost the complete opposite of her brother. Catherine Dewal had eyes that were akin to green emeralds and could be just as hard. Her hair was dark red, long, and slightly wavy. At five feet ten inches, plus boots, she was as tall or taller than most of the men in the room. As she removed her overcoat, they saw a perfectly tailored suit that did nothing to hide the curves of her body.

Colonel Thomas knew what every man was thinking and made sure to make eye contact with each one and dispel any notions they might have. Looking at Catherine now, the Colonel couldn't help but wonder for the thousandth time how she and Albert had ever been related. Albert had been short and pudgy, while Catherine was tall and lean. Albert had a face that only a mother could love, while Catherine had skin like white porcelain and a face everybody loved. Where Albert had avoided sports of all kinds, Catherine had excelled in them all. Where her hair was the color of burnt red, Albert's hair had been short, coarse, and black. The only thing that they had in common was their minds. The few times that the Colonel had been around to listen to the two of them, he had felt like a child in a room full of

28

grownups. When Catherine and Albert conversed, they quickly eclipsed any other people in the room, often heading off on tangents beyond the ken of those around them.

"Catherine" the Colonel began, "Four days ago, a man who works for the DOD was killed and robbed of sensitive information, our information, as he left our office." Colonel Thomas continued to explain the events surrounding Albert, the recruitment of Trace, and the current situation.

"Lloyd, I want all department heads in at nine a.m. for a meeting. I want status on all departments at that point. At eleven, I want to talk to anyone and everyone involved with this Ferand person. I want to know why they killed him and I want to know why they killed my brother." Catherine had assumed command of MIGIsoft like it was nothing new. As people rushed off to do her bidding, she called to the Colonel, "Lloyd!"

"Yes ma'am?"

"I want this Trace person back," she said, "send someone over to the hotel to bring him in for me to meet. I want to hire him.

"Do you have another security test in mind?" Thomas queried.

"Hardly, that's your job. This guy knows more about this than we do right now and I think it would be a good idea to have somebody like him on our team. At least until we learn the rules of the game."

"Yes ma'am!" Thomas was inwardly pleased to hear that he still had a job, and amazed that she had the insight to use Trace.

Trace was in the hotel gym, just finishing his daily workout when he saw Russel walk in to stand at the edge of the padded floor.

"Morning Russell, here to drive me to the airport?"

"No Sir. I have been sent to request that you come back to MIGIsoft for a meeting with the new boss."

"New boss? Has the Colonel been replaced?"

"No Sir, when I say a new boss, I mean new top boss, Ms. Catherine Dewal."

Trace did not follow the technical world very closely, and so he had no idea who was who. He knew about Albert Dewal only because he was in the papers and on TV all the time, but he had never heard mention of a Ms. Dewal.

"Who is she?" Trace asked.

"She is one stunning lady. Sorry, I mean she is Albert's sister. I understand that she spends all her time traveling around the world." Russel explained.

"A real jet-setter huh?"

"Not from what the Colonel says. I mean she looks like one and all, but the Colonel says that she spends her time in places most of us would avoid unless we want to get shot or shoot someone. She is real big on helping kids, supports schools all over the place. Spends much of her time trying to change the laws and how they pertain to children in those countries."

Now Trace was curious, "When you say, 'all over the place', what do you mean?"

"I don't know for sure, but I think that she spends most of her time in South America. When the Colonel started looking for her, he had calls into Venezuela, Argentina, and Brazil, that I know of."

"Interesting."

"Yea, she's pretty easy to look at too. Anyhow, it was her idea to bring you back. She said 'get him', and the Colonel said 'ask him'. After the first time we met, I decided to go with the Colonel's suggestion."

"Well, I appreciate that Russell." Trace responded lightly and with that smirk, he always seemed to have. "But you'll find that I'm pretty easy going, believe it or not, I really don't fight unless I have to, and if I can avoid a fight by meeting with someone, I am more than happy to oblige."

"Thank you, Sir."

" You don't have to call me 'Sir' Russell, my name is Trace. Let me grab a quick shower in my room and change, then I'll meet you in the lobby and you can drive me over to meet the new boss."

"Yes Sir" Russel responded automatically. He had known the Colonel long enough to call him Lloyd, but he still called him 'Sir' or 'Colonel'. It just wasn't right any other way.

Trace simply shook his head and smiled a little as he headed to his room.

"Mr. Kelsi, we got it!" Jeff's voice was ecstatic over the intercom.

"I'll be right down," Kelsi responded, it had only been fifteen minutes since he had last been down to hound Jeff and his little brain trust. At that time, they hadn't been any closer to breaking the code than they had been yesterday. Now they had done it, how was that possible?

"Show me what you've got," Kelsi demanded as he entered the hacker's den.

"We can show you what it says," Jeff answered, " but it will take a while for us to figure out what it is."

"Is this really possible?" The hacker who had broken the encryption was reading the 'mission statement' on the CD.

"That is exactly what we want to know from you people. We know what it is, what we want to know is if it is real and will it work?" Kelsi said.

Forty minutes after Russell had walked into the gym, Russell and Trace walked up the steps to MIGIsoft headquarters. Russell's eyes moved constantly and his body was very tense. Looking for any unusual movement or activity. Trace saw this and was pleased that Russell was doing his best to protect the person who had twice scared the daylights out of him.

"Good man." Trace thought, *"He doesn't hold it against me."*

"Good morning Mr. Conner." The Colonel said as he greeted them at the security desk. "Here is your badge, please keep it on you at all times while in the building."

"Of course, Colonel," Trace answered, "and please my name is Trace."

"Yes, Trace. Did you have a good day yesterday? Do some sightseeing?"

"From the looks of you, I had a much better day and night than you did. After I left the Dewal estate I went to the hotel to check-in, then went to visit some friends and have dinner on the Wharf." Trace assumed that the

31

Colonel knew he meant the famous Fisherman's Wharf in San Francisco, it was only a thirty-minute drive from the MIGIsoft headquarters.

"There are some great places to eat there if you can stand the freak shows that go on all around you," Thomas responded. "Most people want to see the sights when they come up here."

"I thought you did a background on me. Don't you know that I used to live in Santa Cruz and have friends all around the Bay area?" Trace was surprised at this lack of knowledge on the Colonel's part.

"I knew you had friends in the area, as a matter of fact, a Scott's Valley Police officer was the one who recommended you to me." Thomas answered slowly, "I did not know that you used to live up here, somebody missed that in the report."

"Holy shit....holy shit.." seemed to be all that Jeff was capable of saying.

"Well? Is it possible?" Kelsi demanded.

"Holy shit..Yes...No...holy shit." Jeff stammered, "I mean yes it looks like it. We'll have to run their program through some real-time simulations and throw it some curves but this may actually work. Do you understand what this could do, what it is worth?"

"Of course, I do, you idiot, why do you think we stole it?" Kelsi deliberately left out any mention of dead people, the hackers certainly didn't need to know about that or Neko.

"Trace, this is Catherine Dewal. Catherine, this is Trace Conner." Colonel Thomas made the introductions. "Trace has a martial arts academy in Flagstaff, Arizona. That is where we found him."

"Mr. Conner, how do you do?" Catherine said.

"Fine, thank you. Russell said you wanted to meet with me."

"Yes. I want to hire you as a consultant while we try to figure out what happened to my brother and the DOD guy. So far, you seem to have more answers than anyone else."

"Well, I may not be of much more use to you. Not without more information to work with. For instance, I don't know what would be so important that would justify killing two people. Unless..." Trace paused.

"Unless what, Mr. Conner?" Catherine said.

"Please, call me Trace. Unless it was a personal vendetta of some kind. Although that would be unlikely, given that Albert probably didn't know this Ferand very well, if at all."

"Lloyd," Catherine turned to the Colonel, " is there any reason to believe that Trace here wouldn't pass the background check?"

"No Ma'am. So far we have found no problem and his references are impeccable."

"Good. Then fill Trace and me in on the project." Catherine said as she turned back to face Conner. "Right after he signs a confidentiality agreement."

"Yes, Ma'am. I'll have Alan down here in ten minutes with a presentation for you. My secretary will have an agreement here in two." The Colonel turned to the intercom.

"Before I sign or learn anything more," Trace interjected, "We should discuss what our arrangement will be."

"Trace," Catherine looked at him hard, "I have no time to quibble, I need you. Let's say two hundred thousand, that should be enough for at least the next two months."

"Fair enough, but I have a school to run, so no more than six months. At least, not without breaks to care for my school."

"Agreed, the contract will read that three weeks out of every three months are yours?" Catherine asked.

"Agreed." Trace answered, happy that it was such a simple, direct negotiation.

"So, how long will these real-time simulations take?" Kelsi asked, impatient as ever.

"First we have to write a program to simulate a real-time test," Jeff responded. "Then we have to cross-platform it to work with this one. Figure two days to get a preliminary idea if it works at all. About a month to know if it will work like they say it will."

Kelsi was mad, though he tried to control it. "That's too long! We're sitting on something that could be worth well over 500 million dollars. We need to know sooner than that."

"Chill dude," Jeff thought, *"Jeez, these guys have no idea what's involved in this."* Aloud he said, "We're working as fast as we can. We'll cut every corner, but if we tell you it does work when it doesn't, someone's gonna be mighty pissed off. I, for one, do not want to meet the dude that took this stuff."

Kelsi was momentarily panicked, how did Jeff know about Neko? "Why do you say that?" He asked.

"I see the news, Mr. Kelsi. A guy dies outside MIGIsoft headquarters and then Dewal himself is killed in his house. Then we get called in to crack the code on something that obviously came from there. I've read about Dewal's house-fortress, it must have been some very bad people who got this stuff."

Kelsi sighed inwardly, whatever Jeff knew it was just from general information. Nothing specifically about Neko.

"We call it the TFAX." Alan began. Alan Wells was the typical computer geek, glasses falling off constantly, ill-fitting clothes, and spoke to everyone as if he were afraid they would physically hurt him.

"What does that mean?" Catherine asked.

"Kind of a nickname that we came up with, it basically stands for Thermal Fixation, Acquisition, and eXecution," Alan answered.

"Wait a minute," Trace interrupted, "EXECUTION?"

"Originally," Alan responded, "the 'execution' referred to the execution of the program."

"And now?" Catherine pressed.

"Now it's up to the government, what it stands for."

"All right, we'll get back to that," Catherine said, motioning for him to go on.

"It started out as an idea that Albert and I were batting around over dinner. Every time we talked about Saddam or Osama Bin Laden, Albert would constantly gripe about why we didn't just take these guys out. I suggested that if we could've got a thermal fix on him, we could've just bombed their hideouts with them in it." Alan was lost in the reverie of that night. "Anyhow after I said that Albert got that far away look in his eye. You know, the one he would get every time he had a wild new idea."

Catherine and the Colonel both nodded their heads in understanding.

Alan continued, "Albert suddenly said, 'hey, we could do that.' I said 'come on Albert, by the time they could call in a strike, he'd be gone. They tried to fix him.' And he said, 'what if we could tag him with a thermal picture?' That's how this project began, I've been on it for almost a year, it's been easier than we expected actually."

"You're saying that you have developed a way to create a thermal 'tag' for a target?" Trace asked.

"It started out as a 'tag', but we eventually figured out how to create what is essentially a thermal fingerprint." Alan paused to see if everyone was with him. "The problem we had was that a person's body changes its thermal picture every so often throughout the day. To do this, we take two thermal 'pictures', at least twenty minutes apart. From there we can use an algorithm to create the 'fingerprint' based on the time of day in the subject's area."

"How are the 'pictures' taken and how long is the 'fingerprint' good for?" Thomas asked.

"The 'pictures' are taken by a thermal scope hooked to a laptop running our program. From there they are uploaded by cell, Internet, or SAT if it needs to be done quickly." Alan was talking fast now, obviously excited about the project. "As for how long it is good for, right now it is good for about two weeks, we think we can extend that out to a month. Longer if a satellite was targeted to follow and update the 'pictures' to correct for the variances that throw off the 'fingerprint'. Colonel, you understand that would mean that an operative would be well out of the country before the strike and well out of danger."

The Colonel nodded approvingly.

"How good is this 'fingerprint'?" Trace asked.

"T-print." Alan replied, "We've taken to calling it a T-print for short. As for how good it is, right now we can isolate one person out of ten thousand with a ninety-nine percent accuracy. Make it one out of a hundred thousand with ninety-two percent accuracy." Alan beamed, he was very pleased with himself and his project.

"Catherine…" Thomas asked. "Are you all right?"

Catherine Dewal shook her head, with a stunned expression she said, "This is what my brother was doing for money now? Making programs to assassinate people? I just can't believe this."

"Ms. Dewal," Alan replied, "please understand, to Albert this was not about money. In fact, the projected price for our government was to be around twenty million, we have already spent over ten million in the research phase of this. If we are successful, it would mean no longer having to risk troops to stop the worst of people. Bombing milk factories that house chemical weapon manufacturing would be unnecessary, we would be able to have people in the country take the T-print of the head bad guy. A week later the guy would just happen to be the one who got hit by a misfire or some such thing."

"So now we're in the assassination business." Catherine mocked him.

"Ms. Dewal," Trace countered calmly, "Try to imagine what it would have been like in Iraq, Cuba, or Bosnia if we had this then. So many people have died because of these few men and the world's inability to stop them."

"I am not surprised that you would support this Mr. Conner." Catherine's tone was scathing, her eyes like emeralds on fire. "What with Ninjas being assassins and all."

"Yes, Ninjas were assassins. They were usually hired to take out somebody at the top. Someone that conventional weaponry could not get at. Eliminating the need to kill the entire family or town. More often they protected their own. Ninjas did not see then or now the need to kill everyone except the one responsible. I personally believe in cutting the head off the snake, not leaving land mines for the children. In a standard war, it is the common people and children who suffer most, and you know it." Trace's eyes were ice blue, though he spoke calmly, he gave no ground to Catherine.

Alan and the Colonel were speechless. Neither knew how to handle Catherine's accusations, and both were stunned at the way Trace had spoken back to her. The Colonel noted that Trace had repeatedly used the word 'children' when speaking to her. As he watched her, her eyes softened somewhat, Trace had affected her.

"All right," Catherine replied, "for now I will have to think about whether or not this project continues. Mr. Wells, please continue with the briefing."

"I don't know what was taken from Albert's safe, you'll have to get that from the Colonel," he nodded to Thomas, " as far as what Mr. Ferand was carrying, he had the first working version of the program. Not very good, but enough for an evaluation by the government techs."

"What does 'not very good' mean?" Trace asked.

"The T-print is only about one in a hundred and is only good for a day or two at the outside."

"Why was this TFAX sent out with no guard?" Catherine posed this to the Colonel.

"This guy, Ferand, was a regular courier for high-tech items for the DOD, it was decided by his bosses that he would pick it up. They said the less obvious the better, I agreed. The fact is that except for his bosses, Alan and his team, me and Albert, nobody knew he was here or that the TFAX even exists. Much less when Ferand would leave the building. What I can't get is how the killer knew when he would leave." Thomas answered.

"Like I said before," Trace began, "this appears to be the same killer, and he waited at least an hour at the Dewal compound. There is no reason to believe that he didn't just wait here for Ferand to leave, take him down, then go to Dewal's house."

"So, there is still a leak somewhere," Catherine said. "Somebody told him that Ferand would be here."

"Yes," Thomas interjected, looking at Trace "but I notice you're calling the killer a 'him' now. Is there a reason for that?"

"No, it's just more convenient to say that. The fact is, almost everything points to a woman as the killer."

"Almost?" Catherine posed.

"The killer was able to approach Ferand, either very fast or very close, without making Ferand reach for his weapon. He was supposed to be an experienced courier. Men tend to be less cautious about women. Also, the Dewal break-in left little or no evidence to work with. That and the dogs."

"The dogs?"

"Women, especially highly trained women are able to put out very little active energy. What some people feel when they say sixth sense, women tend to be much harder to 'feel', even for an animal. Much like the energy that Ms. Dewal here puts out. We know that one dog was hit with a dart of some kind, but the other one may have just missed the killer."

"You said 'almost', Catherine prodded him again "and what does that have to do with me?"

"The hand spears are an uncommon weapon for a woman to use, they take too much practice and tend to make your hands look like mine." Trace held up his rough, heavily calloused hands. "As for you Ms. Dewal, you naturally have a lot of energy, yet you can control it. Turn it on and off to get the reaction you want. That tells me you have trained in at least one martial art if not more."

"Yes," she replied, "Aikido and Aiki-Jutsu, in the places I travel I sometimes have to defend myself."

"I'm not surprised by the Aikido, the 'way of harmony' seems like a natural extension of your hobby, helping people, I mean. What I don't see is the Aiki-Jutsu, that can be a little harsh." Trace responded.

"Sometimes you have to hurt someone to make them stop. Aikido just wasn't always enough for that."

Trace nodded his head in understanding.

"So, should we be looking for a woman?" The Colonel asked.

"Either a woman or a slight, non-threatening man. Either way, the killer will have calloused hands. So, if it is a woman, she may be passing herself off as a maid or maintenance person of some kind." Trace answered.

"I guess the next question is, 'how much did we lose', Thomas?" Catherine turned her full attention to the Colonel.

"You already know what we lost from Ferand, as far as Albert's safe, we lost the backup and the hard data on the project. Also, about a hundred thousand in cash and some diamonds worth about forty thousand." Thomas replied mournfully, shame at his failure was obvious in the way he answered the question.

I thought you said that Ferand was given the first version." Catherine said, "How could we lose the backup?"

Alan fielded this one, "Ferand was given the first one and the backup was the same. Albert would not let us copy the current version to a disk. He wanted to make sure that it stayed safe."

"Given what is on the TFAX disk the killer got, could they update the program as you have?" Trace asked.

"No way in hell." Alan responded almost gleefully, "we found that the original program couldn't handle the data necessary to fine-tune the T-print. So, we changed the database engine entirely. Remember that was only an evaluation program."

"So, what the killer got is worthless?" Catherine asked.

"Not worthless," Alan responded, "but certainly not worth two lives."

"This is awesome, Mr. Kelsi." Jeff was ecstatic, "this really does seem to work. Man, that guy is brilliant."

"How accurate is it?" Kelsi asked.

"Don't know yet, we're still working on that."

"I need to know that."

"Before you just wanted to know if it would work. Now we need to tell you how well. That all takes time." Jeff said, thinking "Prick".

"Get me that as soon as possible. I can't sell it if I can't market it."

"We're trying. You'll be the first to know."

"Like anyone else would." Kelsi thought. The hackers had their own floor but they were locked in the building and couldn't leave even if they wanted to.

"How many people know that it was an evaluation version?" Trace asked.

"Let me think," Alan answered, "there were Albert and myself, and now you three. I don't believe the Colonel knew before, did you?"

"No," Thomas answered, "not until just now."

"Then we should be able to smoke out your leak if we're careful."

"How so?" Catherine asked.

Instead of answering, Trace turned to Alan. "How long before they figure out it's not the current version?"

"Well, they'd have to beat the encryption first and then a week or so to run real-time trials on it…."

"Assume that they already beat the encryption." Trace interrupted.

"Why?" Catherine asked.

"They knew where to get the disk and the data, so their source is here or the DOD, either way, they probably have the encryption key or have already beat it." Trace responded. "I think they killed Albert to stop the project, not knowing about Catherine. We tell the people here that Catherine is taking charge and the project is going forward. If our 'spy' is here they'll come after her, before they come back for the current version."

"Sure, and we wait for the killer to come after her at the estate," Thomas said.

"Right, only she won't be there. Increase the guards on the outside but have a nice reception inside, make it look good." Trace said.

"What happens if they've figured out it's not the current version?" Catherine asked.

"Then they'll be coming after the program first, then you second." Trace answered.

"The program will never get out of this building," Thomas said.

40

"Never is a long time Colonel. It will get out, there may be a lot of casualties but they will get it. The killer has already proved that. The plan is to catch the killer before they find out they have a test version. Then we can do whatever Ms. Dewal wants with this T-FAX."

"Mr. Kelsi, there's a call for you on line four."

"Thank you, Alice." Turning to pick up the phone. "This is Kelsi."

"Kelsi…, Dewal's sister is here. She's had meetings with the whole company, nothing is stopping. Everything's going to continue like Dewal wasn't gone."

"Calm down," Kelsi spoke sharply, "are you on a safe line?"

"Of course, I'm at the bar about two blocks from the office. I left my cellphone back at MIGIsoft so that it couldn't be tracked. If production continues, we won't get as much for the 'product'."

"I'm aware of that," Kelsi spoke calmly, despite the rising pressure in his blood. "Where is she?"

"She said that if anyone had problems to call the Colonel, but rumor has it she's gonna stay at the mansion."

"Very well, thank you for the update. I will take care of it." Hitting the 'flash' button, Kelsi quickly dialed another number and spoke softly into the phone, "I need you for another job, call as soon as possible."

Kelsi looked at his watch and counted the seconds, he was at forty when his private line rang.

"This is Kelsi."

"This is Neko."

"Dewal's sister has moved into his house, she needs to be eliminated, now."

"Now, is not much time. They will have more security and that will not be an easy thing."

"I'll pay double the fee you got for Dewal, but it has to be in the next two days."

Neko smiled at the phone, he had already decided to do the job, more for the challenge than the money, but there was nothing wrong with getting paid for it. Paid well.

"As you wish. Deposit the money to the usual account, half now, half on completion."

"Of course, as always," Kelsi responded. He would never fail to pay. The thought of Neko coming after him was more than enough to make him pay the assassin promptly and completely. Besides, Neko never failed.

"Why am I here with you?" Catherine asked.

"Because the Colonel needs all the people he can take to the mansion, few people should know about me and I already have a hotel room." Trace answered. "Besides, I thought you might like the company. Your brother did just die."

At the mention of her brother, Catherine seemed to collapse in on herself. Her eyes welled up and she struggled not to cry. "I Can't believe he's gone…he was the best. I know to most people he was just a geek, and to others a rich geek, but he was….he was my brother. God, I miss him." Then the crying started in earnest.

Trace sat quietly and held her when she needed it. At last, she cried herself to sleep. Trace carried her to the bedroom and laid her down. Covering her with the blankets, he checked the window locks and moved out to sleep on the sofa.

Neko, sat in the brush watching the patrols. He planned to come differently, he never used the same approach twice. That was something his father had drilled into him in the jungles of Vietnam. Now, he saw his opening. Moving to the area near where the dogs liked to lie down, he quickly fired two darts into the dogs. The guards wouldn't think it unusual to see the dogs lying there. Using the large bodies of the animals for cover, he cut through the two fences and approached the house unseen. Entering the mansion wasn't any harder than it was the last time, there were more guards but they hadn't proved any more difficult than before.

The mansion was silent, except for a few sounds from the bedroom upstairs. Silently, Neko moved from room to room, watching, listening, feeling. As he approached the master bedroom, he knew something was wrong, she must have a guard or two in the room with her. Noiselessly, Neko stepped into the black room and was bathed in light.

"Surprise asshole!" Thomas said. "On the floor!" As he spoke, one of his men kicked the door closed.

Neko looked slowly around the room, four men besides the one who had spoken, the one he knew from briefs to be the Colonel. All were armed with an MP5 and he had no doubt they were all experts with the weapon.

When Thomas had set up the room, he had his men placed to 'cut the pie', each man had a section to cover, and if they kept to their section only the bad guy should get hurt.

As Neko slowly sank to the ground he suddenly launched himself to the left, putting his body directly between the firing lines of two MP5s. As he had hoped the guards held their fire for just an instant, waiting for a clear shot. An instant was all he needed. Just before he hit the guard, Neko dropped all the way to the floor. He could feel the three-round burst go over him and into his intended target.

Panic! Thomas had him a second ago now one of his men was shot and going down, panic was breaking loose. The assassin grabbed the wounded man's weapon and fired as he dove towards the Colonel. Russell moved to shield the Colonel and took two of the three rounds in the chest and throat.

Neko was up and moving, two down three to go. A quick burst into the light and the room was dark again. Aiming at where the remaining guards had been, he let loose two three-round bursts, and dove to the spot he had just fired into. The last burst had gotten another guard and the final guard fired to where he had seen muzzle flashes. Only Neko was no longer there. With an inaudible sigh, Neko slid out the folding Spyderco knife and buried it at the base of the last guard's skull. Holding the body so that the noise of it falling wouldn't give him away, he waited, listening. Neko wanted to kill the

Colonel now, but he was not giving himself away and Neko could hear more approaching guards.

"Too many to deal with safely, time to go." With that thought, he threw the body forward into the window, and he was gone.

Chapter 6

Trace picked up the phone before it finished the first ring. "This is Trace."

"We lost him, damn it. We had him, had him dead to rights and he got away. He killed three of my men, and it looks like Russel is probably gonna die too. He took two slugs protecting me." Thomas was furious and could barely control himself. "Christ, it was unbelievable. He took out all my men so fast, I couldn't do shit."

"Don't take this wrong Colonel, but why didn't he kill you too?"

"I don't know, maybe he just didn't have the time. I mean from the time he walked into the room until I heard him go through the window was maybe twenty, thirty seconds at the most. Once he shot out the light I stopped breathing until the window broke and I saw his silhouette jump through it. I fired at him and would have sworn I hit him, but we couldn't find any blood or any way to follow him."

"All right, back up. Tell me step by step everything that happened, start with what he looks like."

"Yea, I'm gonna have to do that for the Feds when they get here, better start getting things in order." For the next ten minutes, Thomas recounted the events in order with Trace asking occasional questions to clarify points.

"Okay, I think I've got it. I'll bring Catherine into the office as soon as you get back there with enough people."

"Why don't I send a team over there to bring you both in?"

"Because it's unlikely anybody other than you, me, and Catherine know that she's with me. If you send a team out, anybody watching could follow them to her."

"You're right. I'm not thinking straight, you take care of her, I have to go talk to the Feds now."

"Colonel, why are the Feds coming out. Why not the local police?"

"The government has taken jurisdiction of anything concerning MIGIsoft since Ferand was killed."

"Mr. Kelsi, call on line five."

"Thank you." Turning to pick up the phone. "Kelsi"

"It was a trap, they were waiting for me."

Kelsi felt his blood go cold, if it was a trap who would Neko think set it up? "What happened?"

"I got away, but the girl was not there."

"Are you injured?"

"I was hit twice but nothing that will stop me from completing my job." In truth, he had been grazed on the shoulder and had taken one round through the left side, just below the ribs, through the 'love handles'. Nothing critical was hit and he was able to clean and seal the wounds himself.

"What can we do?"

"I need a list from you as to any hotel rooms charged to MIGIsoft accounts for tonight. I need it now. If she is in a hotel she will not be there later. After the miss, they will try hard to hide her."

"Give me an hour, I'll have it then."

"No more than an hour, I must move quickly."

"I understand, you're sure you're not hurt?"

"Nothing critical."

Chapter 7

"Nothing critical", his mind wandered back to the time he had been shot badly. Neko was seven years old, the child of a Nung mercenary and a Vietnamese woman, he learned of war at an early age. When his mother died, he was three years old. From that time on he stayed near his father, he met the men from America. He learned English from the Green Berets, the SEALs, and of course the CIA men. They were all advisers, and when they left, the Nungs who had been so loyal were left too. Left to fight their way out of a country that wanted them dead.

Neko had been out getting food, taking advantage of his heritage to pass through the villages without question, only this time he was questioned, and when it was clear that the North Vietnamese soldier was going to take him in, he ran. Running away from the village as fast as he could go. He suddenly pitched forward, hit the ground, and ended on his back, the blood pumping from his chest. The bullet had gone clean through. He watched as the soldier walked towards him, and he knew that it was time to die. It was then that he witnessed the true power of his father. As the soldier approached, his father appeared from the brush beside the trail. The soldier swung the rifle around, Neko's father easily taking it from him. Then in what took no more than a minute, but seemed like an eternity, Neko's father beat the soldier to death. His father was armed and could have dispatched the soldier with ease, but this was to be a lesson in pain, then death. First was 'chipping the corners', breaking both arms and both legs. Then to prevent further screaming, the trachea was collapsed. The soldier's eyes widened at the specter of death, his mouth worked spasmodically, but to no avail.

Kneeling to pick up his son, he gently lifted Neko. "Be strong my son, you will survive." As they turned away from the writhing body, Neko saw it jerk twice and lie still.

Survive, he did. Thanks largely to the ministrations of the Nungs and especially his father. Every day needles were laboriously placed and removed, muscles were worked to painful extremes to rid Neko's young body of toxins. It took nearly three months to regain his feet, and when he did, he vowed that, from now on, he would be the one to do the killing.

Neko learned martial arts from his father at a young age, and he never missed a chance to learn from the other Nung mercenaries. By his eleventh birthday, the small band had made its way out of Vietnam, through Laos, and into China proper. The group took up residence thirty miles west of Mengzi. For the next five years, Neko stayed with his father studying the art of fighting and scratching out a living.

Born Song Li, he had been called Neko since he was two years old by his father. Everybody he ever knew called him Neko, when he thought about it, it seemed odd because Neko was a Japanese word for cat, and he had no Japanese heritage. At least none that he was aware of. His father's people hated the Japanese. Neko found this odd too. He understood the principle, but his father and the rest of the Nungs were still loyal to the Americans, it was the Americans that had left them to die. It was the Americans they should hate.

"Trust us," they said. "We'll always support you." They said, and then they left.

Left the Nungs with nothing, in a hostile country with no way to get out. Neko hated the Americans but was careful not to show it, that would dishonor his father. Instead, he buried his hatred in the art of war.

At seventeen, Neko was working alongside his father and the other Nungs, all together they only totaled four now. For the last four years, the Nungs had worked as the bodyguards for a small warlord running opium up out of Laos. Secretly the Nungs detested the drugs but they kept their silence and did their job. Neko was often assigned to go as the personal bodyguard of the warlord's eighteen-year-old son, Yuan Shi. Because Neko was also young, Yuan Shi did not object to his protection, he also enjoyed the fact that Neko had a cruel streak and did not hesitate to follow orders.

That all changed in April of 1987. After a Friday night of carousing in Mengzi, Yuan Shi and Neko returned to find the gate guards missing. Neko knew that the gate would be unguarded only if something had happened. He pulled the Toyota Land cruiser off into the dense brush and bid Yuan Shi stay in the vehicle. Quickly, Neko pulled and checked the Chinese SKS and his

Smith & Wesson .38, moving like a wraith in the brush, he approached the house from the east. Bodies were scattered everywhere, some he recognized as guards for his warlord, Yuan Lo, most he did not recognize. Most of the bodies bore wounds so obviously fatal he didn't bother to check them. On the bodies that weren't so obvious, he stopped to check. Three people he found still breathing, all three he dispatched silently with his crude blade. This was the first time he had killed and it puzzled him that he felt nothing. On the porch of the main house, he found the first of the Nung mercenaries, enemy bodies lay scattered around him like leaves fallen from a tree. He moved on through the house and at each Nung, there was a pile of bodies.

Finally, he found his father's body, lying in front of Yuan Lo's body. There were seven other dead bodies in the room, his father had done well. Neko smiled at that, his father was a warrior to the end. Neko checked all the bodies, none were alive. He returned to the Land Cruiser and drove it to the porch. After taking Yuan Shi inside to see his father, Neko allowed him time to grieve alone.

While Yuan Shi grieved, Neko made a circuit of the safes hidden in the house. One had been found and blown open. The other two were still untouched. Neko began working the locks when he realized that Yuan Shi probably knew the combinations. Grabbing Yuan Shi, he explained that they had to empty the safes and leave, for their enemies would be looking for Yuan Lo's son. Yuan Shi nodded dumbly and spun the combination on the first safe, then on the second while Neko cleaned out the first. Neko ignored the drugs, he knew they were valuable but he despised them, besides there was more than enough cash in American money to take.

As Neko got to the second safe, Yuan Shi was beginning to rant about revenge and how to use the money to hire thugs. Neko turned to face him and struck him hard in the left side, breaking the floating rib loose and puncturing the left lung. Yuan Shi doubled over, his breath coming hard. Neko grabbed the lowered head and twisted, sideways then up and back, the sick, wet popping sound told him when he had gone far enough. Yuan Shi's limp body fell to the ground, Neko leaned forward and watched the eyes as life fled from the body. This too, was a first, killing a man with his hands only, and he was pleased with how easy it had been.

Dragging the body of Yuan Shi out to the gate, he laid it next to one of the gate guards. Methodically he picked up a fallen SKS, checked the magazine, and fired a three-round burst into the body. Then he laid the other guard body on top of Yuan Shi's head. Now if they came back to look for Yuan Shi, they would find him and look no further, thinking they had missed him in the initial battle and had not looked at the gate. Neko dropped the weapon back on the ground and began to clean out the bodies of all cash. When he had finished, he had over seventy thousand dollars in American money and more than enough in Chinese currency to move around for a month or two.

Moving back to the main house he closed the safes and spun the dials. Next, he poured gas throughout the house and set fire to it. As the house was engulfed in flames, so too were all the people who knew him and who he was. Climbing into the Land Cruiser, he smiled as he drove away. He was sad that his father and the other Nungs were gone, but glad that they had died the way they wanted to, in battle. Briefly, Neko contemplated going after the rival warlord but decided there was no point. Were he to kill him, others would only fill the vacuum and it would start all over.

Chapter 8

Trace looked at the Citizen Aqualand watch on his left wrist. Ten minutes before five a.m., nearly two hours since Colonel Thomas had called to inform him of the failed arrest and ensuing debacle. Trace stood, stretched, and moved noiselessly into the adjoining room. Checking Catherine first and then all doors and windows he returned to stand next to the couch. Then he dropped to his knees and began his morning workout, being especially diligent in stretching muscles and joints. He couldn't afford a normal workout, he would be too tired and that could be dangerous.

Forty minutes later, Catherine jerked awake with a muffled cry. Two seconds after that, Trace was next to her. "Good morning, Ms. Dewal. Are you all right?"

"Hmm? Yes, yes, just a dream." She said rubbing her eyes. "What time is it?"

"About five-thirty, when you're fully awake, I have more news for you."

"News? What news? TV?"

"Wake up first Ms. Dewal, I'll start some coffee, why don't you jump in the shower."

"Hmm…okay…good idea."

Fifteen minutes later, Catherine sat in a bathrobe, sipping the strong black coffee prepared by Trace while he filled her in on what had happened at the estate. "Jesus.." She said. "Is this guy human? I mean can anybody be that good or is it just luck, or maybe it's some kind of trick?" She said hopefully.

"No tricks. I asked some very specific questions of the Colonel, and from what he says we have to assume this guy is that good."

"You do know what happens when you 'assume'?"

"In this case, Ms. Dewal, your life depends on us assuming the worst and hoping for the best." Trace responded gravely and turned to resume his workout. Catherine nodded mute understanding and headed into the other room to dress and make some calls.

"Do you have the information I requested?" Neko spoke softly into the phone. He was impatient, the wounds were beginning to stiffen and he would need to rest soon. He knew that nobody else would have been able to get the hotel information in such a short time, but Kelsi had some good sources.

"Yes, it's right here in my hands. Where do you want it?"

"Can you E-mail it?"

"Of course. Give me an address."

Neko quickly read off an E-mail address he had just created during his hour-long wait. He would check it for the hotel information and never check it again. That was always the safest way. The internet made some things so easy, and at the same time made them so dangerous and easy to get careless. Neko always reminded himself that 'careless' led to loss and that he would not allow to happen.

Ten minutes later, Neko had the list in his hands. Five hotel rooms in all, three at the local Holiday Inn. These he immediately discarded, she would not stay there. The last two were very expensive hotels, one of the rooms, at the Plaza Hotel, had been rented to MIGIsoft for two days, the other room was at the Point and was rented yesterday afternoon. Neko gambled that they had set up the new room as a Red Herring. So, he opted for the Plaza hotel.

As he approached the room on the fourth floor, he couldn't believe his luck. There was a room service cart heading his way. Turning like he had forgotten his key, Neko brushed close to the bellhop and struck the man on his neck. The Bellhop went down like a sack of potatoes, Neko quickly dragged the body into the stairwell, where he removed the Bellhop's jacket and donned it himself. Walking back to the cart, he headed for the room where he hoped to find his target this time.

Trace was rinsing the disposable razor when he heard the knock. *"What the hell?"* He thought, heading for the door. Only to see Catherine reaching for the doorknob.

"Don't open that!" Trace fairly shouted.

"Don't be silly," Catherine said with a light laugh "it's only the breakfast I ordered."

As she pulled the door open, Neko moved swiftly to the opening. He could hear a man shouting and knew that he had to move fast. His right hand shot out, the stiffened fingers heading straight for the cricoid cartilage of her exposed throat. At the same instant, Trace had closed the remaining distance, pushing Catherine into a spin and striking the attacker as his hand withdrew.

Neko watched Catherine go backward, knew that he had only achieved a glancing blow, she would survive. The spin had caused his blow to skate off the side of her throat rather than to crush it. As he had pulled the hand spear back, the man in her room had struck Neko's right wrist on the inside and slammed it into the edge of the open door. Neko knew immediately that at least two of the bones in his hand were cracked if not broken from the impact, his right hand was now useless. Without pausing Neko pivoted on his left foot, stepped forward with his right, and dropped low, the stiffened fingers of his left-hand shooting towards the man's heart.

Trace spun hard, knowing that he was too slow. He felt the tearing, like a knife along his rib cage, the blow was tremendous. As he fell backward, he managed to counter by striking with a shuto, a half-folded fist, on the top of the killer's extended arm. Turning the fall into a roll, Trace was immediately back on his feet.

Neko's left arm howled in protest, now it too was numb and useless. Who was this man? Neko had to move, with one hand numb and the other badly injured he could not risk a prolonged fight. Turning he ran from the room.

Trace began to chase after the killer when he heard Catherine gag. Although he desperately wanted the attacker, he had to check on her. A quick check showed that the muscles in her neck were starting to swell, he would have to stay and help her, or she would die from lack of blood to the brain. Kicking the door shut he threw the bolt. Trace then settled into working the muscles in her neck, there was a large red welt where the killer had struck and blood was oozing from the gouges. After thirty seconds of careful pressure and straightening of the muscle, he was rewarded with a scream and a stream of expletives.

"Glad to see I didn't lose you." He said.

"Christ" She coughed, "Why didn't" cough "you stop" cough "him?"

"Well if you had listened to me and not opened the door, I might have."

"Oh," cough "now it's my fault you couldn't get" cough "him?"

"No, but it would've been easier if I didn't have to save your life first. You do know that he almost killed you?!"

Catherine looked at him surprised. "Almost doesn't count. Besides I'm not hurt that bad."

In response, Trace helped her stand and walked her to the bathroom so that she could see the welt on her neck and the bloody lines from the assassin's nails. "You'd better clean those, they'll get infected." He shook his head, he was both impressed and annoyed by her bravado. Next, he picked up the phone and punched in a number. "Get me the Colonel, immediately."

When Colonel Thomas came on the line his voice was tired. "Colonel Thomas"

"Colonel, its Trace. He was here, he almost got Catherine. I need as many men down here as fast as you can. I hurt him, but not seriously and I don't know if he has help somewhere."

"Ten minutes, I'll have the first team there. I should be there in fifteen and I'll have the Feds with me."

"Good. We'll be waiting." Trace set the phone down and reached into his bag, pulling the black Tanto out he jammed it into his waistband, then walked back to the bathroom.

Catherine was sitting on the side of the tub, rubbing triple antibiotic onto her neck. "What's happening?"

"The Colonel's on his way with backup. Until they get here you stay right where you are."

"In the bathroom?"

"Look" Trace turned to lock her eyes in place, hoping to make her grasp the gravity of the situation. "They know where you are. There may be more than just the one. They could have a rifle trained as a backup or they might kick the door down any second. The bathtub is the safest place for you right now."

Catherine's eyes flashed but she held her tongue, despite her bravado, she understood that she could be dead right now. Instead, she nodded mutely and continued to apply ointment.

Trace was glad she didn't answer. As he stood in front of her he turned to look in the mirror and survey his damage now that all the important things were done. Pulling off his T-shirt, he examined the bloody red welt that extended from just left of his heart, across the rib cage to the side of his body. His T-shirt had done nothing to offset the nails on the assassin's fingers and Trace would have some scars to show for this one. It would hurt for a few days, and cleaning it would sting, but there was no serious damage.

When Trace pulled his shirt off, Catherine expected some lame come-on line about cleaning up together. As she watched him examine himself in the mirror, she thought that his vanity far exceeded her own. Turning to face her, she saw the large long bloody line on his side and struggled not to scream.

"Oh god you're hurt, bad."

"No, it just looks bad. Hand me a washrag and the ointment please."

As Catherine watched, Trace soaped up the rag and scrubbed the wound clean, trying not to grimace too much. Then he dried the wound and slathered on the ointment.

"Bastard probably pees on his nails to infect his victims."

Catherine's face took on a horrified look. "Does he really?"

"No, I doubt it. I'm just being overly cautious, and I'm pissed for not stopping him."

Trace knew that he had injured their assailant. Although he wasn't sure how bad, he doubted that the man would be back immediately, but he may have had a partner. By the time the knock at the door came, ten minutes later, he had strung a thin wire from the door handle to the striker plate. Not enough to stop someone, but enough to disrupt their balance and their plans.

"Who is it." Trace stood to the side of the door.

"Mr. Conner, its Syms." Came the reply.

Holding the tanto in one hand, Trace carefully opened the door enough to see Syms and the men with him. "Wait just a second." Trace said then closed the door and undid the wire. Opening the door again he said, "station two men in the hall, another just inside the door. You can come in to stay with Ms. Dewal, everybody else stays out until the Colonel gets here."

"Understood, Mr. Conner. Our orders are that you are in charge until further notice." Syms turned and quickly assigned the men to their positions. Then followed Trace to see Catherine.

Neko cursed softly from the car just outside the hotel lobby. He had hoped that the Dewal woman and her bodyguard would make a run for it. Then he would simply shoot them both with the silenced .22 Ruger, in his lap. He couldn't go back to the room because he was injured, and now he saw what had to be a second team of guards and the Colonel heading into the elevator. Counting the first four men he watched go up six minutes ago, that now made at least nine guards with the woman. *"Not today"*, he thought. He would have to try again later. Still cursing, now in Vietnamese, he pulled out of the parking lot and onto the nearby freeway.

"This is Kelsi."
"The target has not been eliminated." Neko spoke harshly'
"Why, what happened?"
"Not important. I need more information, to finish the job."
"Sure, tell me what you want."
"There was a man with the woman, I need to know who he is, and her location tomorrow night."
"Was he the problem?" Kelsi was surprised that anyone could stop Neko.
"Yes, but he is not an ordinary guard."
"From what I'm told, they're all former military."
"Not this one, he is.......different," Neko said.

56

"Alright, what's he look like, I'll see what we can find."

Neko gave him a brief description, promised to be in touch, and hung up the phone.

"So, we definitely have a leak, how do we find it?" The Colonel asked.

"We can tap some of the phone lines leaving the company, and trail employees." Agent Jares answered, "but it will take your permission, I can get a FISA judge to issue an order, just in case we need to prosecute later."

"You have my permission," Catherine spoke up.

"Yes, tap all our lines," the Colonel added.

"No, that would be a waste," Trace interrupted "whoever is the leak, has something to do with the 'project'. Odds are they wouldn't call from here. That would be stupid. More likely, from a payphone or cellphone, maybe at a restaurant."

"I agree with Mr. Conner," Jares said, "they probably wouldn't make a call from here. If you can specify the lines used by this 'project', I'll get them tapped. I'll try to get taps on nearby phones, and we'll set up surveillance teams."

"Lloyd will get you the names of the personnel to follow and the phone numbers to tap," Catherine told him. "I imagine a court order will be easy enough to get based on 'national security'."

"Yes, I'll get that started right now. It'll take a few hours, so try to keep all the personnel we want to tail, in-house, until we're ready." Jares said while he started dialing his own cellphone.

"Of course," Colonel Thomas answered. "I'll print out associated personnel files, with photos. There are only two phone lines on that floor, and they are 'restricted use', those numbers and call logs will be printed next."

Agent Jares grabbed the stack of printouts and headed out the door.

"Colonel, I think now would be a good time for Alan to leak, to the rest of the project team, what they really lost." Trace said. "Hopefully Jares people will be able to nail the leak for us."

"Why should we tell them so soon." Catherine asked, "why not wait a few more days?"

"Because if they realize they don't have the finished version, they may not try to kill you until they do. If you die, the next person might scrub the project and they would have nothing."

The clock read 6:32 A.M., the phone was worse than the alarm. "Yea, hello."

"Sorry to wake you, I need some help," Kelsi said into the phone.

"Sure," came the reply, and Kelsi hung up.

Fifteen minutes later, it was Kelsi's turn to answer the phone. This time on a secure app. "Hello."

"What can I do for you, sir?"

"We need more information, where is the Dewal woman staying, and who is the new man with her." Kelsi followed with the description Neko had given.

"Ok, I'll see what I can find out. What difference does it make? I mean we got the disk, let's just sell it."

"If MIGIsoft still sells their product, ours drops in value. I don't want that big of a drop, do you?" Kelsi spat out the rehearsed line. He couldn't reveal the real reason.

"No, no, of course not. I better get going, I'll call as soon as I have something."

Chapter 9

"Colonel," Trace began, "how many men do you have? Count the mansion too."

"Let's see, we have twelve staffed here, rotating shifts of three. Fifteen at the mansion, shifts of five, then Russel, Syms, and me. Of course, I've got four down so that leaves, um, twenty-six available. We have about a hundred of the standard security people, but very few of them have any combat experience."

"Okay, here's my suggestion. Leave the dogs and the alarm system on at the mansion. Bring three more men to the office, use shifts of six. Let's not use the standard security people. I want to use every other man to head over to Chinatown, Koreatown, and Japantown. I hurt this guy, not critically, but I did hurt him. I'm hoping that you and your men hurt him too. Hopefully, bad enough that he'll need some supplies, and even more hopefully, from the Asian community. If he does, I want to know. Give your men the description I made, tell them NOT to engage. Try to follow."

"You think he'll go there?"

"It's a long shot, but it's a shot. Maybe we'll get lucky. There's nothing at the mansion to protect, so let's use those men. Oh, and your men look like military spec-ops."

"Yea, so?"

"So, they stand out in a crowd, especially of Asians. Have them wear caps and old clothes, tell them to slouch. Anything to reduce their visibility. Make sure they understand not to do anything but follow if they find him, the best thing they could do is shoot him from a distance, and that wouldn't work well in a crowd."

"Understood."

Chinatown is a wonderful place to find obscure items that most Americans are clueless about their real uses. Herbs, needles, poultices are just a few of the things easily purchased in this small community.

It was items such as this that Neko was searching for. He knew how to administer his own aid, knew his body well, and what it would need. The wrist would need a concoction of herbs and essential oils to promote healing and reduce swelling. The gunshot wounds needed herbs, acupuncture needles, and anti-bacterial poultices. All things he could make from the items he was looking for. Neko was focusing on not limping, which was hard because he was beginning to stiffen up. As he was about to enter the fourth shop for his final needs, he noticed the two Americans. Both of them looked more at the people than at the stores, which immediately made Neko suspicious.

Mark Taylor had been assigned to the mansion and felt responsible for Albert Dewal's death. Russell was a good friend, they had been in Afghanistan together, so Mark was very motivated to find this prick and finish him. Mark was six foot two inches, with pale skin and blonde hair. A fan of working out, Mark was very muscular and stood out like a statue as he scanned the crowds. This made him easy to see in any group, more so in a crowd of Asians. Mark's current team partner was Jesse Beal. Jesse had been a SEAL but had been denied re-enlistment due to a knee injury. He could function fine, just not at the level of fitness the SEALs required. Jesse was five foot nine inches tall, with a dark complexion, and blended in well in most places. Jesse didn't have the height to see over the crowd, so he was checking faces down low. He focused especially on people who had their heads down, which was difficult because many of the Asians kept their heads down and avoided eye contact.

"There," Mark said, excitedly. "Heading into that red and black store."

"All the stores are red and black," replied Jesse, but he could feel his pulse quicken.

"The second store in from the northeast corner."

"Right, call it in?"

"No, I want his ass. We owe him for Russell."

"The Colonel said not to engage, only find and follow. He was very explicit. Besides, this guy took out everyone but the Colonel at the mansion and they had the drop on him." Jesse patiently explained.

"Fine," Mark growled, "call in."

Jesse was still watching faces as he hit the speed dial on his cell. Just then a face lifted and looked directly at him. Jesse dropped his cell, reaching for the Sig Sauer P229 at his hip. His hand had barely touched the pistol when a silenced .22 was shoved hard up against his throat and fired twice. He dropped to the pavement as if someone had removed his legs.

As quiet as the .22 was with the silencer, it still made noise. To most of the people in the area, the sound was lost in all the ambient noise. Mark was not an ordinary civilian and he instantly went to full combat mode at the sound. Then, when the silencer was pressed to the back of his neck, Mark knew he had a chance. Spinning counter-clockwise, Mark swung up his left hand hard, striking the gun and moving it away from his neck. At the same time, he reached his right hand across and under his left arm for the Smith and Wesson .40. He knew that at such a close range he could empty the entire magazine into a target in under three seconds. He never got that far. Like a bad funhouse mirror, the smaller Asian man mimicked Mark's movement and set his palm on top of Mark's hand. Preventing the former soldier from pulling his pistol out. The silenced .22 then swung back and under his chin, two rounds, and Mark joined Jesse on the ground.

Neko moved away from the kill zone. There wasn't a lot of blood, yet, but someone was starting to scream. There would be more teams nearby. He wanted nothing more than to hunt the hunters, to show them he was not afraid, but he was still injured and that would be stupid. The two rounds that had tagged him at the mansion and the debacle in the hotel. His side hurt and wrist throbbed. When the big guy had knocked his hand aside, he had nearly dropped the gun. Were the bones in his wrist just cracked? How bad? How did the man in the hotel hit him that hard? From such a bad angle? How did he dodge the strike? Too many questions.

"Jesse, Jesse...hello?" The colonel said into his phone.

"What is it?" Trace asked, suspecting the answer.

Jesse Beal, one of my guys in Chinatown, is calling me, but he's not there. I can hear voices and it sounds like someone is hysterical, but no Jesse. After another minute of calling Jesse's name, a voice came on the phone.

"Who am I talking to?" The voice said.

"I'm Colonel Lloyd Thomas. Who are you?"

"I'm officer Wilson with the San Francisco Police Department. Do you know the victims?"

The Colonel's head drooped, a silent curse leaving his lips. Trace suspected that he knew why.

"If there are two men down, they are mine. I am their boss. Tell me where you are and I will be there in fifteen minutes." Colonel Thomas went on the describe the men and what they were doing there. He also warned officer Wilson that Agent Will Jares, of the FBI, would be in touch shortly. After giving the officer all the contact information, the Colonel had all the other teams check-in. Nobody else was missing, which was the only good news today. He already had too many phone calls to make to families with bad news.

"Sir!" The frantic voice said on the phone. "It's worse than we thought. They didn't give Ferand the real flash drive!"

"Bullshit," Kelsi replied. "We already cracked the encryption and can see the program, as well as the project description."

"I know that, but it's not the finished product. That was our original program. A 'proof of concept' for the government to review. It is nowhere near as refined as the finished product."

"How much different is it? Can we still sell it as finished?" Kelsi was thinking fast. Could his team adjust the algorithms to use what they already had? Would that work? He needed to talk to Jeff, get some answers. As his mind chased that lead he heard the voice again.

"No way! I know in the early version we used different algorithms. It works but not anything like the finished one. The final version is about a hundred times more accurate and works days later to identify a target. Without those updates, you'd have to target an individual in less than an hour, and even then, the percentile drops dramatically."

"Can you get the new algorithms and we'll just add them in?"

"No, it doesn't work like that. Besides, we also changed the database design. You need the whole thing, compiled and intact. Otherwise, you can't deconstruct it."

"Damn it! Figure out where it is and how I can get it." Kelsi swore, he would have to cancel the hit on the Dewal woman, find a way to get the finished product, and worst of all, tell Mr. Cross.

"Yes sir. I will get back to you as fast as possible." The caller hung up.

"Cancel the second delivery. We will reschedule in a few days." The voicemail said.

"Good." Thought Neko. *"I need to recover for a few days minimum."*

"Understood." Was the only word Neko spoke into the voicemail he had called back.

"You have canceled the 'plan' for Ms. Dewal?" Mr. Cross said with exaggerated patience.

"Yes, Mr. Cross," Kelsi replied, hating these face to face meetings, especially with bad news.

"Do you have a plan for getting the final version? One that won't fail?"

"Not yet sir. Our informant is researching all of that now. Hopefully, we will have an answer in a few hours, so that we can devise a plan." Kelsi spoke quietly, hoping that Cross did not get too angry.

Seventeen minutes after hanging up with officer Wilson, Colonel Thomas and Trace rolled up to the scene of the shooting. Officer Wilson and the other five SFPD officers had parked their cars and positioned themselves to form a fifty-foot perimeter from the bodies. Agent Jares was standing next to the bodies, talking into his phone. He looked up and saw the Colonel, then waved at him to come over. As the Colonel passed the police perimeter, an officer tried to stop him but was waved off by Jares.

"Are these your men?" The agent asked.

Thomas stepped closer, expecting to see a bloody mess. He was surprised that there was very little blood around the two men.

"Can we get closer?" He asked.

"Not until the lab guys finish. The scene is pretty messed up already, I doubt there will be anything useful around the victims, but there is a procedure and we have to follow it. Especially with the national security aspects involved."

Almost an hour and a half later, Agent Jares said "ok, you can look closer now."

The Colonel and Trace both moved in to examine the bodies. They could see the same two small holes, with burn marks, beneath both men's jaws.

"Probably a .22. That's what the lab guys think. We won't know for sure until the medical examiner finishes, but there aren't any exit wounds. So, the rounds are probably still in the skulls." Jares said flatly. "They were both armed, but their pistols were still in the holsters."

Trace noted that Jesse wore a concealed hip holster while Mark had been wearing a shoulder holster under his left arm. Both were empty now, bagged as evidence by the techs. He also noted that there was no other visible damage to the bodies.

"What the hell?" Thomas growled. "How did they get shot there and neither one of them got their weapons out? Mark was one of the fastest pistoleros I've ever seen and Jesse was a SEAL. He was fast as hell too! How could they both be facing somebody and not even pull their weapons?"

"Because they were in life or death, hand to hand combat and they didn't know it." Trace replied softly. "I'm sure they were better with guns than the assassin was, but his skills are not shooting from a distance. From what we have already seen, this killer is beyond an expert in close-quarter fighting. A gun is just another weapon, like a knife. What I don't understand is why he even used a gun."

"Why not use one?" Jares asked.

64

"Because of the noise. Even suppressed, a gun makes noise. The hand spears would have been completely silent. He could have easily crushed all the cartilage and been egressing while the men suffocated. He could have used a knife, bloody, but very fast and quiet, or a hundred other items. All quieter than a gun. Maybe...maybe I hurt him worse than I thought. A gun would mean that he wouldn't have to strike very hard, he only had to move in and press the gun in place. I hope that's the reason. It would make it so much better if I actually hurt this prick!" Trace said this as he ran his hand over the large welt across his ribs and the sore, swollen skin there.

"That still doesn't explain why neither man drew his weapon." The Colonel said again. "The second man would have recognized the noise and pulled before the killer could do them both! They were both combat vets, they would have recognized a suppressed shot. Even a .22."

"It does." Trace replied. "I would bet that Jesse was taken first because he was calling in. There might have been a loud truck or something right then to help cover the shots. Even so, the men are so close that the killer could move between them fast enough to stop the second man from drawing."

"Bullshit!" Colonel Thomas barked. "Jesse was no slouch. I don't even know all his combat history, most of it is 'top secret', but he was fast as hell. Mark, he never left the 10th mountain infantry, but he did three tours in Afghanistan and was the fastest guy I had ever seen with a pistol. He could pull and empty a mag into the center of a target like it was on full auto!"

Trace sighed but tried not to make it too obvious. Then said. "Colonel, when we get back to MIGIsoft HQ, I will show you how he did it. Until then, you have to trust me. I think the killer is really hurt. We need to find him now, while he is vulnerable. We've seen the kind of things he can do when he's at full strength." Turning to Agent Jares, Trace prompted. "Agent Jares, is there anything else you can tell us? Anything at all?"

Jares was silent for a long minute, searching his thoughts. "No..." He said slowly like he was holding something back.

"Really? You're sure?" Trace looked at the FBI man hard.

"No." Jares replied harshly, losing his temper. "Don't look at me like that. I'm FBI, you are nothing. Not even a government contractor. You don't even have a security clearance. Much less a 'top secret'. I don't have to tell you shit. For all I know, you know the killer and you're not telling me! How else do you know so much?"

"Agent Jares." The Colonel interjected in a commanding voice. "You are under orders from the DOD. From the top, I'll remind you, to share information with us. All of it!"

"With you, Colonel! Not this guy. Where did you find him? How does he know so much about the killer? He tells me practically nothing but seems to know exactly what the killer is thinking. We don't have shit! Not jack shit! How does this guy, your 'consultant', know so much? Something is not kosher. I told you everything we have for now. When the coroner's report comes in, I'll share it. Until then, I don't have anything else. Scratch that! I have suspicions about your 'consultant', but nothing else!"

During Jares rant, Trace had drifted quietly away. Examining the area. Avoiding eye contact with the FBI man.

"We'll leave now Jares. Let me know what the coroner finds. As far as my 'consultant', where I got him is nothing you need to worry about. He is clean and I am vouching for him. The reason we went after him is exactly that he is an expert in this."

"Killing people??!" Jares shouted.

"Yes." Was all the Colonel said and walked off, Trace dropped in beside him as he passed, heading back to their SUV.

"He doesn't know anything else. At least, not right now." Trace said, without prompting.

"What makes you so sure?"

"He's mad. Not really at me, I'm just an easy target. An unknown. I'm sure he feels helpless, getting nowhere. I come in, making proclamations, and he thinks there is some information being kept from him. He's frustrated and angry, just like us. You probably understand him better right now than I do, you have lost people to this attack on MIGIsoft and we still know nothing."

"We know one thing for sure." The Colonel breathed.

"What's that?"

"We are going to kill this bastard, from a distance. There is no way we can capture him safely. Then we go after the people that sent him."

"Agreed. Way too dangerous to get close to him. Any ideas on who might be behind it?" Trace asked hopefully.

"Yes, but that's the problem. Corporate espionage, which is what this is, is huge money. If somebody found out about this and could get their hands on it, then auction it to other countries..." Colonel Thomas whistled. "It would be huge, and that's an understatement. If you had access to a satellite with thermal or specialized thermal optics, you could assassinate anybody, anytime, anywhere. Imagine what that would be worth. Bad guys could use it to blackmail countries by targeting specific leaders. Anyway, the number of bad actors that would want this would number into the thousands. We need a way to narrow the list."

"How do we go about that?" Trace asked.

"Well, I was hoping to have a murderous shithead to beat it out of, but that's probably not going to happen now." The Colonel said with a grim smile.

"No." Trace shook his head. "We can't afford to lose one more man trying to capture him. I want to get him while he's injured, I just don't know how. Plus, it would be pointless."

"Bullshit, everybody breaks." The Colonel spat.

"He would break, but not like you think. People like him, people like me, train with pain in a way that is hard to explain. SEALs, Rangers, Delta, and all the other Special Operators learn to deal with pain. To focus it, make work for them. They don't purposely hurt themselves day in and day out. To reach the level this guy has, you have to know what you are capable of, not just endurance, but you have to know at what point one of your bones will break. Because you've done it on purpose. You have to know when you will lose consciousness if you are being choked out. You have to know what you are willing to lose, just to win. You have to get past the concept of "inescapable". It becomes a question of 'what will I sacrifice to win?' Remember, we are talking about the loser dying. For people like this killer, pain gives them strength, it gives clarity and most important, it gives them power." Trace's voice was nearly a whisper as he said this last phrase with conviction.

Thomas shook himself and the goosebumps that had started to form on his arms. He thought of the mansion when they were sure they had the killer, how easily he escaped. How he had run right at a gun trained on his face from a few feet away. What would he sacrifice to win? Anything, the killer will sacrifice anything to win. Not a good thought.

"As soon as we get back, I need to do some calls." The Colonel said. "Then I want you to show me how some ninja could take down two warriors as you think."

"Ok, I assume there is a gym on-site. Maybe some mats?"

"Yea, I'll have the guys set it up."

"Not too much. The mats are for your guys, I'm fine with wood or concrete floors." Trace responded. "Also, I don't think he's a ninja. At least I hope not."

"Why?"

"Cause if he is, we are really screwed."

There were a lot of calls to make. By the time the Colonel got all the remaining security staff back to MIGIsoft's main building, it was almost 7:30 that night. Some of them grumbled about the long day, but they were all combat veterans and had worked many long days without a break. The griping was just routine.

"Why are we all here?" One of the assembled group asked.

"Mr. Conner here is going to explain some stuff to us. Hopefully, show us how some prick got close enough to kill Jesse and Mark without either one of them pulling a weapon or firing a shot." The Colonel replied.

"There had to be more than one bad guy to take them both out." A large man said. "Mark was fast as lightning, nobody could beat him on the draw."

"This is exactly why I asked for all of you to be here." Trace began. "You all need to have a better understanding of what I'm warning you about. Especially about keeping your distance from this guy. He's like nothing you've ever seen before."

"BULLSHIT!" The large man screamed. "We've all seen combat, some of us have seen a lot! Seen every piece of shit dirtbag there is. Then we killed them."

There were emphatic nods around the group, along with a few "Fuck Yeah!" and a "Hoo Ya" or two.

"What is your name?" Trace asked, walking closer, looking up at the big man.

"Trace Conner, meet Luka. Luka was also a SEAL. He is the second-fastest pistolero we have. Only Mark was faster." Colonel Thomas began.

"Barely faster," Luka said, as he pushed even closer to Trace. "Sometimes I won, sometimes he won. He was good, so was Jesse!"

"Great. Who is the third?" Trace asked.

"That would be Kevin here. Former Cav Scout, two tours in Iraq and one in Afghanistan. All tours under fire." As the Colonel said this, a man about five foot eleven inches stepped forward. A touch shorter than Trace but almost twice as wide.

"Does anybody here think that I am stronger or more fit than Luka or Kevin?" Trace said as he scanned the group. "Because I am not. I guarantee that I am not going to beat either one of them in weights, distance, or endurance." After a slight pause, he added. "But, I will kill them both before they can shoot me."

Laughter broke out loudly in the group and Trace smiled.

Chapter 10

"The Dewal woman has us working on the program, but there is no way I can copy it. It's a huge program and the security guys on our project are very tech-savvy here. They watch us all the time. On top of that, the system monitors for any downloads and records the user ID. If I try to get it, they'll know it was me." The spy said quickly. "I have no idea how we are going to get it out. Mr. Kelsi, they have locked the building down even tighter than before!"

"Stop using so many names on the phone. You can't just get it out on a microSD?" Kelsi asked, his head pounding, trying to come up with an alternative.

"I'm on an internet VOIP phone, the app itself is encrypted, we're safe on that score. As far as a microSD, a disc, a thumb drive, or anything else, no. They are making us use "clean room" protocols when dealing with this program. They are even running jammers to block any signals coming in or out of that building. You have to get your phone from security and walk about a hundred yards away just to make a call. It sucks!"

"Brute force?" Kelsi pondered aloud.

"Maybe, but the people the Colonel hired all look like real badasses. I wouldn't want any of them mad at me."

"We have our own badasses..."

"That's up to you sir. Tactical stuff is not my wheelhouse unless you're talking about HALO."

"I thought the program was complete," Kelsi said, ignoring the video game reference. "Why is she having you work on it at all?"

"It is, but she says she wants us to run every piece of the software for glitches. Especially since it's going to run on the government computers. She wants every possible computer-related problem planned for in advance. The one that we gave that Ferand guy, would have worked fine on their computer."

"Smart," Kelsi replied. " Gives an excuse for a delay and makes use of the time. Call me back as soon as you have any more information. No matter the time!"

"Yes, s..." But the connection had already been broken.

"We have to make a few assumptions, but we are going to base this exercise on the distance the victims were from each other." Trace began his explanation. "I want to put a phone in Kevin's hand, just like Jesse had and Luka will stand six feet to the side and behind Kevin. Both of you, please empty your weapons and remove the magazines. I want you to be using a weapon and holster that you are used to. I will be using a 'red gun'." Trace was referring to a plastic, red gun used for hand to hand weapon training.

As the two former soldiers moved into their positions, Trace moved in front of Kevin, five feet away.

"What are we supposed to do now?" Kevin asked.

"You hold the phone up like you're making a call, and whenever you want, drop the phone, pull your weapon and shoot me." Trace replied. "Luka, you wait until you hear either me or Kevin say 'bang'. Then you draw your weapon and fire. Everybody understand?"

Both men nodded their understanding. Trace relaxed and waited. For those watching, they saw Kevin let the phone drop and move for his weapon.

Trace moved. His left palm pushed flat against Kevin's wrist. Pressing it against his ribcage and preventing him from pulling his weapon free. Trace's right-hand rose up and pressed the red, training gun at the bottom rear of Kevin's jaw. "Bang! Bang" Trace barked.

Luka had seen Kevin move but then almost immediately there was the "Bang! Bang!" Luka went for his weapon, moving in a blur.

After 'killing' Kevin, Trace performed a 'yoko aruki', a cross-stepping technique that cleared Kevin and closed the distance to Luka in a fraction of a second.

Luka's hand made it to his gun and it was almost out.

Trace switched the red gun from his right hand to the left as he moved in. His right hand dropped on to Luka's weapon hand just as it cleared the holster, pinning it against his chest and safely off the shooting line. His left hand jammed the red gun up and into the big SEAL's throat. "Bang! Bang!" Then he stepped back and away.

Luka was stunned and gagging a little, from the red gun that was moments ago, jammed into his throat. He looked at Kevin, whose weapon was still in his holster. How the fuck did that guy do that? "That wassh..bullshit!" He choked out. "That little fuck cheated!"

"Yes, Luka. That's the point." Trace said looking around the group. "We told Luka what to expect, he and Kevin were both ready for it. Imagine if I had just appeared in front of Kevin and initiated, instead of letting Kevin move first. Luka managed to get his weapon clear of the holster, but still 'died'. There are a whole host of variables that we still don't know about how your friends were killed. We used the ones we knew and then went with the worst-case scenario for me to overcome. Luka and Kevin still lost."

"You already knew what you were going to do. That gave you an advantage." Kevin said.

"Yes and no. I had no way of knowing when you would move, if you would pivot or slide to the side. I let you tell me."

"I didn't tell you anything," Kevin growled.

"You did, you just didn't know it." Trace looked around the assembled group. This is where he was most comfortable, teaching what he knew best. "What did you guys see? Anybody call it out."

"I saw Kevin drop the phone and go for his weapon, then your red gun was against his throat and you were moving to Luka in a blur. I saw Luka go for his weapon, then it was over." Colonel Thomas said.

"This little shit pulled something.." Luka reached out with his left hand to push Trace, but it never made it there. An instant of excruciating pain, then he was on his knees and it felt like the bones in his left wrist were being ground together between a vise and an anvil.

Trace moved so fast, Luka never saw anything. Neither did the rest of the group. Reaching up with his right hand, he wrapped it over Luka's left. Rolling it clockwise into 'hon gyaku', the 'base reversal', Trace then aimed his index finger at Luka's heart dropping him to the ground in pain. This hold caused the small bones in the wrist to grind against one another, creating excruciating pain. Trace maintained the hold to make a point. "Did anyone see me move? Or was it just Luka you saw move?" To Luka's credit, he was trying to fight the pain, so Trace had to keep a good amount of pressure on the joint to keep him in place. Luka had a pained grimace on his face but was not making any sounds.

"I only saw Luka," Kevin said from less than eight feet away.

"Exactly." Trace made eye contact with every man in the group, lastly, he met Luka's eyes and released his grip. "You have all trained to be fast and accurate, but not how to keep your moves from being telegraphed. Whenever one of you goes for a weapon, there are dozens of small body movements that the human eye can pick up. We call them 'tells'. In my art, we practice for years to get rid of our 'tells'. That allows us to move faster, or at least it looks like that. Because everyone saw the big shoulder movements on Kevin, they never saw me move. Same thing with Luka, I was moving toward him, but the lift of his shoulders, the twisting of his body, his right elbow pistoning back for the draw, his larger size, all of that 'visually' over-powered my movement. The human eye is incredibly good at picking out movement, I just moved less visibly than these two." Trace pointed at Luka and Kevin.

"All of you are hardened warriors. You have been trained to fight with weapons and have no equal in squad or platoon fights. This opponent is not like that. He doesn't use weapons, he IS the weapon. Anything in his hands is an extension of that weapon. Like a suppressor added to a pistol. The suppressor doesn't make the pistol deadlier, just more effective." Trace had all their attention now, so he drove the point home. "You cannot beat this enemy in close! You must have distance! At least fifteen feet, preferably more. If he gets inside that range you are dead! You guys need to take this warning to heart. If I could take out two of your fastest, then he can. He did! I personally would prefer we shoot him with a .308 from two hundred yards, but that might be difficult to do in a busy city, especially one with a lot of Asians in the population."

Trace held his right hand out to Luka to help him back up. "Sorry about that. I have immense respect for you guys. I never served, so I have no idea what it's like. I just needed to make sure you guys all got this point hammered home."

"Yes sir," Luka replied rubbing his left wrist gingerly. "You did. I thought my wrist was gonna explode any second there. How did you do that? With the finger-pointing thing and all?"

"Later Luka. We don't have the time to teach it right now."

"Roger that. I will hold you to that. It's a shame you never served. You would have made a badass SEAL!"

"Ha....I'm sure I would have rung the bell right away. That's why I do Ninjutsu. I don't have to work as hard or be in as good of shape!" Trace smiled and the big man returned the smile.

"So, what do we do now?" Colonel Thomas asked while he and Trace walked towards the Colonel's office.

After a very long pause, Trace responded. "Nothing. We play defense. We pull everyone in tight and hope that we get another lead from the FBI, DOD, or something else. I hate the idea but we can't send men out like that again."

"You showed them how dangerous this killer is. The men won't take that lightly."

"Maybe, but even so, we barely have a description. Mine sucked. He could be standing right next to your men, they wouldn't even know it. No, we need to hunker down until we get better intel. We sent them out based on my suggestion and because of that, two of your men are gone forever. That's my fault. I, we don't want to lose any more men."

"That's crap and you know it." The Colonel replied. "None of us, even you, could have known how dangerous this guy is. We all take our chances. Don't get me wrong, I will raise a toast to my men and I will grieve for them. I'll ache with their families, but they wouldn't want us to take the blame for it. That's not who they were."

"After what he managed at the mansion, both times and when he came to the hotel, I should have known." Trace mumbled, mad at himself.

"Tell me, Mr. Conner," Colonel Thomas said in his most authoritative voice "how many times have you hunted killers like this one?"

"What? Never. This isn't what I do."

"Then how could you know better?" The Colonel said more gently. "You're learning, just like us, how to deal with an assassin like this. You understand his methods and his skill set. That's why you're here. Giving orders is my job, my responsibility."

Trace nodded, but he was not convinced. He had spotted the original signs at the mansion. He had been briefed on the first capture attempt. He had actually gone up against the assassin. It was his fault. He shouldn't have suggested they try to catch him. Stupid..stupid...stupid.

Chapter 11

"The final version is only in the server on the fourth floor, where we work on it, in the main building. I don't see how we could get a copy out or destroy the original." The spy blurted out.

"There has to be a way. Think!"

"I'm trying sir. I just don't see a way, unless they try to move it out and we can intercept it again."

"Could we go in by force?" Kelsi asked. Not sure if his spy had the necessary knowledge to answer this. For that matter, Kelsi didn't either. He had no idea what a direct assault would entail, but he had access to people who did. This was not a job for Neko, it had to be brute force. "Never mind. What I need you to do is write down the security procedures, how many guards are in the building, which computer and where is it in the building? Windows nearby, power outlets, circuit panels, and" Kelsi tried to think what else an attacking force would need, "exits. Mark all the exits."

"I will try sir. It will take a while. Do you want me to email it?"

"Do it right now. Yes, email it but not from anything that can be tracked to you."

"Sir, I do computer security, you don't have to tell me."

"Send it out as fast as you can." With that, Kelsi disconnected the call.

"Colonel, it's been three days. The FBI still doesn't have anything?" Trace was antsy. Not used to sitting on his hands. "They didn't give us anything helpful on any of the attacks. Could they be withholding information?"

"No, Trace. I doubt that. Agent Jares might not care for you, but he has all the brass breathing down his neck and wants answers as much as we do."

"I doubt that. He's not in the line of fire. To him, it's another assignment, an important one, but nothing more. What about Catherine? Have you been able to talk her into disappearing back to where she came

76

from?" Trace said this, only belatedly looking to see if she was anywhere nearby.

"No, haha, I'm not convincing her to do anything. Nobody is. Nobody ever has. You obviously haven't spent much time around her or redheads in general."

"I've known a few of them." Trace said with a wistful look. "Can't say I understood them. Can't say I got much sleep with them either."

Colonel Thomas had just taken a sip of his coffee as Trace said this and immediately spit it out as he burst into a laughing fit. Timing being what it is, Catherine chose this moment to stride into the Colonel's office.

"What's so funny?" She asked.

"Trace was just telling me a story about some night operations." Colonel Thomas tried to cover. Which only made Trace snicker.

"What?!" She demanded, looking at Trace now.

"If you really want to know, I was telling the Colonel about my previous encounters with redheads." Trace replied calmly.

"Let me guess," she began, with a withering look, "they were all nympho.."

Her words were cut off by a shrieking alarm. Colonel Thomas began moving and seconds later the gunfire started. Grabbing Catherine, the Colonel simply picked her up and carried her across the hall to Albert's office. Pulling a hidden lever, an entire wall of books swung open. Thomas unceremoniously threw Catherine inside the safe room and slammed the bookcase back in place. "Lock it down. Don't come out unless you hear me or Trace." He turned to see Trace at the office door.

"Gunfire is below us. Sounds like it's moving up from the lower levels." Trace said quickly. "What do you want me to do?"

"Grab some radios from that shelf. With Catherine in the safe room, I can investigate. You stay on this floor. Protect Catherine." As he said this, Thomas reached into his desk, pulling two pistols out, he tossed one to Trace, at the same time, Trace tossed a radio to him. There was already confused chatter coming from the radios. Thomas activated his radio. "This is Colonel Thomas, what's happening?"

"Sir, control room, tangos breached the manned security on level one. Looks like all our men are down on that floor. Multiple gunshots. The tangos are moving up the stairs and in the elevators."

"Do you have a count? How many tangos?" The colonel asked calmly, with command in his voice."

Trace had already pulled the slide back far enough to verify a round in the pipe, then he dropped the magazine and checked it. Full. Ready.

"I don't know sir, they moved fast, efficient. There has to be at least ten."

"Get me counts. How many in the stairs, how many in the elevators? Teams two and three, leave your floors. Harden up the fourth floor. Put your principles in their safe rooms."

"Sir, team two lead, we are engaged. We cannot egress to the fourth."

"Copy team two, get your principles safe, then your men. The tangos will want to clear the floors as they go. Try to move up if you can."

Team two lead did not respond and the Colonel hoped it was because of a radio issue. Just then the elevator opened to his right. Gunfire erupted from the inside as soon as the doors opened a crack and continued until they were fully open. As he rolled into his office doorway. Four men moved out, professional, competent, hardened warriors. The man in the front of the stack was a giant. At least six and a half feet and three hundred pounds. Thomas knew he was screwed, all he had was the Sig in his hand and Trace across the hall. He could see Trace just behind the doorframe, a calm look on his face, his left hand up, three fingers extended. As he watched, Trace dropped one, then two fingers. When his third finger went down, Thomas fired. Hitting the frontman dead center. The big man didn't even stagger, he swung his m4 toward the Colonel, but then Trace was there. He moved in tight against the lead man, firing a round down into the man's left knee, then one up under the jaw. As the big man began to crumple, Trace grabbed his tactical vest at the shoulder and twisted the big body to his left, clearing a line to shoot the second man in the throat, while using the big body to protect him from the third man. Colonel Thomas's second round went through the third man's bicep, entered his armpit, and continued across his chest. Destroying lungs and arteries.

The last man in the stack had a straight shot at Trace and pulled the trigger, putting three rounds into a target that wasn't there anymore. Trace had only moved a little, just barely enough to get off the shooting line. Pivoting to his right, instead of shooting the last man, Trace's hand shot out, going past the left side of the gunman's head. As Trace pulled the pistol back, he angled his wrist at ninety degrees and rolled the hammer under the assaulter's helmet, hooking it in the nerve point beneath the man's right ear. Pivoting back to his left and dropping to his right knee, Trace used the leverage and the hooked point to throw the attacker over himself and into the metal door frame. Despite the helmet, the last man was knocked unconscious.

Colonel Thomas rose from his kneeling position at the door and headed for the stairs to assist his team one level down.

Trace stepped quickly into the elevator, pulling the 'emergency stop', locking out the elevator. That only left one elevator and two stairwells to cover. One down and one up to the roof.

"Piece of cake." He thought sarcastically as he went about verifying the first three shooters were dead, then securing the last one.

"Fifth floor clear. Coming down the stairwell." The Colonel called over the radio as he descended the stairs. "Team two, status?..... Team two lead, respond!" No answer. *"Damn it!"* He thought. "Team three, status?"

"Sir, team three lead, principles in the safe room. We are with team four and are hardening the entries." Kevin responded so calmly, one would think this happened all the time.

"Team four lead, respond."

"Sir, team four lead." Luka came back in a sharp voice.

"Luka, start destroying computers. I want you to personally stand next to the server. Make sure you have enough rounds to completely destroy it, but only if you know we have lost. Also, position crossfire elements on the elevator. Tangos used it to get to the fifth floor."

"Yes sir!" Luka pointed to Kevin and then the elevator. Kevin moved two members of team three to crossfire on it. Luka and one of his team began moving swiftly through the cubicles and tables meticulously dispatching computers. Under other circumstances, *"this would be great fun,"* he thought as he moved and fired.

Colonel Thomas arrived at the fourth-floor landing only moments before the four-man assault team coming up. Bullets chased him through the fire door. At that same moment, the elevator began to open on to the fourth floor. The assaulters tried the same technique as the team on the fifth floor had, unloading on full auto as soon as the doors cracked. Team three waited calmly, professionals. With their weapons trained on the space, they held fire until a target appeared. Three of the assaulters were killed with the first five rounds from team three. The fourth attacker hid behind the edge of the door, effectively shielded. This worked for him until Kevin simply walked up, reached his pistol around the corner, and stitched rounds from knee height to head height, killing the last man.

As the team four men shot the last laptop, Luka stationed himself next to the server. He was itching to get in the fight. Waiting to kill a computer was not the same thing, but he knew it was important. He could just see the far edge of the stairwell door from where he waited. He saw one of team three and the Colonel. He knew that two of his team were there also but couldn't see them. He could hear the firefight going at the elevator, but it wasn't visible from his location either.

"Back away from the door!" Colonel Thomas bellowed. "There's no reason to think that they don't have breaching charges. Get clear!"

As the four men moved back from the door to cover, the door blew in. Rounds started coming through like a burst beehive. Then Luka saw the grenades. He identified them in a brief glimpse, he threw his hands to his ears and turned his back to the brilliant flash. When he turned back, the first attacker was coming through the twisted door frame. A burst from one of his team dispatched the first attacker. A second attacker dove through the frame firing toward his unseen team. Luka saw the Colonel's Sig buck twice, killing the second attacker, but the third and fourth were already through the door. One fired at Colonel Thomas and the other fired at the team three man with Thomas. Luka saw the Colonel launch over a file cabinet, part of his own power and partly from the rounds that tore into his left shoulder and upper arm. Luka fired at the fourth shooter and noted with satisfaction that his head exploded in a red spray. He swung his weapon to take the third attacker when his team four man, that had been shooting computers, put three rounds into the tango's upper chest and throat.

After a few moments, the men at the elevator shouted "clear". Kevin reached in and pulled the emergency stop, adding that alarm bell to the cacophony of alarms and approaching sirens. After checking the landing, the team three man who had been with the Colonel yelled "clear".

Luka ran over to check on the Colonel, who was lying on the floor, bleeding profusely. "Sir, are you still with me?"

"Yea, Luka. I'm still here. Fuck, that hurts." He groaned. "Put a man on the server. We still might have to destroy it, if there are more of them. Call control, can they see anymore?"

"Control, team four lead, anymore Tangos?"

"Team four lead, I can't see anymore. I rewound the footage and counted twelve total. Do you have a count?"

"Control, hold one. Kevin," Luka called out, "how many tangos you got?"

"Four" was the reply, "all dead."

"Larry, how many over there?"

"Four, all toast."

"We got four on the fifth floor also." The colonel said to Luka. "Trace took one alive. I don't think we should tell the authorities about that one." He winked, then sighed. "Take three men, clear the rest of the building. Go down first. Cops should be here soon, sirens are close. Then go get the last one from Trace and lock him in one of the safe rooms until the authorities are gone."

Luka and Larry dragged the Colonel over to the server, where Larry applied pressure to the wounds and kept an eye on the landing. Kevin took his two men from the elevator and formed up with Luka. A quick glance told both of them that the two team four men that had been at the stairwell door were dead. It took the four men ten minutes to clear floors one, two, and three. Luka had Kevin wait to meet the SWAT team. He then sent the other two men to release civilians from the safe rooms on all the floors and check for injuries. Lastly, he went to the top floor.

"Mr. Conner? It's Luka. We're all clear on the other floors." Luka said this as he looked at the line of three bodies on the floor. Confusion spread across his features as he tried to visualize how it went down up here. "I hear you got a live one."

"Yea," Trace replied, "over here."

Luka walked around the office door to see a Tango lying on his face. Although the man was still unconscious, Trace had secured his hands behind his back with paracord. Luka looked at the cord, the joint positions, and the unusual knots questioningly.

"It's very convenient when they bring their own restraints. I don't normally carry that on me." Trace said shrugging.

"Y'all are gonna have to tell me what happened up here. Seems like a good story. In the meantime, Colonel wants this Tango stashed in a safe room. Away from the cops."

Trace nodded his head. Of course, cops had to follow rules, lawyers, and all that. While we still need answers. "Is everybody ok?" He asked.

"No. We lost a bunch of men. The Colonel is hit and is gonna need medevac and serious wound care. He'll probably be out for at least a week, maybe longer."

"Are we secure enough to get Ms. Dewal out of the safe room?"

"Yes, we have men pulling all the civvies out of the other safe rooms now. So, we can let her out too."

"Great...any idea how we do that? I saw the Colonel swing a bookcase open, but no clue how he did it."

"Hmm..," the big man said, "I'll go ask. Never even seen the safe room on this floor."

"Catherine..it's Trace Conner. It's safe to come out. Can you find the release?" Trace yelled loudly.

"You don't need to yell, Mr. Conner." Her voice came from a speaker hidden in the books. "There is a microphone, so I can hear you just fine. Can you step back a little, so I can see you on the camera feed, please?"

Trace did as she asked, looking around for the hidden camera. He didn't find it before the bookcase swung open. Luka dragged the still unconscious attacker to the safe room and threw him in without any pretense of being nice. Noting with satisfaction how the man's head bounced off the floor, this time with no helmet.

"Luka, we still need to question him." Trace scolded the big SEAL.

"Let me do it, he'll talk."

"No doubt, but I'll wait in the safe room with him until we have the building to ourselves again. Then, we can question him. I'll keep him quiet too." Trace said and then pulled the bookcase back into place with a quiet click.

Turning to face the big SEAL, Catherine demanded. "Mr. Luka, is it? Where is Lloyd? The Colonel."

"This way ma'am, he's hurt. He should be getting evac'd right now."

Chapter 12

"What do you mean I can't shut it down?" Catherine demanded into the phone pressed to her ear. "It's my company and my people are dying for this project." She paused, " We have over ten million already in this and you're gonna threaten me with a breach of contract? You're a prick, you want it that bad, you come to get it!" With that, she slammed the phone down.

"Catherine," Thomas began, "try to relax a little. We'll figure it out."

"No, Lloyd, I am going to shut it down. My brother is dead, our people are dead. We've lost what, twelve people including my brother?" She demanded with tears welling in her eyes and her voice cracking. "Now you have to go into surgery, Russell is still down. How many more do we have to lose? Maybe the government will force us to give them a program, but we can always give them the old one and tell them it never got any better."

"I've been coordinating with Luka. He'll keep the main building locked down. There are police, FBI, and DOD personnel there. The building will be safe for a while. Nobody would try anything right now." He sighed out, having expended most of his energy talking to her.

"We didn't think anybody would have tried to attack our main offices, but they did." She countered.

"Not true," Lloyd interjected, "Trace must have. It was his suggestion that we pull everyone from the mansion and put them at HQ. Otherwise, we would've had fewer men on site and probably would've lost everything."

"Speaking of him, where is he?" Catherine asked.

"Luka said he was following a lead. Not sure what that was. Said he'd tell me after surgery. If Trace hadn't been on the fifth floor with us, I'd be dead for sure, and maybe you too. You should have seen the way he moved through that tango stack. Like he was water or a dust devil. Then he just sent the last guy flying through the air, like the guy was made of paper or something. Spooky to watch." Lloyd mumbled the last.

"Rest Lloyd, sounds like the drugs are starting to affect you. I'll see if I can find our 'Ninja' and coordinate with Luka on security until you wake up."

"They failed!" Kelsi said into the phone. "You promised me that your team could do this! I paid you half up front! According to my police contacts, they are all dead and they made one hell of a mess of the job. Killing everybody they crossed. I thought they were supposed to be professionals!"

"They were." The man on the other end of the line said in a British accent. "They were all experienced soldiers, turned mercenary. I have used them for a long time, this will hurt my business considerably and cost me a fortune to replace them."

"You better not be asking for more money! They failed!" Kelsi screamed into the phone. "How the hell am I supposed to get anything from those computers now? What if some of them got caught? Then what? SHIT!"

"As you said, they are all dead. Even if one or more was caught, they won't talk. They couldn't if they wanted to, they were only told to get the tech and the computer you specified, nothing else. Besides, it would be the FBI doing the questioning. Civil rights and all that."

"You are awful calm about this. I don't want to go to a federal penitentiary!" Kelsi yelled.

"Relax," the man said calmly, "I am the only one who knows who you are or how to get hold of you. None of the men I sent know who I am. All contact with me is blind."

"What the fuck does that even mean?! 'Blind', they wear blindfolds or something?"

"Nothing so melodramatic. We have never met face to face, the contact system is not direct and only the leader and his second even know how to initiate contact. I am far more concerned about their failure. It seems that you may have provided me with erroneous information, leading to failure."

"Or they weren't as good as you think and they were just outmatched!" Kelsi shot back.

"Possibly, maybe both. You told me that they were 'armed security'. They must have been more than that or many more men than I was told."

"Call it whatever you want. You failed!" Kelsi wanted to tell him to expect a visit from Neko, but that wouldn't accomplish anything. "The agreement was 'second half on completion', so don't expect that half!"

The man on the other end sighed loudly. "As a gesture of goodwill, I will forego any additional compensation for the loss of my team."

"*Like I care.*" Thought Kelsi, but said aloud, "Good. I'll contact you if I need more done. Just find a better team for the next time."

"Mr. Conner?" Luka yelled at the bookcase. "Mr. Conner!"

"Easy Luka," a voice emanated from the shelving, "the microphone pickups are plenty strong."

"Sir, the police and Feebs have all moved outside the building. I think it's safe for you to come out."

With a quiet 'click', the bookcase swung out. Trace exited the saferoom to stand in front of Luka. "How is the Colonel?"

"In surgery, last I heard," Luka replied.

"How does it look for him?"

"I ain't a doc.."

"Yea, but you have seen combat. Tell me your opinion." Trace said.

"Didn't look too bad. He's messed up, for sure. Looked like a round in the shoulder and one in the arm. Didn't see any bubbles or shooting blood, so they can probably fix him up pretty quick."

"Good thing you were there to save his ass."

"Think he'll remember that when I ask for a raise?" Luka joked. "Speaking of saving his ass....what happened up here? I told the Feebs that the Colonel took out all three bad guys. Wasn't much of an explanation and they wanted a better one."

"Sucks to be them, eh?" Trace asked with a smirk. "Anyhow, I need you to get video security to look through the recordings for anyone in a lime green shirt."

"Lime green? Why?"

"Our friend in there, says they were told not to kill somebody in a 'lime green shirt'. I don't know if that was their mole or if it was somebody they thought they needed for the project. He doesn't know either."

Luka leaned around the corner to see the only survivor from the assaulters, staring back toward him with huge eyes. "Damn, Mr. Conner, what did you do to him?"

"I told him that 'real big guy' out there, said he had a cute ass and wanted to spend some alone time with him. After that he just started singing like a canary, the only problem is that he only knows one song."

"That's not funny, man," Luka growled. "What should we do with him now?"

"Give him to the Feds, tell 'em we found him hiding in a roof access or something. They can try longer to break him and we can't afford the manpower to guard him." Trace replied. "Besides, I'm sure he doesn't know anything else."

"How can you be so sure?" Luka let the question hang, seeing that Trace was not going to answer it. Grabbing the bad guy, Luka looked quickly for new burn marks, cuts, bruises, or some other visible sign of torture, but was relieved and baffled to not find any. Turning to take the man down to the FBI, Luka could see the man was terrified of Conner. Luka raised a questioning eyebrow at Trace.

Trace looked back blankly as his mouth twisted into that same smirk.

As he marched the prisoner away, Luka looked back to Trace. "I don't need the videos. I know who was wearing a lime green shirt."

"Agent Jares," Catherine began, pointing at the monitor between them. "We want to focus the security on this man. Ken Tellu, he is on the project design team. His specialty is security and encryption." She let the information speak for itself.

"So, if this is your mole, he is going to be very hard to catch red-handed," Jares replied.

"Definitely," Catherine answered while Trace stood a respectful distance and kept his mouth shut.

"Why do you think it's him?"

"We aren't sure it is. I heard one of the bad guys say, 'remember to grab the guy in the lime green shirt'." She lied. "That day, only Ken Tellu was wearing a lime green shirt. Plus, it makes sense. The encryption on the program would take months to beat, unless they had a little help, like the key or a hint. Ken would've known that."

Jares looked flatly at Trace as he said, "you heard them say that?" Obviously not believing her.

"Yes, I'm crystal clear on that." Catherine stared the agent down. "One hundred percent."

"Okay, then. I'll move the entire surveillance team to cover this one man?"

"Yes. That would be good."

"What about your pet killer over there? He doesn't have anything to say today?" Jares tried to provoke Trace.

"He's not my 'pet killer'. So far, he has saved my life and..." Catherine trailed off.

"And?" The agent demanded.

"And, he is a consultant." She said defiantly.

Trace looked at the agent and a small smile crossed his lips, but not a sound.

"Mr. Conner.." Catherine began.

"Trace, call me Trace."

"Trace, Lloyd thinks you knew we were going to be attacked. Is that true?"

"No. Not at all. I was much more concerned with the assassin coming for you again. It never crossed my mind that they might send in a whole team like that." Trace shook his head. "They were just shooting everyone, I don't understand that. Makes no sense to me..."

"No, it doesn't." She said, struggling to hold back tears. "Almost all the people we lost had family, many of them had young children. Now their mommies and daddies, husbands and wives, are gone for this stupid program! I can't even get rid of it! Did you hear about that?"

"No, why not?"

"The DOD says they will sue us for breach of contract if we don't deliver the program, but they won't come to get the fucking thing! We have to take all the risk and we can't get rid of it!" She screamed, pounding her fist on the table.

"Maybe this gives us a path.." Trace said, pondering.

"How so?"

"Give me a sec. Let me think it out."

Wanting to scream but trying hard to hold it back and be patient, Catherine just watched him. She knew patience was not her strong suit, but she knew so little about this. If only her brother were still here, the two of them could figure it out, together they could solve any problem.

"We think Ken is the spy, what if we force him to make contact?"

"How do we force him to do it?" She asked.

"He's the encryption guy, right? We get him to help us pull the hard drives that have the program and put new encryption on them. He'll think he's still trusted, but he'll have to let the enemy know that we pulled the drives and they left with me." Trace said slowly. "We make sure he knows that I have all the copies of the program. That should keep everybody safe here. There won't be a reason for them to come here again." Picking up speed as the plan coalesced in his mind. "I leave, nobody really knows me. It will make it very hard for them to track me. Maybe, I can stay mobile long enough for the DOD to accept the program. Then I'll deliver it myself."

"I can't ask you to do that. They'll kill you to get the program!"

"They'll TRY to kill me. I'm pretty hard to kill, ask my brother." Trace replied with a big smile, that just as quickly faded from his face. Replaced with a sad look. "Seriously, if they send the same killer, I stand a better chance than anyone here. Your security team is top-notch, but they can't protect all your people. If I take the T-FAX, the danger should leave too."

"I don't know. Trace." She said his name hesitantly. "I just..I'm not sure. The DOD will have a stroke if they find out. You aren't even cleared for the project."

"Technically, you weren't cleared either. I agree it's a little crazy, but not insanity. Insanity is defined as 'doing the same thing and expecting a different result'. Keeping it here is insanity. We need to do something different. Let's run it by the Colonel, I'm not a tactician and I want to get his view on it. Maybe ask Luka and a few of the other combat guys for ideas too."

"Okay," she replied slowly, "he should be out of surgery by now. Let's go over to the hospital."

"I don't like it." The Colonel said flatly. "You'll be all alone, no backup. If that psycho finds you and grabs it, we won't even know."

"That's why we have Alan here. I propose we put an 'Easter egg' in the program. If someone tries to open it, it will self-erase." Trace answered.

"Easter egg?" The Colonel asked.

"An 'Easter egg' refers to something that is hidden in a program to find later during usage," Alan answered. "That's not technically what a 'self-erase' would be, but close enough for our discussion. If we hide it in the Python code, it would look like a simple data fetch request."

"Hide it in the Python?" The Colonel asked.

"Python," Alan answered, "is a coding language. We are using it in part of the T-FAX to fetch historical data for the algorithm."

"You can do that for sure?" Catherine asked.

"Yes, it's very simple. I already wrote it at Mr. Conner's request." Alan said. "I just need a few minutes to add it to the program."

"Well...I like that part, but why not just use Luka and the other guys to take it to a military base?" The Colonel said. "Some of the guys still have privileges and we can hunker down there."

"The closest bases are San Joaquin and Camp Parks." Trace replied. "I thought of that too. San Joaquin is such a busy place, with all the equipment moving in and out. We'd never be able to control the people around it. Camp Parks is Army and a former prison camp, so security would be vastly better, but the enemy must have people in the DOD and possibly the military. If we could get it on a Special Forces base like Coronado or something, that would be great. I just don't see the military letting us bring an armed force of our own on to a restricted base."

90

"Ungh...." The Colonel grunted out, putting his hand on his shoulder. "Hand me my phone, I'll start making calls to old buddies still in, who can get us that permission. Although, you're probably right. I doubt we can get that permission..... Okay, Alan, put the 'Easter egg' in. Make sure you do it with nobody around except Luka. IF I can't get permission for a SF base, we'll go with Trace's plan."

"I have some other suggestions for the plan, but we can discuss those later." Trace said looking at Catherine. "So, if Catherine gives us the ok, we should move forward."

Catherine nodded her head. "I still think it's too dangerous, but you're right about our people. I just don't want to lose anymore, no matter what it costs us."

"Have you figured out what you're going to tell the DOD?" Colonel Thomas asked.

"I don't plan to tell them at all." She said. "If they find out and whine, I'll say that I asked them for help and they didn't come to get it, so, tough shit."

"That part doesn't make sense," the Colonel stated, "they could bring in any of the SF teams or a platoon of marines and securely take the program away. Somebody in the DOD must be blocking assistance to keep the program out, where it's vulnerable."

"I was thinking that too." Trace said. " There must be more than the spy in MIGIsoft. Somebody had to pass on the pickup date and description of Ferand. If we can get one string to pull on, maybe we can get more of it to unravel."

"How are we ever going to hand it off to the DOD, if someone there is blocking it?" Alan asked.

"Let's start by getting it away from MIGIsoft. I want to take the drives, not just copies. Then there won't be any incentive to send someone to MIGIsoft's HQ." Trace continued. "I'm going to start contacting other Ninjutsu senseis around the world. Someone with the skill this killer has must train consistently. It's possible he crossed paths with someone I know."

"So?" Catherine asked. "Can't he just do his training alone? Workouts and all, like I saw you doing?"

"Katas, kamaes, and so on, yes. But when it comes to keeping that level of skill up, you need real bodies to train against." Trace answered. "In his case, he needs highly skilled opponents to practice with. There are lots of choices around the world, but percentage-wise, that's only like .0001 of the population. Somebody I know may have crossed paths with him. I hope."

"Once before," the Colonel began, "you said we're screwed if he is a Ninja. What did that mean? Can't you take him if it's your art?"

"First, there is more than one Ninjutsu school. Some are still hidden from westerners and even from the Japanese." Trace went on. "In my school, we teach seven different styles. Two of those are actually historic Ninjutsu, the rest are karate, jujitsu, or bone-breaking styles."

Catherine shivered at the mention of a 'bone-breaking' style, then interrupted, "but you stopped him at the hotel. You should be able to do it again."

"I came out of nowhere and surprised him, I got lucky. What worries me is that my second strike should have broken at least one of the bones in his forearm. I'm not sure it did. That takes a lot of skill to prevent that." Turning back to the Colonel, Trace said, "Second, you guys think I can do amazing stuff. To people outside my art, I can, but inside my art, I'm not even technically a 'master'. Every time I go to Japan to train with the Grandmaster, he kicks my ass, like you beating a two-year-old. I've never been able to touch him and he's over eighty! The 'master teachers' can do mind-boggling stuff, even to me."

"Again, so?" The Colonel asked.

"So...if he is at that level in another Ninjutsu school, he'll beat my ass in nothing flat."

"Then you shouldn't do this," Catherine stated flatly.

"I have to. We don't know who or what he is. I still stand a better chance than anybody you have. Also, I'm thinking that a day or so after I leave, Colonel Thomas sends Luka, Kevin, and another man or two to help watch my back. Give me an advantage."

Colonel Thomas nodded his head. "Yea, I like that. We can set them up with some spotting equipment and other electronic gear to monitor you."

"Don't forget the long gun." Trace said seriously. "I would still rather put a hole in this guy from a few football fields away. Testing my skill against him just for vanity is stupid."

"Agreed." The Colonel replied. "I'll have Luka talk to the guys, see if any of them have done 'sniper school'. I don't remember it, but maybe one of them had the training and left it early, or something. Of course, my memory right now is a bit muddled."

"Good. You make those calls and I'll start making arrangements to get out of here with the program. Just in case you can't get it on to a SF base." Trace said, turning to leave.

"I don't understand why you had me rent such an old beater," Luka said, as he looked at the 2008 Ford expedition.

"Because I didn't want a vehicle that might have a GPS or locator on it." Trace answered. "We don't know how well connected the enemy is, and I want to make it as hard as possible for them to find me. Hopefully, the Colonel will call me in a day or two and say 'swing by Coronado and drop it off'. I doubt it, but we can hope."

"They can use your phone," Luka responded.

"I plan to pull the battery and sim card before I leave. They shouldn't know who I am, that's why everybody referred to me with a fake name. That should give us some time. Speaking of which, make sure the security guys all keep calling me Trace or Mr. Eldridge. Especially around Ken Tellu."

"After today, it won't matter." Catherine began, "at the end of today, I'm giving everybody on that team a month off, and then we'll re-assign them to completely different teams and areas, all separate from each other. Hopefully, this will all be done before they come back."

"Bye Catherine, stay safely out of sight until we know that the story about me leaked." Turning to Luka, "see you soon."

Pulling his cellphone out, Trace popped the backplate off and pulled the battery and sim card out. Dropping them into separate pockets, he climbed into the expedition.

"Goodbye Trace, please be careful," Catherine said, with a slight catch in her voice.

"What did that mean?" Trace wondered.

"Watch your six," Luka said seriously and stood back waiting to escort Catherine back inside the main building.

"We pulled the hard drives and they're gone." Ken Tellu said quickly into the phone jammed against his ear.

"Gone? You mean the product is gone?" Kelsi asked.

"That's exactly what I mean. They had me change the encryption key, then they pulled the drives out, handed them to this guy, then him and the big security guy left." Frantic now, Ken went on. "The entire program was on there. Without those drives, we don't have anything!"

"Who was this guy?"

"I don't know, some consultant. They kept calling him Tres. You know, three in Spanish."

"Did he have a last name?" Kelsi queried, trying to be patient and get as much information as he could. "What does he look like?"

"Now that you mention it, the big security guy called him 'Mr. Eldridge'. Yea, that was it Tres Eldridge. About six feet tall, dark hair, white skin but tan, blue eyes, good shape....um...I don't think he's a soldier like the other security, but it looked like they respect him."

"Did you see what he was driving, a license plate number?"

"It was an SUV, white, at least a few years old. I don't know what the license plate was. I couldn't just walk out and look! Oh, wait...I remember the logo on the SUV was oval-shaped." Ken said quickly.

"So, a Ford SUV? Small, medium, or large?"

"I would say medium. Definitely not small, but not as big as the giant ones the company has here. Could probably hold six or seven people."

"That'd make it a white, Ford expedition. Not new, ten years old or more?" Kelsi asked.

"I would say about ten years old, but I'm not a car guy."

"Alright, if we can't find this guy, can we grab some of the other people from the project and just make it from scratch?" Kelsi asked, looking for options.

"Grab who?" Ken shrieked. "Your kill squad executed most of the people who did the framework. They all worked on the second floor, I heard that everybody on that floor was killed. Then Albert created the critical algorithms. Without those people and Albert, no, there's no way."

"None at all? You're sure?"

"NONE!" Ken screamed into the phone. "Everybody is dead! Do you hear me? Dead! I thought I was dead! I thought they were gonna kill me too!"

"Relax," Kelsi said soothingly, "the team had orders not to kill you. That's why I had you wear that ugly shirt."

"Understand this, Kelsi, if you don't get those drives, we did all this for nothing."

"I got it. See if you can get me any more info on who this consultant is." Kelsi pressed.

"I can't. At the end of the day, they sent us home. Told us to take a month off and recover from the attack. By the time I go back to work, this will be all over. I don't want to go back to work, understand me?" With that Ken hung up.

Freshman special agent Scott Mills knocked on the doorframe to Agent Jares office. "We got him!"

"Ken Tellu?" Jares asked.

"Yup. We couldn't actually hack the phone, it's one of the new Samsung Galaxy units, but we were able to turn on the mic and listen to everything he said."

"I want to hear the recording."

"Should be hitting your inbox, right about....now." Mills said and pointed at the computer on Jares's desk.

Sure enough, there was an email just arrived bearing an audio attachment, with a computer assigned date and time stamp. Jares had to acknowledge electronic receipt, then saved the file to his local drive. Once done, he clicked on it to open the file and turned up the speakers on his computer.

"Do we know who 'Kelsi' is? Where he works?" Jares asked.

"Not yet, this just happened. We are researching all of Tellu's past schools, groups, jobs, fan clubs, comic con visits, Facebook, Twitter, and any other rock we can kick over." Mills answered. "So far, no luck, but we just started."

"Keep on it." Jares instructed, "we need more answers ASAP."

"Now that we have proof, should we go pick him up?"

"Not yet. I want to keep him in play a little longer. I don't think he's a threat and I'm afraid picking him up will tip our hand. Just keep capturing anything we can and find out who Kelsi is."

"Yes, sir." Agent Mills said as he went back to his cubicle.

"So, you gave this program, that everybody wants so bad, to your pet killer?" Jares asked Catherine.

"How do you know that?"

"We recorded the conversation talking about it."

"Then Ken was the spy," Catherine announced triumphantly. "Are you going to arrest him?"

"Not yet. We're gonna keep gathering intel on him to make a strong case. I'm calling so that you keep him away from anything critical."

"I told everyone to take a month off. He won't be near anything." She said.

"Even so, keep him segregated from important information. I want to keep him in play, just in case." The agent repeated. "Where did your pet killer go? That's government property, you gave him."

"I couldn't get the government to come take it, so I got rid of it to protect my people. If you want to take it, by all means, I'll have Trace bring it to you. They've only killed what, twelve people so far? I'm sure you can handle it." She replied sarcastically.

"Why give it to him?"

"My 'pet killer' as you call him, seems to be the only one capable of staying alive against this invisible enemy. If we knew who we were facing, maybe we could go a different route."

"Speaking of invisible enemy," agent Jares interrupted, "do you know of anybody named 'Kelsi'."

Catherine paused for so long, Jares wondered if she had hung up on him. Then she slowly said, "no...I can't think of anybody by that name. I'll ask the Colonel when I go back to the hospital. Maybe he has crossed paths with someone by that name."

"Good, keep me informed of where your 'consultant' is."

"No."

"What?" Jares replied indignantly. "I need to know where he is with the program."

"I'll let him know that you care about his welfare, but he decides to share his location with you or not. Besides the spy in our shop, there has to be somebody in the government working against us. Why else wouldn't they come to get the finished program? In fact, I bet that if you try to get permission to take the program yourself, you'll be told no, and given some bullshit reason."

"The government is corrupt? Helicopters and black SUVs? It's all a conspiracy? Come on Ms. Dewal, there has to be a legitimate reason for that. I just don't know what it is. I'll make some calls. Keep your man close."

"Goodbye Agent Jares." With that Catherine ended the call.

Chapter 13

Trace had driven east for about an hour and decided the risk from his phone was minimal. The enemy either had him already or didn't. Using the phone shouldn't make much difference. Putting the battery and sim card back in, he accessed his contact list and started calling other Ninjutsu dojos around the world. He gave each a description of the killer and his strikes, asking them to talk to their students as well. He finished making calls as he rolled into Lake Tahoe. He hadn't talked directly to all the other Senseis, but those he couldn't reach, he left a long message for. Trace planned to head south from Tahoe, back to Arizona. It was a far longer drive to get home, but the roads were more isolated and it would be easier to spot a suspicious vehicle following him. It was late fall and the mountains he would be driving through already had some snow. The Ford Expedition had a great four-wheel drive and, if needed, he could use that advantage.

At seven a.m. the next morning, Trace was eating breakfast in the small town of Walker, California. Not much more than a rest stop, he was refueling both the Ford and himself. He had pulled off highway 395 into the woods just before midnight, then crawled in the back and folded all the seats down for a mostly flat, though not comfortable rest.

The tired, pregnant young waitress had just delivered his egg scramble when his phone began to ring.

"This is Trace." He answered.

"Trace, this is Karl Paz in Croatia. I am returning your call." Said a voice with a heavy accent.

"Stitches! How are you old friend?"

"I am well. When will you stop calling me by that ridiculous name?"

"Hahaha...that is not gonna happen, my friend. When you get twelve stitches from the Grandmaster himself, you get stuck with the name."

Karl had a dojo in Rijeka, Croatia. A city on the Kvarner Bay in the northern Adriatic Sea. Karl had earned the nickname 'Stitches' during training in Japan, years earlier. While acting as 'uke', ('victim' as the Ninjutsu people defined it), for the Grandmaster, Karl had tried to 'counter the counter'. Meaning that he had tried to do a counter technique for the one the Grandmaster was demonstrating on him. Much to everyone's delight and laughter, the Grandmaster had simply redirected Karl's left fist into his own right eye. Splitting the skin open above that eye so bad that it required twelve stitches to close it again. Trace had made a similar mistake once and the Grandmaster had broken his collar bone. Fortunately for Trace, nobody had thought to nickname him 'chicken wing' at the time.

"God, there really is something wrong with us," Trace thought as he remembered all this in a flash. *"We must be sick to keep doing this."*

"Do not remind me," Stitches said in very good English, "I see the scar every time I look in the mirror. You could have taken a few minutes to make it look better."

"Hey now, it's not my fault you were cheap and didn't want to leave training to have a real doctor stitch that up. Besides, I was the only one who had a sewing kit that day!" Laughing now, Trace continued. "I did the best I could, maybe if your face wasn't so crunchy, I might've done better!"

"Hahaha," with a big laugh, Stitches said, "I miss you old friend. When are you coming to Rijeka again to teach a seminar for me?"

"Come on Stitches, you don't need me to teach to your students. I can't teach them anything that you don't know."

"Not true, my friend. You have a natural skill. Something that most of us do not. I know techniques and can teach, but there is something about the way you....flow? I think that is a good word for it. Like the Grandmaster does, it is very natural to you, and you are an excellent teacher."

"Thank you, that is very kind of you to say. Although, I am a very long way from the Grandmaster. We need to schedule a trip back to Japan together. Spend some time drinking at that Irish pub in Kashiwa!"

"That would be very good. Very good." Karl replied.

"So why the call Stitches?" Trace asked.

"Ah..yes. I listened to your message and it reminded me of someone who visited my dojo about a year ago. The description was close enough, but not very precise. What was specific was the way he used hand spears."

"Go on." Trace urged.

"He came in and attended the classes for about a week. He understood the techniques quickly, then he asked if anyone would spar with him. One of my fourth-degree black belts, Ivan, agreed. They decided that bruises would be allowed but no permanent injuries. The class watched for about fifteen minutes after the regular class. Ivan moves very well, he is young and has been training hard for about five years. Still, he was unable to make many successful attacks. This man never allowed Ivan to deliver any attacks with force, but I remember that he used hand spears a great deal. He always slowed the impact at the end, so as not to hurt Ivan. Afterward, he was very polite and thanked Ivan for training with him."

"What was his style like?"

"Many of the kamae he used looked like Kung Fu, but not as rigid. More organic. Very much like some of the Pencak Silat I have seen." Karl said slowly, referring to the Indonesian fighting style. Pencak Silat was a general term for the Indonesian arts but had a very distinctive look.

"Interesting, do you think his style is a combination of those?"

"Doesn't our style reflect all our previous training to some degree?" Karl asked. "I studied four other arts before Ninjutsu and you studied what...seven? Since starting this, how many others have you investigated?"

"Good point." Trace said but he was thinking of all the other arts he had studied before and after starting Ninjutsu. How much did those affect his own personal style?

"Any chance you have a name or phone number?" Trace asked.

"I will have a name and signature on the waiver form he signed. However, one of the students had been walking past him as he answered the phone after class one day. He said, 'this is Neko'. All of us assumed that he was Japanese. We talked about the name and that is why I remember it. That and he didn't actually speak any Japanese. Do you think this could be the man you are looking for?"

"Maybe....any chance there is a picture?"

"Please, Trace. You know that none of us like pictures, why would we take one of visitors?" Stitches responded indignantly.

"Yea, just thought I'd ask. Can you get me that name from the waiver? I doubt it's real, but it might help."

100

"For you, my friend, I will look. It may take some time as I do not know who I am looking for."

"Thanks, Stitches, I really appreciate the help."

"No problem. Come to Rijeka, if you don't want to teach, we will take the boat and do some more diving." Karl teased him, knowing how much Trace loved to scuba dive.

"I will do that. It may be a few months, but I will definitely do that. Goodbye Stitches."

"Goodbye Sensei." With that Karl hung up. Trace was flattered that Stitches referred to him as Sensei. Trace had never been Karl's teacher, but it was a sign of great respect from his friend.

"Hung Wong," Trace said into the Bluetooth earpiece.

"What's hung long?" Luka asked. Catherine, Luka, and Kevin all sat gathered around the phone in the center of the Colonel's hospital bed.

"That's the possible name for our mysterious killer. I'm sure it's bogus, probably just a funny one he made up. 'Neko' is the more likely name. He was overheard answering a phone call and said, 'this is Neko'." Trace said.

"Neko?" The Colonel asked.

"Neko is Japanese for 'cat'." Trace responded.

"So, this dude is Japanese?" Luka said.

"We don't think so. He spoke English, but no Japanese and no Croatian, we have no idea if he speaks other languages." Trace quickly explained how he had contacted other Sensei around the world looking for the killer. That Stitches had called him back and provided this lead.

"Are you sure this is him?" Catherine asked.

"No," Trace replied, "Stitches is going by my crappy description of his looks and his style. What little we know. The fact that he used hand spears while sparring and what looks like a fake name, makes me think it might be him. As I told the Colonel when we first met, hand spears are not that common."

"So, an Asian guy that uses hand spears during a sparring session. That's what we have to go on?" Luka asked doubtfully.

"Yea, I know it's not much. It may be completely off base. Nicknames are as common in the martial arts world as in the special force's community. Hell, every one of my students has a nickname, and an Asian guy that can use hand spears could still number in the thousands," Trace replied.

"Ok, so what do we do?" The Colonel asked.

"I was hoping that you SF guys have crossed paths with some spooks in the past. Any chance you have numbers you can call? Maybe ask them if they have ever heard of a killer that goes by 'Neko'?" Trace asked hopefully.

"I can call some people I know." The Colonel said.

"I might know a 'Smith' or two, I'll talk with the other guys, see if they know any." Luka Said.

"Catherine, you travel in circles the rest of us don't..." Trace began.

"What is that supposed to mean?" She shot back.

"It means you know people from a different social spectrum than we do." Trace replied. "Simple fact. Talk to people you know, charities, company owners, state department reps, and so on. Ask anybody you can. We're shooting in the dark here, so we might as well use a scattergun."

"Fine," she grumbled.

"What are you gonna do now?" The Colonel asked.

"I just got back to Flagstaff. I'm going to call the other dojos back, with this new information and see if we find any other links. I'll also call Agent Jares, give him this info and let him know where I am."

"Why?" Catherine asked. "He obviously hates you, he might be the one leaking information from the government side."

"Anything is possible at this point, but I doubt it. He didn't get brought in until after Ferand's murder, so I think that's unlikely." Trace responded. "He might unwittingly pass information to the government leak, but...I am kind of hoping for that."

"What!?" Catherine gasped. "Why would you want that?"

"If we can get Luka, Kevin, and our sniper moving now, I can pick them up from the airport in a few hours. If I call Agent Jares after they are in the air, we'll have plenty of time to get our team set up and prepped for the killer."

"Are you insane!?" She shouted at the phone. "If he surprises you, you're as good as dead!"

"I appreciate your concern." Trace began, "but we need to get a handle on who we're up against. That's why I want Luka and his team here. If we can draw this killer in and take him out, maybe, just maybe, we can find out who is behind this."

"What's to keep him from just shooting you from a distance?" Luka asked. "You hurt him, he might not want to tangle with you up close."

"I think he will." Trace answered. "I feel like it may be a point of pride with him. Mind you, I'm not positive, I have no desire at all to test my skills in a life or death fight. That's why I want a sniper. As far as him shooting me, he'd have to get inside my house anyway. The walls are six-inch-thick, rebar, and fiber reinforced concrete. I tested it, nothing short of a .50 can punch through. Thermal doesn't work, or it shouldn't, because of the heat sink qualities of the wall. The windows are all shatterproof, he could break them but it would take at least an hour to smash a hole big enough to crawl through, plus they have metal covers for when I travel. He'll have to come through a door."

"Were you always expecting something like this to happen?" Luka asked.

"Haha..no. Maybe a zombie apocalypse, but not a honed killer. I make extra money doing construction, dojos don't make any. When it came time to get a house, I pulled some favors and built the most energy-efficient thing I could. It's small but the benefit is that it's a fortress too."

"Well, if we're all agreed, we need to get the team moving and start making calls." The Colonel said.

They all nodded, Catherine last of all, but finally did.

"Um, guys....I'm on the phone here. Is that a yes?" Trace called out.

"Yes," Catherine answered with finality, "it's a yes."

Chapter 14

"Well Kelsi, what's your plan?" Cross asked. "We've spent a lot of money on this, but it appears that you lost it."

"Lost it, would imply that I had it, which I did not." Kelsi thought irritably.

"Sir, I have people looking everywhere." He answered out loud. "Our contact in their accounting department is looking for any reported expenses that might indicate where this 'consultant' took the drives. Our contact in the DOD is blocking receipt of the program until we can get it and is watching for any information on the government side."

"Listen to me very carefully, Oswald." Cross began in that nasally, irritating voice, using Kelsi's first name, which he hated. "If you fail to get this program before MIGIsoft puts it in DARPA's hands, there will be no future for you here. Or anywhere else."

Kelsi knew full well that 'no future' meant no future at all. He would get a visit from Neko or somebody like that. An assassin. He began, "Sir, the Defense Advanced Research Project Agency.."

"I know what DARPA stands for, Oswald!" Cross interrupted, actually raising his voice.

"Of course, Sir. Since our contact is a Deputy Director of DARPA, there is still a chance she could get us a copy of it after they have received it."

"And what will be the value then? Right now, we can get ask $500 million-plus. Once DARPA has it, the value plummets. That also assumes we can even get it. No. We need it and there can't be copies anywhere else!"

"I have every possible resource on this. Neko is standing by, ready to go anywhere we need it. If our contact just keeps stalling, we'll get it. We just need time." Kelsi answered.

"I'm not sure we have time. Oswald." Now Cross was using Kelsi's first name just to irritate him. "What's our exposure from the South African team?"

"From reports so far, they were all killed. None are in the hospital, so we are secure, if somewhat disappointed. We did spend $200,000 as a deposit, but they only knew to grab a person wearing a lime green shirt. Tellu was the only person who knew what to take. The team didn't even know they were there to steal the program."

"At least that's good news. Do you know why they failed? A twelve-man team seems like more than enough to get what we needed."

"We are not sure what happened. Either MIGIsoft's security was much better than we thought or Tellu didn't give us all the information or it was flawed. He's a computer guy, not a physical security type. He may not have known how important some information was. We're still getting reports, but they're slow. Our police informants aren't placed high enough to get it quickly. The FBI took over the site fairly quickly but we don't have anyone in the Feds. We'll have to wait for the report to trickle back through the DOD."

"Agent Jares, this is Trace Conner."

"What are you trying to pull, Mr. Conner?"

"Excuse me? I'm calling to give you my location and pass on some information I got." Trace replied.

"I want to know what your game is." Agent Jares said angrily. "Who are you and what qualifies you to be in the middle of my investigation?"

"You already know my name, you probably ran it, so you should know everything there is to know. As far as what qualifies me...I have been teaching this art for about twenty years. I've trained hundreds of students, some military, most not. I have a skill set that you don't."

"Killing people. That's your skill set?" Jares shot back.

"Do you have some record of me killing people that I am unaware of? Has a complaint been filed I know nothing about?"

"Don't get smart with me asshole! I can make your life hell!" Jares said.

"Look, Will..." Trace purposely used the agent's first name to irritate him, "I received some information that might be a link to the assassin. Do you want it or not?"

"It's probably bullshit, but sure, wow me with your mystical knowledge and all that crap."

Sighing, Trace relayed what little they knew of Neko, as well as his own location.

"That's it? An Asian guy, Hung Wong, and Neko? This is total bullshit, Conner! I think you're playing everybody. I don't know how yet, but I think you're in this." Jares growled.

"Will..why would I call in? I have the drives. I'm in Flagstaff, effectively out of your reach. Why should I tell anyone, let alone the Agent in Charge, where I am? Think about it. If I just wanted the program...I have it. Think man!"

After a long pause, Jares said, "I'll put a call into the Flagstaff field office. Let them know you're there."

"If I remember correctly, there is only one agent in that office." Trace said.

"Fine, I'll call the Phoenix office and see if they can send some people up there."

"If you're thinking about security, don't. I'll take care of my own. I don't want this assassin killing any more people."

"We're the FBI! We don't hide from killers!" Jares fairly shouted.

"I'm not telling you to hide. I'm asking you to investigate. Run down that lead, see if it goes somewhere. I'm on my home turf here, I have the advantage." Trace said.

"Fine. I'll let you know if this 'lead' has any legs, but don't hold your breath and don't go anywhere."

"Agent Jares?" Trace said calmly.

"Yea?" The surly reply.

"Never threaten me." With that, Trace disconnected the call.

"I'll threaten you as much..." Agent Jares realized that Trace was gone.

The phone on his desk was ringing when he walked into his office. Kelsi looked at it and considered ignoring it but saw that it was an internal call. Picking up the receiver and punching the button, he said. "Kelsi"

"Mr. Kelsi, it's Jeff."

"Yes, Jeff, have you tested the program finally?"

"Yes sir, well no...that's not why I called." Jeff stammered out. "Sara called me. A charge came through on one of their company credit cards for a car rental return and final bill."

Jeff was referring to Sara Bellis, a young mother of two who worked at MIGIsoft in the accounting department. Sara never finished college, she barely finished high school before getting pregnant with her first child. After giving birth to a little boy, the father got her pregnant again almost immediately. Promising to take care of Sara and the children, the handsome, intelligent, older man quickly dropped everything and disappeared. Forcing Sara to move back in with her parents, putting off college indefinitely. One night, Sara had stopped to have a few drinks with coworkers in a bar near MIGIsoft's offices.

Jeff was trolling the bars near MIGIsoft, looking for employees that he could befriend and gain access to what was going on at MIGIsoft. Sara wasn't ideal, she worked in accounting, but Jeff began talking her up anyway. He played it shy and Sara was enjoying the attention. She knew she wasn't ugly, but she wasn't a raving beauty. Since Jeff wasn't sure what would be gained from someone in accounting, he let her set the pace. Sara punched the gas. Before the night was out, she had convinced the self-proclaimed 'shy nerd' to have sex. Things progressed and soon Jeff was asking her about MIGIsoft's financials. After the first time, Jeff put two thousand dollars in her hand for some information that Sara thought was worthless, she was trapped. She realized that the attraction had been phony, but she consoled herself with the extra few thousand Jeff gave her every month. Now she passed on all types of information she still thought worthless, like hotel room stays and now, rental cars.

"Tell me she doesn't have your real phone number." "Kelsi said.

"Of course not, the number she has goes to a burner phone. I check messages and call her back. I wouldn't give her my real number."

"Fine, tell me what you have."

"So, Sara says a final bill came through for a rental of a 2008 Ford Expedition, which was returned in Flagstaff, Arizona. The gas tank was only half full, so they added an extra charge for topping it off." Jeff said triumphantly.

"Is she sure about this?"

"Mr. Kelsi, I can't push her too hard. She is totally freaked out by the shooting at their main building. She was demanding to know if what she had given me before, had anything to do with that." Jeff answered.

"And what did you tell her?"

"I assured her that I only try to keep track of MIGIsoft's financials so that my investors are confident about the company. I told her that the things she tells me about don't show up in profit and loss statements, but it is a good way to track how a company is really doing. Blah, blah, blah...and so on. I also pointed out that nothing she has told me would have helped some crazy gunmen storm their headquarters. Don't worry, she's not that smart." Jeff replied.

"Good. Sorry, I'm getting so used to incompetent people that I forget you're not one of them." Kelsi said.

"Oh, and on the program, we should have the system ready tomorrow and then we can start running tests, day after that."

"Fine, fine." Kelsi had not bothered to tell Jeff or the team that it didn't matter. They were going to have to start all over when the final program came in. This was just keeping them busy and out of his hair for now. "Thank you, Jeff."

"Goodbye"

"Bye." As Kelsi hung up the desk phone he pulled his cell and opened the 'red phone' app. Dialing a number from memory. When the call was answered, he said, "I have an address for you in Arizona."

Chapter 15

Trace was waiting for the small chartered plane at Flagstaff Pulliam Airport. Big commercial planes didn't come here, but that was just as well. The three former soldiers had gear that no airline would have let them carry on anyway.

"Luka, Kevin...good flight?" Trace asked, looking at the third man.

"Good enough, would have preferred a jet, but we're trying to stay low profile and all," Luka answered, then turned to the other man. "Trace Conner, meet Larry Reed."

"Mr. Conner, " Larry said.

"Call me Trace, like I keep telling Luka....you look very familiar."

"I was at the demonstration you gave with Luka and Kevin, I just didn't get to talk to you then."

"Oh, right. Of course, sorry." Trace said.

"No worries sir," Larry said amiably.

"You're my sniper, I take it?"

"Yes sir. Scout sniper school." Larry answered proudly.

"Don't take this wrong, but you seem kind of young to have done that and be out of uniform. Marines tend to hold on to snipers after they put all that time and money into their training."

"Yes sir. I joined at eighteen, did a tour in the sandbox, saw a little action and then I put in for sniper school. I was accepted, busted my ass, and thirteen weeks later I graduated. Two days after that I got so stupid drunk that I wound up in jail with multiple assault charges. The Corps decided they didn't want an idiot like me running around with one of their M40A6, so they sent me off for a dishonorable. Fortunately, I had saved somebody important in Iraq. I was still kicked out, but at least I got an honorable discharge." Larry finished.

"What are you shooting?" Trace asked.

"This here," Larry started, beaming like a proud parent, "is an MPA 308BA bolt action rifle. Custom made by Masterpiece Arms. I can nail a fly at 800 yards. A little farther if I have to."

"I don't think we'll need that much distance. The spot I'm thinking of is about two twenty-five or two fifty yards.

"At that distance, I can pop individual grapes out of a bunch," Larry said confidently.

"Good," Trace replied, "Cause if you miss, one or more of us may wind up dead."

"Yea," Luka mumbled, "let's not do that."

Neko looked out the window as the Boeing 737 circled on approach to land at Sky Harbor Airport in Phoenix, Arizona. He had always believed that all of Arizona was a desert. Something akin to the Sahara. This isn't what he saw, even in the desert, there were countless mountains. In the far north distance, he could see mountains rise up to block the view. He wondered if that was Flagstaff. Looking down he saw swimming pools dotting the landscape like morning dew on a fresh cut lawn. Bright green lawns, golf courses, and parks. So different from the land of his birth. No jungle, no canopy of trees to block the view of the ground, no swarms of mosquitos and other insects to attack and infect you with diseases.

As the plane taxied to the terminal, Neko powered on his phone. The bullet wounds were sewn and healing nicely. His left arm was still sore but had mostly healed, thanks to the treatments he had administered himself. His right arm was finally back to full strength. He wondered how he would kill the man who had inflicted that damage and caused him to fail for the first time in his professional life outside of China. He wasn't really angry, but his honor had to be satisfied. Neko held no silly ideas about having a 'fair fight'. He would kill the man, any way he could and that was it. He wondered briefly if he would have time to inflict some real pain on this 'Trace Eldridge'. As he looked down at the screen and began to shuffle towards the front of the plane, he saw a message pending. Logging in to the secure phone app, he heard, "the target's real name is Trace Conner. Eldridge was a fake. The home address is....." Neko smiled, time for the hunt.

"Nice place, Trace." Kevin said, "Hey, look at that. I'm a poet."

"Ugh..." Luka replied

"Thanks, but it's just a simple box really." Trace said. "Kitchen to the left, bedroom, and bathroom to the right. This is the living room, spread your gear out here."

As the three men began to pull equipment out, Trace said, "There's a big pot of chili in the kitchen. I hope none of you are vegetarians. Once you're fed and kitted up, we'll go to the spot I picked for overwatch, see if you like it. I'm hoping that this killer doesn't think I'd have a sniper."

"I won't miss." Larry said, "besides, I saw how you took out Kevin and Luka. I'm sure you could take this guy up close."

"Larry, a lot of ex-girlfriends have accused me of being egotistical. I prefer to think of it as confidence, but I don't have that much. How about you just put a big hole in his head for me?"

"Sir, yes sir," Larry replied with a laugh and a heel click.

Neko climbed into the rented Jeep. According to the GPS, he had a two-hour drive to his target. That meant he had time to make a few stops. The first stop was a Harbor Freight Tools store to pick up a folding knife, a hunting knife, and a few prybars. The next stop was a Big 5 sporting goods to get some outdoor gear. His information said that Flagstaff could get snow at this time of year, although it was still early. Neko was not good with the cold, so he wanted to be prepared for it. As he shopped, his mind drifted back in time.

Neko had been in Bosnia in 1993. He was in his early twenties. Having arrived there after leaving China. He still had some money and could have gone elsewhere, but the war had drawn him here. It didn't take long for one of the Generals to make use of his skills. Neko didn't care which side won, as long as he was allowed to practice his trade. It didn't matter who he killed, woman and children were just targets to him, albeit, not challenges. As his skill progressed and his technique refined, he was given more and more difficult assignments. He always succeeded, his legend growing. This was a double-edged sword, the more his legend grew, the more work he would get, but it also made him more of a target. What he didn't like was the winter. Bosnia was cold, often at zero degrees Celsius. Neko knew that places like Russia were worse, but zero degrees seemed ridiculously cold to him. This time he would be prepared for the cold.

"Yea, Trace," Larry said. "This looks good, nice sightlines, good coverage for us."

"Good. I'll leave all the external lights on. I don't know if you have night optics, but I can light it up pretty well." Trace said.

"Can someone outside cut the power?" Luka asked.

"Technically, yes, but it's difficult. I don't think this guy will do that. Taking out the power would alert me." Trace answered.

"So, we set up and just wait?" Kevin asked.

"Yea, sorry I don't have a better plan." Trace replied. "We just don't know enough to guess when or even if, the killer will come here. I'm betting he will but I have no idea how long we'll have to wait."

"Ok," Luka said, "we'll do shifts. One man on the gun, one man spotting and covering and the last man rests. We can do this for at least a week, I know I've done worse, with less."

"Oh yea," Larry said.

Neko was amazed as the scenery around him changed from cactus to hills, then hills to mountains. He had to pop his ears several times as he went up in altitude. Much to his surprise, his destination was listed as more than two thousand meters above sea level. Amazing, everyone told him that Arizona was just a hot desert. Giant pine trees soared up around him, sometimes blocking the views of the mountains that continued to rise as he drove north on Interstate 17.

Trace's hand shook visibly as he reached the key towards the top deadbolt. His mind racing, wondering what else he could do to prepare for Neko. As time progressed, Trace became surer that Neko was their foe. As he drove back down to his house, Luka called him.

"I just got a call back from a guy I met when I was in the teams. He's doing security work for some Saudi's. Mostly bodyguard stuff." Luka started.

"Saudi Arabia?" Trace asked.

"Yea, but this guy's principal travels a lot. I mean, a lot." Luka replied, "anyhow, about a year ago, the rest of the men on the principle's security team started getting really nervous, jumping at shadows and all. When my buddy asked what was going on, he was told that they had received a tip that a killer known as 'Neko' had been hired to kill their boss's son."

"Anything happen?"

"As a matter of fact, yes. Two days later, two of the security detail and the son were all dead. The guards were killed with a knife but... the son had 'no visible marks' on him." Luka emphasized the last part. "My buddy was assigned to the father, so he only got secondhand information."

Trace went over all this in his head as he was opened the front door. Once inside he turned the locks, and wondered, *"what the hell am I doing? I'm not a professional soldier. What makes me think I can take this nut job?"*

His heart hammering now, he went through the house, making sure all the security shutters were down and all the door locks were on. *"I've never been in combat, what am I thinking?"*
He didn't feel bad about the few men he had killed, they were bad, very bad. The ones at MIGIsoft's HQ were just killing everyone, for money. He knew that the hotel fight with Neko and the gunfight at MIGIsoft had happened so fast that he didn't have time to think, his training had kicked in and his body had responded without any direction from his brain. But now....now he had plenty of time to think about how stupid this was.

"Fuck..what was I thinking? So stupid..." As his anxiety grew, he tried to reason it out in his head. *"If I didn't do this, more people would die at MIGIsoft. Nobody else has a clue as to what they face in this killer. At some point he'd get the program and who knew how many would die?"*

Trace knew he had unorthodox skills, he knew that he could do things that he couldn't even explain. *"Can I really beat this guy? I've been training for the better part of three decades, but Neko has probably been killing for that long. He's been at the pro level for years and here I am, the rookie, just starting out."*

Trace nearly jumped out of his skin when his cellphone vibrated in his pocket. *"God, I'm never this high-strung normally."* He thought as he fished the phone out, hitting the call answer button. "This is Trace"

"Trace, it's Catherine, how are you doing?"

"At the moment, I'm questioning my life choices." He said.

"What do you mean?"

"Well, I'm thinking that if I had just sat on a couch and watched sports, I probably wouldn't be trying to protect something worth over $20 million and I wouldn't be waiting for an assassin to show up and try to kill me for it."

"It has to be worth way more than that, for someone to go to all this effort and expense." She replied.

"That doesn't make me feel any better." He said.

"Sorry, so just destroy it."

"We can't. Besides what it would do to your company, the people after it won't believe it was destroyed. They'll keep coming and the bodies will pile up. I really don't like this, but I don't see any alternatives." Trace said. "Did you call for something besides my mental health?"

"Ah, yes. We have some information for you. First mine, then I'll hand you to Lloyd." She began, "I reached out like you said. Oddly, I got a call back from a friend who is the director of an aid organization in Somalia. He said that a few years ago, they were having a problem with one particular warlord, who kept intercepting their medicine shipments. He openly complained and one night an Arab man, he thinks it was a Saudi, handed him a paper with the word 'Neko' and a number on it. The Arab said that this Neko could get rid of the problem, for a fee. I know it's not much. Sorry."

"No, it's not much, but it fits with what I was thinking." Trace said.

"Here's Lloyd."

"Trace, I got a call back from a friend that works with the ATF, mostly tracking gun smugglers and arms merchants." The Colonel began. "They were working in Turkey, this is about ten years ago, he said. They were tracking one particular dealer that was selling American service weapons on the black market. He didn't go into too much detail. Only said that this dealer died suddenly."

"Cause of death?" Trace asked.

"A missing head...apparently. After questioning local syndicate members, he learned that the deceased dealer had put a hit out on someone named Neko because he didn't want to pay him."

"Shit," Trace breathed.

"Not what you were expecting?" The Colonel asked.

"Unfortunately, it's exactly what I was expecting, but that doesn't mean I like it."

"Well, be careful and watch your six. Here's Catherine."

"Trace, all this sounds bad. I can have Lloyd hire more people, I'm sure Luka knows some more SEALs that would be willing to help you." Catherine said quickly.

"I would love that, really I would, but the best chance we have to bag this guy is right now. If we bring in a whole bunch of shooters, we may wind up with another mass shooting like at MIGIsoft. We just can't do that." Trace said. "As much as I'm regretting this now, I still think it's the best shot we have."

"Alright, we'll keep digging. Let me know if you need anything, anything at all. Be careful Trace." With that, she disconnected the call.

"We got movement," Kevin said.

"Hope it's not more Elk," Larry said as he looked around through the scope. The Elk here were huge, so were the mule deer. He wanted to come back here and hunt them. Maybe Trace could help him out with that later.

"Coming in from your two o'clock, it's a man and he's moving very stealthy," Kevin said while kicking Luka out of his sleeping bag.

Larry zoomed in on the figure as it approached the back door. Taking a knee, the figure pulled something out of a pocket.

"Trace, we got a bad guy at your back door. He's Asian." Luka called over the radio, then said, "everyone go to voice activation."

They all did, except for Trace. He was afraid that they would hear his thundering heart over the radio. He looked at the clock, 4:04 a.m. He must have dozed off around one a.m. Keying his radio, Trace said, "if you have a shot, take it!" As he continued towards the back door.

Larry centered the crosshairs on the assassin's head, breathed out slowly, squeezed the trigger, and said, "Bye shithead."

Neko felt the invisible push. Just enough that the bullet passed by his head, but too close. He knew that it had grazed his scalp, he felt the burn. As he looked in the direction of the shooter, he felt the push again, this time the bullet missed by more than an inch. He never fought the push, it had saved him too many times. Then he was moving fast, into cover. Closing on the sniper.

"What the fuck?!" Larry had seen the target's head move just as he had squeezed the trigger. Reaching up he worked the bolt, centered on the head again, this time the face because it was looking right at him, breathe, squeeze... "fuck!" He moved again. Then he was gone.

"What's going on out there? Is he down?" Trace asked over the radio.

"Negative, Larry missed, twice," Luka answered.

"Exfil now!" Trace came back.

"We ain't leaving you alone and we ain't running." Luka came back.

"Listen to me! Evac RIGHT FUCKING NOW!!" Trace roared. "He's coming for you because that's what I would do! Throw everything in the truck, head out a couple of miles. I'll call if I need you."

Kevin and Larry looked at Luka who was pissed. After a moment he nodded and they all grabbed gear, threw it in the truck, and peeled out, heading for the main road. The whole time, Luka was mumbling about leaving a man behind.

Neko arrived in time to see an old pickup truck, the color of chocolate chip cookie dough, peel out of the dirt, and on to the paved road heading away. That explained the missing truck from the satellite photo. Only the Jeep had been at the house. Neko had attributed the missing truck to the Google photo being a few years old.

"Stupid....very stupid.." Neko mumbled in Vietnamese. "Arrogant, lazy, and stupid. They almost killed me. I should have checked for snipers, I should have taken more time to scout, should have been more thorough."

He touched his scalp on the left side and felt the blood, a large gash, he would have to fix it to avoid leaving more DNA evidence. *"I'm getting very tired of being shot."* He thought, *"when this is over, I'm going to go back and kill all the security people that work for MIGIsoft."* He knew this was just a fantasy. Not only was it unrealistic, but it would expose him to law enforcement far more than would be prudent.

This consultant, Trace Conner, had almost killed Neko, twice. *"I must give him more credit. This is the second time he stopped me. The second time I fell into a trap. If not for my sixth sense, I'd be dead."* He thought. The Russians he had worked with in Georgia had called it his sixth sense. Neko knew there was a Chinese word for it, his father had told him once, but that was a lifetime ago and he couldn't remember it.

"Okay, tell me exactly what happened." Trace ordered.

"I had him dead to rights, easy shot at two twenty yards. I squeezed the trigger and at that exact instant, he moved." Larry answered. "I sighted in on him again, after I chambered a new round, squeezed the trigger and he moved. Which was really weird because he was looking right at me when I fired."

"There's no way he could have reacted to the sound of the shot," Kevin said.

"No, the bullet takes less than a second to travel that distance." Larry continued. "the sound would have arrived after that."

"Damn, that's what I was afraid of." Trace said.

"What's that?" Luka asked.

"In Ninjutsu, we call it 'kidzuki'. It's the ability to sense an attack as it happens, without being able to see it." Trace replied.

"Bullshit!" Larry put in.

"Maybe, but you just saw it happen, twice." Trace said. "I've seen master teachers do an entire class blindfolded, with the attacks coming from behind them. They never get hit. It's eerie as hell to watch."

"It's just an illusion, some kind of trick maybe." Kevin offered.

"No, in the field you guys call it the sixth sense. Guys with a lot of combat experience seem to be able to just know when something bad is about to happen. We call it 'kidzuki', which translates as "awareness". We train for it, with it. In fact, demonstrating the ability to use it, is one of the tests to get your teaching certificate. Learning to feel that energy, to let it push you is critical to our training."

"You can actually feel that energy?" Luka asked.

"Feel is a poor word. It's not something you can describe easily. When it happens, you can't miss it. I personally believe that it is a leftover from our primeval brains. A connection to the world around us that we don't perceive with our usual five senses."

"So, this guy is one of your Ninjas?" Larry asked.

"I'm still not sure, although, with that skill level, I probably would have run across him at some point in the last twenty years." Trace answered. "Other arts talk about it, but most treat it with so much skepticism, that they never really learn to use it. Regardless, this killer can use it and he uses it well. Him looking straight at Larry means that he has absolute faith in his ability, for good reason."

"I saw some blood on the door frame, I think Larry winged him at least a little." Kevin put in.

"Yea, I noticed that too. Maybe he'll get a terrible infection and die for us. Wouldn't that be nice?" Trace asked.

"Think he'll be back soon?" Luka asked.

"I don't think so. Not today anyway. He'll need to doctor the wound, then he'll do drive-bys, looking for cops and other security. When he finally does come back, he will look very carefully for hidden snipers."

"I can just get farther away, where he can't find us." Larry offered.

"No, that won't work. We know now that he has the ability to use kidzuki. That means a round from far away will take even longer, give him more time to move, it'll never work. In fact, a premeditated strike of any kind won't work. It's the 'intention' that he senses. At this point, I have no idea how we are going to take him off the board." Trace said as he plopped onto the couch, exhausted.

"Is there any way to negate this ability?" Catherine asked after hearing the report from the team in Arizona. She wasn't as skeptical and Trace attributed this to her Aikido training.

118

"If there is, I've never heard of it. Maybe the master teachers or the Grandmaster know a way to defeat it, but even if they told me today, it probably takes time to learn and control." Trace responded. "To be completely honest, I never even thought that he might have this skill. Ego, I guess."

"Then what do we do?" Catherine said.

"That's the reason for this conference call. I am open to ideas. Anything at all." Trace added.

"Could we bring in one of the master teachers to help?" The colonel put in.

"No. We would have to prove that he was from one of our Ninjutsu schools, gone bad. Otherwise, they never leave Japan, we have no way to prove that and I still doubt it. The system we use tends to weed out psychos. I'm not saying it couldn't happen, I just don't think so."

"The system didn't weed you out." Luka put in.

"Hahaha...very funny." Trace said.

"It was another trap," Neko said flatly, no anger or animosity.

"Shit, how did they know?" Kelsi asked, wondering now if there was a mole in his company, working for MIGIsoft. No, that was ridiculous. Only Jeff and himself knew about the Flagstaff lead. He hadn't even told Cross.

"No doubt they simply set up and waited, hoping that your spies would pass the information."

"And maybe find my spies in the process." Kelsi thought. Out loud he said, "what are you going to do now? I still need those drives."

"I understand. This Conner fellow is not to be underestimated. Twice now, they have almost killed me. That must not happen again. For now, I will watch for law enforcement. After that, I will begin to hunt for hidden opponents. When I feel that I have eliminated all other opposition, I will face Mr. Conner, kill him, and take the drives." Neko said with no emotion in his voice.

Kelsi felt a chill as he listened to Neko. *"This guy is on a whole other planet."* He thought. *"I never want him after me."*

119

"Jares" Came the answer on the phone.

"Special Agent, it's Trace Conner."

"Ah, good. I was just about to call you. It appears your mystery man does have a history with the FBI." Jares said.

"Really? I'm so surprised?" Came the sarcastic retort from Trace.

"Yea, yea. I'm not gonna apologize if that's what you're hoping for."

"Hardly, please tell me what you found out." Trace said, less sarcastically.

"An FBI team was in Georgia, the country by Russia not the U.S. state, investigating the murder of a negotiator. The Georgian government believed it was the Russians and asked the U.S. to send over a team of investigators. Lots of boring details, then the important part. An anonymous source said that 'the Cat' had been sent to kill the negotiator because he had insulted one of the Russian team. In a different interview, this source said the man sent was called Neko."

"How was the negotiator killed?" Trace asked.

"That part is weird too. He was found sitting up in bed, staring at the tv. No obvious signs of trauma or foul play." Jares answered.

"I'm assuming the autopsy came back with a ruptured heart or another critical organ?"

"Correct. None of the agencies involved thought to look for skin oils in the clothes." Jares said.

"Wouldn't matter. Even though it's a fast death, it's not instantaneous. The victim would have thrashed and fallen out of bed, or at the very least messed up the bed. No, Neko may have killed him in bed, but then he staged the body."

"The FBI team thought the same thing. Why would he stage it?"

"I have no idea, maybe it was a request from the employer." Trace asked.

"I suppose that's possible, at this point anything is possible. Anyway, the team never found Neko or any more evidence to follow."

"Okay, well this fits with the other small pieces we've been getting. Is there any chance you could get us in touch with a facial sketch artist? Several of the guys here got a good look at him when he tried to come in early this morning." Trace said.

"Wait, what?" Agent Jares barked. "He was there?"

"That's actually why I was calling, to fill you in on what happened." Trace began, "at 4:04 a.m....." and retold the events leading up to this call.

"You know that using a sniper in the U.S., even in wild west Arizona, is still considered murder, right? I mean, what if your guy had hit him? What would you have done then?" Jares demanded.

"Well, I probably would have called you sooner." Trace quipped.

"Not funny, asshole."

"Look Agent, if you have a better idea of how to deal with this killer, I'm all ears. I guarantee he'll be back, and I have no idea how I'm gonna deal with him."

"Give the drives to the government. Let us deal with him." Jares replied.

"Great. When and where?" Trace asked.

"Well...did I forget to mention that I ran that up the chain to DOD? Word came down from on high that I was not allowed to take custody of them. 'National security'..blah..blah"

"That doesn't make you suspicious?" Trace questioned the agent. "Since when does the government not trust a special agent to hold on to evidence?"

"Yea, I'm beginning to believe there might be somebody dirty in that chain. Somebody with some real pull, who is probably getting everything I report...."

"Right,... then voila', the killer shows up at my door after your report goes in. Seems a little too coincidental to me, but I'm not a trained investigator." Trace said, trying to inject as much sarcasm as possible into the comment.

"I got the hint," Jares replied sharply. "There could be other explanations. MIGIsoft had one spy, there could easily be others. They do have hundreds of employees. Everybody just assumes it's the government that is corrupt."

Trace snickered, "not sure I even need to respond to that one..."

"Ha..you so funny," Jares replied irritably.

Chapter 16

DARPA Deputy Director Alicia Parks pulled out the burner smartphone. Using her Red Phone app, she dialed a number and waited.

"Yes?" Kelsi answered.

"Kelsi, I just got a report. The program is with a consultant in Flagstaff, Arizona." She said in a rush.

"I know, I already have a team there to retrieve it," Kelsi replied coolly.

"How do you know already?"

"You don't ask and I won't tell, okay?" Kelsi replied.

"Right, of course. Will they have it soon? I can't keep blocking receipt for much longer."

"The first attempt was a trap. My team escaped but will return and succeed." Kelsi was quite confident of this.

"I've been using the vetting process as the reason for not taking the program, but that can't last much longer. At some point, they are going to figure out that I am actively trying to block receipt." Alicia was very agitated.

"Hmm...maybe you shouldn't."

"What? Why not?" She asked.

"If for some reason, my team is unsuccessful in obtaining it the next time, you could order a pickup to take it safely into DARPA's control. Only, we have a team replace the DARPA team and take it ourselves. It would make you look proactive. Help shift the scrutiny away from you." Kelsi mused aloud.

"I like it. I like it. Some of the security guys here are real self-righteous pricks too! I wouldn't miss a few of them." Alicia brightened. "This program, this kind of power shouldn't be in the hands of this President. It must be stopped."

"Save me the political rant," Kelsi interrupted, "You're doing this for the money."

"Just make sure I get the money." She said, all business now and disconnected.

"I don't know about you guys," Trace stated, "I'm exhausted but still wired as hell. Is this what combat is always like? How did you guys ever get any sleep?"

"You either get used to it or you take a lot of combat naps," Luka answered. "In the teams, there were a lot of times where you just didn't have the men to pull actual guard duty, so combat naps became the norm."

"In the corps," Larry put in, "we just went until the physical side won out over the mental shit. Eventually, everybody gets tired enough."

"Well, I have a solution I know will work for me. Any of you guys want to go spar a little?" Trace asked. "We can run over to my Dojo, work out some kinks."

The three men looked at each other, nodded and Luka said, "Sure, plus I think we should stay together, with a professional assassin in town trying to kill us."

Fifteen minutes later, all four men stood on the edges of the mat at Conner's dojo. Trace had changed into his simple black Gi, worn and with a few small tears in the fabric, a worn black belt wrapped around his waist. Looking at the other men, he said, "Who wants to go first?"

Luka stepped towards him, "That would be me."

"Don't go easy on me, Luka. I want you to really come at me." Trace said eyeing Luka's stance, balance, and form. Luka was at least four inches taller than Trace, he had a longer reach, more muscle and easily outweighed Trace by forty pounds. Luka stood in a modified boxer pose, he began bouncing just a little. Trace relaxed, letting all the visual cues come in at once.

Luka stepped forward and slightly to his left, pivoting just a little, he shot out with three quick jabs at Conner's head. Trace stood in the Bear posture, his feet positioned at shoulder width, balance equal side to side and front to back. His hands open, held just in front of his face, and slightly to each side. From this posture, Trace easily swatted away all three jabs with the palm of his left hand. Luka then came with a long shot from the right-hand, not too much energy, testing the response. Luka repeated this combination

124

three times, on the fourth one, the right fist came with his entire body behind it, intending to take Conner out with one shot.

Stepping directly at the fist, using his left palm on the outside of Luka's right arm, Trace pushed the incoming missile just far enough to the right to slide past his right ear. At the same time, Trace shot his right hand, in a hand spear, into Luka's exposed armpit. Hitting the brachial neural plexus there. In a microsecond, Luka's brain thought he had hit his target but something went wrong, a second after that his brain registered that the right arm no longer responded to commands.

"SHIT!" Luka roared and turned back to face Conner, swinging his left fist hard at Conner's right side. As he did this he stepped forward with his leg, putting his considerable size behind the blow.

Trace dropped his right leg back, but as he did, his left foot came up and the rigid toes struck Luka's left leg, just above the knee in the 'teardrop' muscle. Luka's leg collapsed completely, also useless now. Trace turned and looked at the other two men, "Who's next?"

"Wait," Luka said, "What the hell did you do to me?"

"The shot to your armpit hit the nerve bundle there, not too hard, but you won't be able to use that arm for about ten minutes. When it does come back, it will be some of the strangest pain you've ever had. The shot to your leg fragged that controlling teardrop muscle. The leg just collapses, you can't stop it. That will bruise, but it'll come back faster."

"What did you hit me with? Steel rods?" Luka gasped.

"In the armpit, I used a hand spear, the leg was my toes."

"You can make your toes that hard?" Luka looked at Trace's bare feet.

"I can actually punch holes in a wall and kick steel drums over with them. That's why my hands and feet look so rough. A lot of training."

"I'm next," Larry said.

He had switched to sweatpants and a t-shirt like the other men. Almost the same size as Trace, he moved forward cautiously. Adopting a stance like an MMA fighter, Larry was closer to the ground, his vital parts protected. As he came in closer, he launched a low right kick, Trace simply pulled his left foot back. Now Trace had dropped into a straight-line posture, his left foot forward, his right foot back, and angled ninety degrees from his

125

left. With about sixty percent of his weight on his back foot, Trace could easily lift and move his leading left foot, to defend or guard. Trace's left hand was straight out in front of him, held pointed at Larry's eyes, his right hand back by his chest and relaxed.

Larry tried to knock the hand that was pointed at his eyes out of the way but Trace just kept bringing it back in line. Larry switched to a combination, a low right kick, then a left low punch, and a high right punch. Trace dropped back to his left, changing the forward leg and hand, easily blocking the strikes, then fell back to the right side, resuming his original posture. Larry threw a high right punch, then dove low, wrapping his arms around Trace's leading left leg. Trace drew this leg back as before, Larry came with it, Trace dropped all his weight and brought his right elbow down on the other man's exposed spine. Striking with a 'shukiken' means using the point of the elbow. Trace didn't want to permanently damage the other man, so he flattened out the strike a little.

Larry felt a sledgehammer strike his spine and for an instant, he believed that he was going to be paralyzed for life as everything from his shoulders down went numb. Struggling for breath, all he could do was watch Trace pull his leg away and step back into the same posture he had been in a second ago.

"Just breathe." Trace said with a smile. "It will come back, but you'll have a good bruise there and it'll hurt for days."

"I can't feel anything." Larry breathed.

"You will and then you'll wish you didn't." Trace said sympathetically. Then turning to Kevin, "ready?"

"Nope," Kevin said, as he looked at the other two men on the floor.

"Come on." Trace urged.

"Nope. Not gonna happen. I'll shoot you from here, but I'm not getting in close."

"Hahaha...smart man. The Navy guys always told me that you Army soldiers weren't that smart." Trace laughed.

"Nobody has ever dropped me that fast. Hell, I don't even remember the last time someone beat me." Luka said. Dragging himself to a wall and propping against it.

"Ungh.." Larry agreed.

"Maybe I'll just throw Kevin at you and then hit you while you're tangled up," Luka said.

Smiling broadly, Trace replied. "Yes, you could try that......shit, that's it." His face changing into a scowl.

"What?" Kevin asked.

"How we beat Neko. I have to tie him up."

"Tie him up? Like with a rope?....Everybody else that got that close wound up dead." Luka put in.

"Yea....that's the part I don't like...we'll have to think this out." Trace said very slowly, thinking.

Since Kevin wouldn't spar with him, Trace headed over to the heavy bag, pondering as he struck the bag with vicious combinations. Using a different strike with every blow. Extended knuckles, then a palm strike, followed by a shuto, a backhand strike, then a hand spear, thumb knuckle strike into a rolling strike designed to break bones. In between these were the kicks, toe strikes, heel strikes, inside and outside foot strikes.

The assembled men watched the flurry of blows against the bag for several minutes, then suddenly Conner launched himself straight up, both feet shooting forward together, the toes drilling the bag near the top, almost six feet off the ground. Conner then dropped back to his feet and fluidly into a back roll, coming up into the straight-line posture he had used against Larry. The landing and roll were so smooth that there was virtually no sound.

"Are you stupid or just plain crazy?" Catherine asked.

"Did you come up with a better idea?" Trace replied. All four men were gathered around Trace's phone at the edge of the mat, still at the dojo.

"So, he just kills you and takes the drives. Then what?" She demanded, not waiting for a reply, she continued. "You're dead, we lose the drives, the company goes under, everybody loses!"

"Easy Catherine," Trace said calmly, "I'm not wild about this idea either but let me explain."

"Please do that." The Colonel's voice came through the small speaker.

"First, he can't kill me until he gets the drives. Otherwise, he might not find them at all. They're buried in the forest and the forest here is huge, hundreds of square miles. Second, I'm going to be wearing level IV body armor with plates front and back. This will protect my heart and the most important organs."

"Neko doesn't know the drives aren't there and he could just smash your throat as he did to Albert." With the mention of her brother, Catherine choked up.

"The lower strikes are what we call 'hidden strikes', much harder to block. If he goes for my head, in any way, those are easier to counter. Nothing's guaranteed, but it will give me a better chance." Trace responded

"So, you're going to grab him and Larry tries to get a headshot?" The Colonel pressed.

"No, that would never work. If Larry was set up close enough, Neko would find him, plus the situation will be very fluid. It'll be hard enough for me to grab him, much less hold him in a specific place so that Larry could get a headshot. Also, a .308 round could go right through Neko and my vest, or my head....." Trace finished.

"Then this won't work either," Catherine said flatly, trying to end the discussion of this madness.

"The plan is for Trace to hold him," Luka answered for the group. "I'll bust in, I have the most CQB training, put a three-round burst into the bad guy. Once I hit him, Trace lets go and I hit him again. Body shots at less than twenty feet, simple."

"What's to keep the bullets from going through Neko and hitting Trace." The Colonel asked though he thought he knew the answer, he wanted it said aloud for everybody's benefit.

"Yes sir, I'll be using subsonic nine-millimeter rounds. Hollowpoint, they should mushroom inside the bad guy, but if one goes through, Trace's vest will stop it." Luka said.

"I don't like it. Too much risk. We have to find another way." The Colonel said.

"I hate it." Catherine agreed with the Colonel. "Why can't we get the FBI to put in a team and wait for him?"

"Let's assume he fell for that and didn't spot the agents, which I highly doubt. How many of them will die because they will try their best to take him alive?" Trace continued. "Remember, if he doesn't have a gun, they'll try to arrest him. They are bringing plenty of weapons to him, for him to use. Some of them will have families. No, we can't let that happen."

"Well, this plan is a big, fat NO." The Colonel said adamantly.

"Sorry, you two, this isn't your call. We're here, the killer's here, he'll probably be back in a day or so. Besides, isn't it a rule in special ops that you don't question the man in the field?" Trace asked triumphantly.

"No, not really." Luka piped up.

"Oh, well, then it's a good thing I wasn't in the military. I suck at taking orders." Trace looked around his group and they all nodded. "We're doing this."

There was a prolonged silence on the other end of the phone. Finally, the Colonel came back on. "Check in every 2 hours. If any of us hear anything, we need to share it immediately." With that, he ended the call. Catherine had not said anything more.

"How are we gonna set up?" Larry asked.

"I'm thinking of a spot for you that's probably over a thousand yards out." Trace began.

"I probably can't hit him at that range."

"I know, it wouldn't matter, he'd have plenty of time to move once he felt you take the shot. No, we set you up with a spotting scope and you're our advance warning." Trace said. "Luka and Kevin will be in a rented SUV, sitting in an open garage about a quarter-mile away. When Larry sees that Neko is about to enter, he calls out. Luka and Kevin haul ass over to my place, kick in the front door and Luka shoots him. I'll try to hold him with his back to the front door. Kevin covers the back of the house in case he bolts that way."

"Simple, I like it," Kevin said. "Open garage?"

"House belongs to one of my Black Belt students. You can leave the door up, if Neko drives by, he'll only see an open garage. Unless he's driving with infra-red optics, he won't see you guys."

"We can't be any closer?" Luka asked, "I don't like being that far away. It'll take a bare minimum of a minute for us to get there. A lot can happen in combat in a minute."

"We can't risk you being any closer. If he finds you, we're blown, this may be our only chance to take him out." Trace replied.

"Why can't we hide in the house?" Luka pressed.

"You're gonna hide in the closets for days? We have no idea when he'll come back, if he sees more than one person, I doubt he'll come in." Trace said.

"I still don't like it." Luka groused.

"Mr. Conner, I have some more information." Agent Jares began.

"Agent Jares, you can call me Trace. After all, we're friends now."

"HA," the agent snorted, "and you can call me Agent, or special agent."

"Understood. What do you have for me?"

"Before I start, anything else happen there? Any bodies to report?"

"Nope. Been absolutely quiet for two days now. I know he's been out there, I've felt him a few times. He's being very cautious." Trace said.

"Felt him? More of 'the force' crap?" Jares mocked.

"Believe it or not, Special Agent, I don't really care what you think."

"Fine. I hope you're right. I hope whatever you have planned, works." Jares said.

"What's the new information?" Trace prompted him.

"I set up a search to watch all law enforcement reports with any mention of 'Neko'. Of course, a lot of the ones from San Francisco PD in the Japantown popped up, most were actually about cats. However, one from Chinatown came in. An informant said that one of the enforcers from the Three Dragon Triad had been threatening shop owners. Telling them that Neko was in town. That their families would get a visit from him. 'Like the old days', was a quote. The informant didn't know anything specific about who Neko was, but the enforcer is not native. He moved from Hong Kong about fifteen years ago."

"So maybe Neko worked in Hong Kong for the triad at some point? Trace asked.

"Yea, that was my thought," Jares answered. "We keep a team in Hong Kong to watch international gambling and other bad stuff. I'll get hold of them, see if they can shake any information out of HK about Neko."

"That would be great. The more we know, the better."

"I'm just hoping it will give us a line on who is farther up this particular chain. We still haven't had any luck finding a 'Kelsi' and we can't crack the Red Phone app that they're using."

"Well, when Neko shows up, I'll ask him. I'm sure he'll tell me." Trace said in a sarcastic tone.

"You mean if he shows up."

"No. He'll be here...at some point. I have the drives, they're hidden, he has to talk to me. Please make sure that goes into your report. I would prefer he not just kill me and look for the drives."

"Yea, it'll go in the report and I'll verbally tell a few people up the line. Good luck Conner." Jares said, then disconnected.

Chapter 17

The waiting was driving everyone crazy, on both sides. Everyone except Neko. He controlled it. He watched, waited, and searched. Nobody hiding within a half-mile. He knew there might be a sniper farther out than that, but he would feel the shot if they took one. Besides, he had a plan to deal with that. If there was one that far away, it took time to set up the shot, he had to pause long enough to let the sniper see him, range and fire. He wasn't going to do that his time around. There were other houses within a half-mile, but he couldn't search them all and they wouldn't have a sign up stating their location. He would move swiftly, get in, and get out with the drives or with the consultant.

It was the fourth day since his last attempt. The wound on his skull had closed nicely, only requiring some superglue and time to seal up. Neko knew the best high point within two miles had a good view of the back door but only limited of the front. The front was brightly lit at night but the back door had plenty of dark shadows to hide in. He moved forward slowly, staying hidden. Once he moved, he had to move fast, with no pauses. Checking the equipment he had with him one more time, he began a mental countdown. He would beat the consultant this time.

"Movement at the front door! It's him!" Larry called over the radio.

"Shit!" Trace thought.

After four days he was beginning to think he was wrong and Neko wouldn't come again. Trace had been sitting at the kitchen table, closer to the back door. He got up and began moving towards the front door. A Sig Sauer in his right-hand.

"Wait!" Larry called, "He just ran away from it!"

"What the hell?" Trace thought as he moved cautiously toward the front.

"We're moving," Luka called out over the radio.

Conner was within fifteen feet when the door exploded in, throwing him backward. Landing on his back, he continued the momentum, rolling over onto his hands and knees, not fighting the tremendous energy. Stunned, he looked up to see Neko rush through the shattered door, a Beretta in his extended right hand, pointed at Trace's head. From this distance, he couldn't miss. Trace moved very slowly, ears ringing, he raised his right hand off the ground first. Neko moved closer.

"*Come on, closer..*" Trace thought, willing it.

Neko moved within five feet, not close enough. As Trace slowly raised his left hand, he looked up at the killer. Getting a real, close up for the first time.

"Neko, I presume," Conner said.

A slightly surprised look on his face. "You have learned my name. I am impressed." A very slight British accent, almost undetectable. "And you are Trace Conner, sometimes called Trace Eldridge. Where are the drives?"

"Buried in the forest. Kill me and nobody will ever find them." Trace eyed the killer, about five foot nine or ten. Lean, hard, Trace was a little larger and heavier, probably a bit stronger.

"Perhaps, where is your team?" the assassin asked coolly.

"What team?" Trace tried to play dumb, although he knew he was a terrible actor. As he did, he moved his head side to side, as if he was trying to crack his neck. There, about three inches from his left foot, a nice chunk of the door. As he continued to move his head, drawing Neko's attention, he moved his left foot over it. Curling his bare toes over the splintered edge.

"I will begin by shooting your elbows, then knees, and so on, until you tell me," Neko said as his pistol aimed at Trace's left elbow.

"Any chance you'll tell me your real name or who hired you?" Trace probed.

"I will tell you, just before I kill you."

"Okay then, I don't want to know." Trace tried to joke.

"Where are the.." Neko began.

Conner pretended to stagger, his left foot coming up and forward, just enough to release the gripped wood, sending it flying toward Neko's face.

The killer easily batted it aside with his left hand. As Trace's left foot landed forward of where it had been, bringing him within striking distance of the gun hand. Trace's raised right hand, knuckles extended, slammed into the inside of Neko's right wrist. Trace's left hand, with knuckles extended, slammed into the small bones on the outside of Neko's right hand, causing the gun to flip backward and into Neko's face.

Instinctively closing his eyes, Neko moved his head to dodge the weapon. Too slow, it hit him on the left side of his face, just below the eye. Tearing open the skin. Conner was still moving, the right-hand whipped a back fist into the right side of Neko's face, next to the killer's right eye, a strike meant to crack the weaker bone of the temple region, but the angle wasn't quite right and the bone didn't break.

"Thirty seconds." Trace thought as he pressed the attack. "Have to keep him busy for at least thirty more."

Neko could feel Conner on him, pressing the attack. Neko dropped his center of balance lower, shooting out a left-hand spear and then a right, into the soft areas at the base of the lungs. Not to kill Conner but slow him way down.

"Uhnn." Trace grunted. Even through the body armor, the blows were tremendous. His mind wondered briefly how bad it would have been if he didn't have it on, but there was no time for that. His right knee came up to his own chest and then fired the flat bottom of his foot out, smashing into Neko's chest. Trace continued the stomp kick, sending the killer flying backward. As he finished the stomp, Trace extended his toes, driving the rigid end into the xiphoid process, the cartilage at the base of the sternum, just above the heart. A final blow intended to cripple the opponent. It was at that moment, Trace Conner realized they had failed.

"Chi trich!" Neko cursed in Vietnamese as he sailed back, going over something. He let the momentum go, not fighting it, rolling and was back on his feet, moving towards the consultant. Ready to put the larger man down hard.

"He's got a SAPI plate!" Trace thought.

He called out loud, not sure if his radio was still transmitting or even if it was on him. "He's got a SAPI plate and armor!" Referring to the Small

134

Arms Protective Insert that is usually placed in a pocket on the front and rear of body armor. Trace knew that the subsonic nine-millimeter rounds Luka was using wouldn't punch through that. Still, Trace closed on him, not thinking about what he was doing, just moving.

"Conner is also wearing a vest." Neko thought as he launched a low kick at Conner's right knee.

Trace saw the kick, shifting his weight off his right leg, pulling it back. Trace shot the stiffened toes of his left foot out, going for the teardrop on Neko's right leg, he missed. The strike landing below the target on the hard bone inside the knee.

Neko grunted, letting his left leg fly away and absorbing much of the impact. As it did, he let it fall, onto the side of his left knee. His right foot swept around low, taking out both of Conner's feet and sending him tumbling backward.

Trace landed hard, doing a rear break fall. He gained his feet at the same time as the killer.

"Forty-five seconds," Trace thought, *"come on Luka, hurry."*

Neko came forward, moving in a stance that reminded Trace of Pencak Silat. He understood what his friend had seen, but it wasn't quite right. It wasn't pure Silat, it was a mixture of others. His left hand shot forward in a fist, blindingly fast.

Conner parried with his left, but too slow. The blow clipped his right ear and spun his head some. The next blows came twice from the right, hammering the bones of Conner's hip. Neko was so fast, Conner couldn't block all the blows. Trace twisted counterclockwise, taking the strikes, grunting in pain. Using the pain to reinforce himself, he drove the extended fingers of his right hand into Neko's exposed neck. Then rolled his elbow up and into the bleeding cut under Neko's left eye, trying to open it more.

Neko gagged and pulled back for just an instant. This consultant was good, better than anyone Neko had ever faced.

"Not good enough." Neko thought. His left elbow coming up under Conner's chin. The fight was close and brutal now. The blows were given and received. Then Conner moved all the way in, using a head strike and going

135

for Neko's nose. Neko dodged the blow, taking it on his right cheek, feeling the skin split there too. Then Conner was on him.

Trace snaked both his hands through the killer's armpits, up and over his back. Chest to chest now, Trace's iron-hard fingers hooked under Neko's jawline on both sides, using his thumbs to dig into the nerve bundles on the assassin's neck, pinning the head back, forcing Neko to look up at the ceiling, trying to use the incredible pain to restrain him long enough for Luka to show up.

Neko felt the pain, intense pain, shooting through him. It hardened his resolve, strength growing. His head was pinned in place by Conner's grip, he couldn't move it at all to look around. He attempted to strike Conner, but the hold limited the strength he could bring to bear. Still, he hammered the sides of Trace's head, right and left.

"Come on Luka." Trace thought, *I don't know how long I can keep him here.*

Neko felt the invisible push, danger from behind him. He tried to move, but the consultant held him. Pulling hard clockwise, almost falling, he felt the first round hit his vest in the rear SAPI plate, the second round in the right side of the vest. The third round hit Conner.

"Fuck!" Bellowed Trace, the nine-millimeter feeling like a baseball bat. "Go for the head! He's wearing armor!"

Luka hesitated, "did Trace just say 'go for the head'?" The two men were moving so fast, he couldn't risk a headshot, even this close. He knew he'd already hit Trace once.

Neko used Trace's physical response to the round he took, bending both their bodies to his right. Neko just barely managed to pull the second Beretta from his back. He rolled it around his body and fired three rounds into Conner's vest from inches away.

Trace gasped, losing his grip and staggering back, blocking Luka's firing line. Neko dropped low, staying in front of Conner, using him as a shield, he shot under Trace's still slightly raised left arm. Once, twice, he struck the new, much larger man. Conner's body was protecting the assassin, but not the new shooter. Neko pushed Trace back, into the bigger man. As he did so, he fired three more rounds into the new combatant. The big man grunted with each blow, then finally a small cry escaped him and his weapon dropped free, falling a few feet from Conner.

Trace heard Luka's cry and the weapon clatter. From the corner of his left eye, he saw it fall. Neko was still in close, Trace dropped his left arm, pinning Neko's pistol and pivoting counterclockwise, away from Luka. Trace dropped his whole body now, letting the assassin's gun hand move up just below his own armpit. He clamped his arm tight on the weapon itself, pivoting back clockwise. He felt the killer's trigger finger break as he completed the weapon strip, losing both the gun and his grip on Neko.

Neko's index finger howled in pain. His left hand shot forward, hitting the inside of Trace's left leg, then right leg. Folding the consultant's legs and dropping him to the ground. Much to Neko's consternation, the consultant fell, executing a ground drop then rolling for the much larger man's weapon. Neko saw Conner's hand grab the free weapon as he started the roll. A glance told Neko that his own weapon was too far away, and Conner was coming up out of reach also. In a microsecond, he made his decision, flying over the much larger shooter in the doorway and out of the small house. He felt the first two rounds fly past his head and the third hit the top of the rear SAPI plate, pitching him forward and off his feet. He continued the momentum and rolled, coming back on to his feet instantly and into a full run into the forest.

"He just came out the front. Neko's bolting." Kevin heard over the radio. He was still positioned outside the back door, where he had been waiting for the killer to emerge. Something had gone wrong, as it always did. Trace's radio had gone silent as he and Luka were closing in. Then a second later, they heard an explosion. Luka still went to the front and Kevin to the rear, as they had planned.

Trace launched himself over Luka and out the shattered front entry. As he passed the fallen SEAL, he saw the copious amounts of blood on the floor and Luka trying to stem the flow, bright red, an arterial hit. Cursing loudly, Trace took one last look out at the forest, where the killer had disappeared and backed up. Without a tourniquet, Luka would bleed out in a few minutes. The big man was trying to stem the blood flow with one hand but was not faring well.

"FUCK!" Trace screamed, then, "Kevin, get in here, now!"

Kevin heard the shout, first out loud then over the radio as Conner leaned in and keyed Luka's radio. He moved quickly in a combat crouch, weapon scanning in front as he moved. "Larry, where is Neko?"

"I don't have eyes on him, he went straight out into the forest and disappeared." Came the reply.

Kevin arrived at the front door, took a knee, and scanned all directions. Seeing nothing he hollered through the front door. "Trace, I'm here."

"Come inside, help me move Luka back so I can treat him and you can cover." Came the reply instantly. "He's hit, an artery, I need to stop it. Call Larry down, we need to get Luka to a hospital." Short, flat, calm, clipped answers, like he had done this before.

They pulled Luka back and Kevin took a knee inside covering the front door. Conner hit a switch on a security panel and the two windows that had been open, sealed closed with the metal shutters. Four minutes later, Larry skidded to a stop, the rear door of his rented SUV lined up with the front entry. Trace and Kevin grabbed Luka, who was cursing loudly now, and hauled him into the backseat. With an enormous cloud of dirt, Larry spun the SUV in a one hundred eighty degree turn and took off. Trace was behind him, holding Luka's damaged arm and giving directions to the hospital. To help offset shock, Luka's legs were out the window on the rear passenger side.

"Somebody give me a phone. Mine's somewhere in the house debris." Trace said.

Luka used his good hand to reach into his tactical vest, as he grabbed his phone, he felt the shattered screen. "Mine took a round, no good." He said.

"Trace, here," Kevin said, handing his phone over the seat.

"Thanks." Conner began dialing.

"Lieutenant Alonzo, who am I speaking with?" Came the voice on the other end.

"Fuzzy, glad I got you, this is Trace Conner."

"Sensei, we're headed to your house. Got a few reports of an explosion and gunfire. Are you doing some special training there?" The Flagstaff police lieutenant asked. "You didn't answer your phone."

"No, listen to me carefully Rob. Somebody very bad just tried to kill me, he may still be near my house. Don't leave any officers alone. Just sit on the house. I'm calling a contact in the FBI, I'm sure they'll take it from you." Trace said, referring to the Flagstaff Police department.

"I'm sure we can help."

"I'm serious Rob, this guy is the most dangerous person I've ever come across, you know what that means. He almost killed me, he wounded one of the guys with me. We're on our way to the hospital, so you'll be getting a call for a gunshot wound soon."

"The Feebs were in our office a few days ago. I think they're at the Little America Hotel, off of I-40. Is that why they're here? Because of you?"

"Yea Rob, I'm doing some stuff for the Department of Defense, that's all I can say about it."

"Alright, Sensei, can you give me a description of the guy?" The lieutenant asked.

"Better than that, the Feds will have the sketch we did a few days ago. Asian male, between thirty and fifty, about five-ten, and one fifty-five pounds or so." Trace answered.

"Is this why you haven't been in class the last few weeks?"

"Yea, Rob. Listen, be careful, and don't leave any officers alone. Gotta go and thank you."

"Sure Sensei. We'll wait for the feebs, then I'll come to the hospital." The lieutenant said and then disconnected.

Neko had watched the man come from behind the house and move inside. He was an experienced soldier. Scanning, alert, competent, and a real danger to Neko at that moment because he had no weapons of his own. He had climbed a Ponderosa pine about thirty feet beyond the tree line, at twenty feet off the ground, he could see the front of Conner's house easily. He waited and watched, after a few minutes, an SUV slid to a stop. The large shooter he'd hit and then jumped over to escape was helped into the back seat. Conner ran around and got in the other side, as soon as his door closed, the SUV spun around and roared off in a cloud of dust. Neko climbed down, intending to search the house anyway, but that changed when he heard the first siren close by. He turned and ran into the forest, escaping.

The head wound from the sniper had torn open, he had gashes on both sides of his face and he could feel the swelling and tenderness where Conner had pummeled his temple. No, he couldn't let the police see him, he couldn't let anyone see him. As he ran, he went over his injuries. Besides the bruised and cut face, he had what felt like cracked ribs from the round he took in the side. His left leg was very stiff on the inside of the knee, no doubt swelling at the spot Conner struck him. His chest and back ached under the SAPI plates from the stomp kick and the other rounds that hit him.

He had failed. They had almost killed him again. They had underestimated him, but he had still underestimated Conner. Thinking about the tactic, Neko actually laughed. This Conner fellow was a lunatic. Neko didn't fault himself for not foreseeing this tactic, it was so crazy, he couldn't believe somebody had even tried it.

It only took him ten minutes to reach his rented Jeep, jumping in, he started it and headed north, away from the sirens. According to his GPS map, there was a town called Tuba City up there and eventually, he could make it to Salt Lake or head Southwest to Las Vegas. Both had major airports.

The call to the Colonel came first because Trace didn't have agent Jares number memorized. After a quick explanation, Trace waited while Colonel Thomas got the agent together with them on a conference call. Just as agent Jares and the Colonel came on the line, the nurses began to take Luka into the emergency exam room.

"Hey, Trace." Luka called, "let's not do that again!"

"Yea," Trace smiled, "let's not. See you when you get out."

"Let's not... what?" Jares asked. "Did you get him?"

"No," Trace answered, "it went sort of like we planned and then fell apart. Murphy's law, I guess." He went on to explain to the others about the breaching charge, Neko's entry, and as many details as he could dig out of his memory. Although the whole fight, from the explosion to the frenzied hospital ride, took less than seven minutes, the storytelling took more than twenty.

"How badly hit is Luka?" The colonel asked.

"I know it was arterial, I don't think the humerus bone was broken. At least it didn't feel broke. That guy's arm muscles are like iron cables though, so it's hard to tell. I know he took at least one round to the vest, his phone was hit. Not sure how many others he took. So, he probably has some bruising and maybe a cracked rib or two."

"How many hit you? Catherine's voice, Trace hadn't even realized she was on the call.

"I honestly don't know. Feel like I was a punching bag for Mike Tyson and a semi. Neko hits like a mother. If I hadn't been wearing the vest..." Trace trailed off, wondering now just how badly bruised he was.

"So then, you probably have a few cracked ribs too?" Catherine pressed.

"Probably." Trace replied.

"Do you think Neko is injured badly enough to need a hospital?" Agent Jares asked.

"No. His injuries were more visible, I hammered his face good. He's bleeding a lot and in an hour his face will be swollen and bruised, but I doubt we got anything vital. Pretty sure I broke at least his trigger finger on the right hand, but none of this will stop him." Conner finished.

"It'll make him a lot more visible, especially to law enforcement and the slight British accent you mentioned might have something to do with Hong Kong," Jares added.

"Yea, well Flagstaff is a city, but not a huge one. I'm sure he's already gone. Sitting on I-40 and I-17 as we do, he could go any direction and hit an international airport in a few hours. You couldn't put roadblocks on the highways, that'd be thousands of cars... We lost him." Trace lamented, "Sorry."

"Go back to the fight," the Colonel said. "He shot you what, three times? Inches away? Does that mean he decided to kill you?"

"Yea, I think it was three, but no, he wasn't trying to kill me. He would've known the instant his first strike hit, that I was wearing body armor.

His second strike would've removed any doubt, just like I knew he was wearing it when my kick landed." Trace replied. "He just used the bullets to make me let go. A very effective technique, by the way."

"How long before he tries again?" The Colonel asked.

"It will be at least a week before he could move around here unnoticed. Maybe longer, but he'll know that law enforcement has a description. I'm betting he's gone and won't be back." Trace said.

"Think they'll try to send another team to take the program?" Catherine asked.

"That's what I'm afraid of. A lot of innocent people here..."

"I did tell you that it was a bad plan," Catherine stated emphatically.

"Yea, it probably wasn't the best." Trace replied, fingering all the bruises that might indicate cracked ribs. "But, in my defense, Neko definitely didn't expect it and nobody died."

"True, but we're running out of combat qualified people to help you." The Colonel said.

"What are you going to do now?" Jares asked.

"Colonel, is it possible to bring Alan into this discussion?" Trace asked. "I want to run something past him."

"Hold on, I'll call him. Then conference him in, if he answers."

"Agent Jares, I need you to put almost everything we discuss on this call into your next report, just as fast as possible." Trace said during the lull.

"You want our government leak to get the intel quickly?" Jares queried.

"I'm counting on it. I don't want the opposition sending a team here like they did at MIGIsoft's offices. No reason for innocent people to die." Trace responded. "I plan to be moving within the hour."

"What about your man there in the E.R.?" Jares asked.

"I'm gonna leave Kevin here as security for Luka. I'll take Larry with me, as backup."

"Wouldn't Kevin provide more help to you than Luka?" The Colonel asked, coming back on the line. "Alan is on the line with us now."

"Yes, and I'd really like to have Kevin with me, but until Luka is safe somewhere else, I'd feel better if Kevin stayed with him." Trace continued. "I think we have to switch to a cat and mouse game. I'll be the mouse. Alan, are you there?"

"Yes, Mr. Conner." Alan Wells replied.

"Is there any way at all to reconstruct the program at MIGIsoft? Think hard, any way at all?" Trace asked.

"I don't see how..." Wells spoke slowly, thinking it out. "Our people destroyed all the ancillary computers that might have had anything on them, there were no other physical backups that I'm aware of and you took the server drives. No. Especially without Albert. He personally wrote the algorithms, there aren't any copies of those either."

"Good." Trace breathed. "I need you guys to bring in Ken Tellu. Alan, you ask him to help you recreate the program. Tell him that I just took off after the last call and nobody knows where the drives are. Tell him you think I've gone mercenary and might try to sell the drives, but the company has to give the DOD something. Make sure he understands how hopeless it is to rebuild the program, I want to make sure the word gets back to this 'Kelsi' person. That way they won't try to take people or stuff from MIGIsoft."

"I can do that,... traitorous bastard," Wells answered. "Who is Kelsi?"

"We don't know yet." Answered agent Jares. "I see where Conner is going with this. Hopefully, Tellu will get in touch with Kelsi again and help us get closer to finding out who he is. There are a lot of Kelsi names in the SF area. So far, we haven't had any luck."

"Did you already rule out Oswald Kelsi, over at Terrace software?" Wells asked.

"Oswald Kelsi...at Terrace software..?" Jares said as he scribbled a note. "I don't remember seeing that name on the list."

"I met Oswald about five years ago. I think it was at the last Military Defense show we displayed at. He was spending most of his time 'headhunting' at the different vendors." Wells quickly continued. "Which isn't unusual, everybody does it. I know he talked to me and a few others that were working the booth, taking each to lunch and stuff. I know he talked to Ken. Maybe more came of that than I thought. We all said that none of us were interested in switching to Terrace."

"So, Terrace is a DOD contractor as well?" Jares asked.

"Yes, they are." Catherine put in. "They had the tank targeting software, I think it was for the M1A1 back before 2001. After 9/11, DARPA came to Albert, on behalf of the DOD and asked him to create new targeting software. He was doing some really groundbreaking stuff with GPS locating and Geotags. DARPA thought it had practical applications for targeting. It kicked off MIGIsoft. He created it, they bought it and we had the contract for about ten years. Albert used that time and money to spread into just about every other application there was. When we lost the tank contract, it was such a small part of our business, that he didn't care."

"Tellu was with Albert, way back then," Wells added.

"Yes, and now that I think about it, Albert gave him the option of company shares instead of money at that time, because the company was still cash poor. Tellu refused, he wanted the cash. Over the years Albert paid him very well, but he would've been rich if he had taken the shares. Many of the company employees from back then took stock and have already retired." Catherine finished.

"Come to think of it," Wells said, "Ken did complain a lot about how much Albert made, but he stopped griping about it a year or two back."

"Think maybe he made a deal with this Oswald Kelsi?" Jares asked. "If they are a DOD contractor, anybody that works for them in those areas must have a DOD clearance. So, we should have information on him. Do you know anything else about him?"

"Not really, I only had that one conversation with him," Wells answered. "I just remember the name, because I thought it was strange. I remember that there were whispers back then that he was mob-related, but I have no idea if it was true. He might not even be at Terrace anymore."

"Could that be Chinese mob?" Trace asked, thinking there might be a link to the Chinese Triads in Hong Kong.

"I'm sorry, I just don't know. It was a rumor I heard." Wells said.

"I'll track that angle." Jares put in. "And don't worry Conner, I'll leave out any mention of Kelsi in my report."

"I was hoping I didn't have to say that." Trace said. "Okay Allen, you'll have to do some acting on this. Really convince Tellu that I've gone off and want to sell the drives. Maybe leave your phone available for him to see my number, I don't know, tell him that Catherine told you to keep calling me till you get an answer..or something."

"It might be more convincing if I use Ms. Dewal's phone or the Colonel's. I could tell him that we don't want an unknown number popping up on your end." Wells replied.

"Whatever you think will sell it best, then get out of there. The longer a scam runs the better chance it will fail. I just want him to know that the program can't be recreated, I have the drives, I've taken off, that I might be willing to sell them and that he gets my number." Trace said.

"Then you're hoping to get a call from this 'Kelsi' offering to buy the drives?" The Colonel asked.

"Yea and if we're lucky, Agent Jares will be able to grab this person and finally roll this thing up." Conner finished.

"I really doubt it will be that easy," Jares said. "The opposition has a lot more information than we do and seems to be a step ahead of us."

"No, it probably won't be, but it's a shot." Conner continued, "I was hoping to get something off of Neko, he did call me by my real name by the way, not the Eldridge pseudonym. Other than verifying his description and the slight English accent, I got nothing besides pain from that encounter."

"So, they definitely have more sources than just Tellu," Jares said.

"It would seem so. Colonel, can you have someone run the records and see who in the company would have known my full name? Secretaries, doorman, security, operators...I don't know...maybe we're missing something simple, besides the DOD leak."

"Yes, I can do that." The Colonel replied.

"Are you really taking off with the drives?" Catherine asked with a worried note in her voice.

"Yes. I'm not gonna tell you guys where I'm going either. I'll update you when we get somewhere. Don't worry, Larry will keep me from getting suddenly rich." Trace quipped.

"I don't like it." Jares put in.

"Me neither." Said Catherine.

"I don't either." Trace agreed, but the only way to keep everybody else safe, including all the other employees and their families at MIGIsoft, is to paint a big ole bullseye on my back and hope I can keep moving fast enough to not get hit...again."

Right then, Lt. Rob Alonzo from the Flagstaff Police Department walked through the outer doors and made a beeline for Conner.

"I have to talk to the local police now, Agent Jares, please get some of the FBI over here as well." Hanging up and turning to face Lt. Alonzo, Trace said, "Fuzzy, how does my house look?" Fuzzy was the nickname Conner had given Lt. Alonzo after he showed up for his second class wearing fuzzy socks. He had a penchant for the things, Trace had given him the nickname before he ever found out that Rob was a police officer. Being politically correct was never Conner's forte' so he continued to use the moniker on the officer.

"Messed up, Sensei. Furniture, glass, guns, broken shit and blood, just about everywhere in the living room." Fuzzy replied.

"Any chance you grabbed my phone and pistol before the FBI showed up?"

"I grabbed your phone, that's not super pertinent to the investigation, but I couldn't remove any weapons. Big no-no."

"Well mine, the Sig Sauer, was never fired. It shouldn't be part of it." Trace huffed.

"Not my call, Sensei. The FBI has it now, along with all the other ones still there. Maybe you can get it back later. "I need to file a report, what can you tell me?" Fuzzy asked.

"Nothing really, Fuzzy. Toss all of it to the FBI, let them deal with it." Turning to the other men in the waiting room, "Kevin, you stay here with Luka. Babysit his big ass. Larry, you're going road tripping with me."

Fuzzy did not look happy as Conner left dragging the former Marine along.

146

Chapter 18

"It was another trap, but they failed to kill me again," Neko announced as the call was answered.

"I'm guessing that you lead with that statement because you failed to obtain the objects," Kelsi replied.

"This is true. This Conner fellow created an ingenious trap. It almost worked even though I surprised him with my own variation. I barely escaped alive."

"Christ, Neko! We need those drives! Can you go back and finish?"

"No. Conner did an efficient job of damaging my face. It will be far too obvious if I am seen anywhere near the area. I also have a broken finger, at least two cracked ribs, and multiple lacerations. I must stay out of sight for at least a week."

"Damn it! This isn't Hong Kong anymore, I can't call up a bunch of Triad hitters to help out, like last time." Kelsi growled angrily.

"No, you cannot," Neko said, his mind drifting back to Hong Kong, a lifetime ago.

Hong Kong, China, July 1987

Neko arrived in the gambling mecca with a pocket full of money. It had taken months to make his way here, past the guards and fences. He paid bribes and snuck past barriers on his way. Like all young men, he thought he would just go to the tables, put some money down, and get rich. After all, James Bond did it in every movie. As it turned out, it was very hard to get rich gambling, but quite easy to get poor.

The gambling establishment was owned and run by the Three Dragons Triad. The Triad didn't object to a seventeen-year-old gambling, as long as he lost. After almost three weeks of losing and spending, Neko was broke. His last two hundred dollars in American money lost to roulette.

Angry now, he screamed at the dealer. Insisting that they had cheated him. Two young men arrived to escort him out of the casino. Neko knocked both men out in a few seconds. After that, three men arrived at the table. Other patrons hastily cleared away. Neko smiled, this is what he did best, not gambling, fighting. In short order, Neko had disabled the new arrivals. Moments after that a middle-aged man appeared and asked him to please leave. Neko attacked the man, planning to take out all his frustration on him. Much to his surprise, he found himself face down on the floor, a foot on his neck. The older man allowed him to rise and Neko launched a furious attack. The man easily blocked all the blows, before hitting Neko so hard on the bridge of his nose, that he practically flew backward. Two of the men that had been defeated earlier, were up now and grabbed Neko off the floor. They drug him towards a rear exit, intending to punish him for their failure.

"Wait!" The older man commanded.

"Sifu...we must teach this whelp a lesson he won't forget." One of the men replied.

"No, I claim him as mine. He will go with me, I will speak to our master about him. Cuff his wrists for now."

Obviously irritated, the man bowed his head. "Yes, Sifu."

"Why did you save me? I deserved to be beaten." Neko asked the older man. While he held a wad of paper towels against his bleeding nose.

"You have great potential. You easily bested our security team, that is no easy feat."

"You beat me even easier. They must not be that good." Neko replied.

"On the contrary, I have never seen any of them beaten before." the older man switched to English. "Do you speak English?"

"Yes, the Americans taught me when I was very young."

"Good. Your training will be in English."

"Training...is that what you call torture and beating?" Neko said irritably.

"No, training is to improve your skills and give you a job."

148

"As a security guard at a casino? No thank you. I can do better on my own."

"No, not merely security. Your skills would be wasted. You may not have realized this, but this casino is owned by the Three Dragons Triad. You made many enemies on the house floor. If you do not work for them, you will be against them and hunted. Eventually, they will find you." The older man said.

"So? I beat them before." Neko boasted, but dread had begun to seep in. It was one thing to have a fight and leave, but another thing entirely to have a triad after you.

"Training will be in English because we both speak it well and many of the triad do not speak it at all."

"Why? What difference does it make?" Neko asked.

"We are both outsiders. You are not Chinese, at least not full blood Chinese. They will consider you an outsider like me. We can never be true triad members, but we have our uses."

Neko looked more carefully at the 'Sifu'. He was definitely not Chinese.

"Probably Indian or Thai." Neko thought, but he wasn't sure. Out loud, he asked. "What did you use to beat me? It was so easy for you."

"Most refer to it as 'Pencak Silat', although this is a broad term, applied to all the different styles from my islands. It is actually a derivation of Silat Melayu."

"The guards did not use it," Neko observed.

"No. Being Chinese, they want to know a Chinese Martial art. I am well versed in them. I teach the majority of triad muscle Wing Chun. Bruce Lee made it a very popular style. Most of them could not grasp the subtleties of Silat."

"But you think that I can? Why do you want me to change, if I am as good as you think?"

"Not change. Add to or alter if you will. Silat is very effective against the Chinese arts, as you have seen. I want to add these skills to you so that you may become a 'last resort weapon' for the triad. No normal security or collection work. You will be sent on special, difficult assignments."

"Now we are talking." Neko thought, both excited and scared. *"What would necessitate a 'last resort weapon'? Why would they need that? They are one of the biggest triads in China."* Out loud, he asked, "Is this not your job? This last resort?"

"Yes, it is. But I am getting older and as the teacher for the triad, I am more important than you are." Sifu replied bluntly. "The head of the Three Dragons will pay you well, although you can no longer gamble in China."

"That's fine," Neko grumbled aloud. "I'm not good at it anyway."

"Then you agree to the terms?" Sifu asked. "Providing the Dragons head approves, of course."

"Yes, I agree," Neko said seriously.

For the next two years, Neko trained with Sifu. He also helped to train new triad muscle in Wing Chun. Occasionally he was sent to deliver a message to a gambler that had failed to pay a debt or tried to run away from it. Sometimes this meant that he had to go into China proper, crossing the border into communist-controlled areas. Kelsi sent Neko on these tasks.

Oswald Kelsi was the triad's 'operations officer', as he liked to call himself. A former analyst for British MI-6, he had gotten bored doing analysis and the money wasn't very good. Kelsi had approached the triad and offered his services to them. The Dragonhead saw the immediate benefits and hired him. Kelsi had originally passed the qualifications for a field agent but had nearly died when he froze on the first assignment. Only his field trainer's swift reaction had saved him. Shaken, he resigned from fieldwork immediately and was placed in analysis in what was then British controlled Hong Kong. After three years of parsing intelligence for no personal gain, Kelsi decided to branch out. He had watched the triads, he knew them all. Three Dragons were the largest and had the most potential. The Dragonhead did not hate foreigners, as so many Chinese did, but used them to promote the rise of his triad. Kelsi saw this as an open invitation and applied.

Three Dragons and the communist Chinese government already had an agreement, which allowed triad members to 'sneak' in and out of the country. The government got information and money from the triad, while the triad was allowed to chase deadbeats inside china.

That all changed after the Tiananmen Square massacre in 1989. Under intense scrutiny from human rights organizations, first-world governments, and the ever-present media, China had to find a way to deal with outspoken critics and revolutionaries. Three Dragons triad filled this role nicely. In exchange for a promise that the triad would retain its casino and related underworld business after Hong Kong reverted to China in 1999, the triad would deal with the voices that denounced the communist regime.

For the next three years, Neko dealt with these critics for the Chinese communists. Sometimes he had a conversation with them, convincing them that it was in the best interest of themselves and their families to change their rhetoric. More often, he simply killed them. Neko had become adept at ending lives while leaving virtually no evidence of the murder. His hand spears were like knives, easily shredding internal organs. Then the local government would pronounce the deaths as natural causes or accidents. Everything was going well for Neko, the triad, and the communists until early in 1992.

"Her name is Wei Shin," Kelsi said. "She's becoming a real problem for Beijing. They want her gone."

"Dead gone?" Neko liked clear orders.

"Yes. It needs to be an accident. She is very popular already and her death will make her a martyr for the cause if they can blame it on the communists."

"I understand." With that, Neko left for Beijing and Peking University.

Neko spent the first week blending into university life. He went to classes, made friends, and pretended to be critical of the communists. This was easy, he was twenty-two now, the right age for college and he had lived in a capitalist atmosphere for the last four years. His second week was spent trying to get closer to Wei Shin. This was not nearly as easy. She had a personal retinue that consisted mostly of men that were slightly older and didn't attend classes. Neko assumed this was her personal security, surprised that she even had it. Halfway through his third week, he made his move.

Breaking into her room while she was out at a small gathering of anti-communist believers, he waited, not even sure if she would be back.

When the door finally opened, it was by one of her security, performing a sweep of the room, before allowing Wei Shin to enter. This was a problem. Neko was under strict orders not to kill anyone other than Wei Shin and it had to look like an accident. Neko couldn't leave without being spotted, so he attacked the bodyguard and rendered him unconscious. He then left through the window he had used to enter the third story apartment and climbed down the brick facade. The rest of her team quickly deduced there had been an intruder and moved Wei Shin to a new, safe location. Fortunately, people like her had to be heard to be effective. Neko spent two more weeks locating Wei Shin's new apartment. Having reported his first failure to Kelsi, he had asked for special items that had arrived that morning. Armed with these extra tools, he climbed the balconies of the new building to the fifth floor this time.

Neko moved inside, having easily defeated the lock on the balcony door. No security in the room this time. He moved to the bedroom and closed on Wei Shin. Even though he had not made a single noise, she stirred, turning over and facing him, then her eyes blinked open. She screamed and reached under her pillow, producing a small Makarov .380 pistol. Neko should have been moving already, should have been at her side, and disabled her before she could scream. Before she could pull out a pistol. He had the skill but not the ability. He stood there frozen. She was stunning, absolutely stunning. Dark eyes, a soft mouth, blue-black hair that cascaded around her face and shoulders, she was like a goddess brought to life. Neko simply stared, knowing in that instant that he couldn't kill her. It would be akin to destroying Michelangelo's 'David' or a Monet painting, he just couldn't do it, she was breathtaking.

She stopped screaming but held the pistol level, pointed at his chest. "You are here to kill me, aren't you?" She asked.

He merely stood there, drinking in the sight of her. He knew it didn't make sense to spare her, Kelsi would send somebody else to do it, she would still die. Beijing had ordered it, nothing could change that. As the argument raged inside his head, his reverie was broken by the front door bursting open.

152

Two men rushed at him. Neko turned and met them at the bedroom door, using it to force them to attack one at a time. Neko easily subdued them, killing both. He kept expecting the gun behind him to go off, waited for the bullet in his back, but it didn't happen. Even after he had killed the two men. He was turning to look at her again when a third man entered the apartment. This one was pointing a gun in Neko's direction, but with virtually no firearm discipline. Neko was about to move forward and kill the third man when he saw a fourth and fifth man in the hallway beyond. The fifth man also had a gun and Neko knew it was time to leave. Turning, he sprinted for the bedroom window, the first man fired, Wei Shin screamed again. Firing wildly, the first man followed. A round burned a furrow in the top of his left trapezius muscle and a round whistled by his right ear, then he broke through the window. As he did, he grabbed the lower edge of the frame, cutting his hand on the glass, and swung back towards the next, lower balcony, below the living room. He fully expected the shooter to lean out the window and keep firing, he did, but none of the rounds hit, and soon, the gun was empty. Neko continued his frantic climb down and escaped into the chaos of Beijing and the population of almost eleven million people.

Oswald Kelsi was furious. Neko had failed, again. It didn't seem possible. Wei Shin was making public statements about the attempt on her life, blaming Beijing. The communists were furious. The triad was in real trouble.

"What the fuck happened?" Kelsi practically screamed. When he got angry his English accent came on strong, most of the time it was turned way down and he sounded like an American. "Do you have any idea what you have done? How am I supposed to fix this now?"

Neko was injured, but he didn't expect any sympathy. The triad and Kelsi didn't operate like that. He had failed. He also knew that if he was sent back, he couldn't kill Wei Shin. It just wasn't possible. Unfortunately, this also meant that his future in Hong Kong was over. The triad would have to sacrifice him to appease the communists and still kill Wei Shin. Neko stood silent, saying nothing.

"Never mind. I've already ordered a team of enforcers to go and finish for you." Kelsi was calmer now. "You've been an amazing talent for us, but Beijing wants you punished."

"I understand." No other movement from Neko.

"That would be a waste. I hate to waste an asset, that I might need in the future. I'm going to give you a name. He is a General in Serbia. I believe he will have a use for your skillset. Something big is happening there."

Puzzled, Neko looked at the older man. "I do not know where Serbia is."

"Well, that is about to change. You had better leave right now. You will need to travel very far to get there and you cannot cross China anymore. Every communist soldier and party official will be told to watch for you. I know that you have money, so this name is all the help I can give. Keep in touch. I may be able to bring you back in a few years." Kelsi finished.

The team of enforcers that Kelsi had sent to kill Wei Shin, killed her and everyone nearby. An absolute blood bath and Three Dragons triad took the blame, publicly claiming that she had failed to repay her debts. The communist government made a big show of denouncing the murders and asserting that this lawless attitude would not be allowed. The triad would be punished. They never were. Beijing gave the triad more power, while the world heaped anger and hatred upon them. In a few years, the world forgot about the issue and followed a shiny new atrocity happening in Bosnia.

Traveling first to Japan, then south, through the islands. Into Indonesia, where he spent many weeks visiting Silat schools on different islands. It took Neko five months to make his way to Serbia, then finally Bosnia to find the General. It was now August of 1992 and the Bosnian war was in full swing. Neko smiled, time to get back to work.

Chapter 19

DARPA Deputy Director Alicia Parks looked around one more time, before hitting the call button on the red phone app. She was nervous, but she was also greedy and greed trumped nerves, as it almost always does. Well paid by DARPA, she still wanted more. She knew she was too smart to be caught by the gumshoes at the FBI. No, her concern was the whiz kids that ran the data collection at the NSA. They weren't supposed to tap her calls, but that didn't mean they didn't just grab it along with millions of others. She had met some of these 'kids' as she called them. Many worked for her at DARPA. It was strange to have them talk above her head about things she barely understood. Often, they had to dumb it down for her, which she found particularly insulting. Rather than try to learn more, she just chafed at their superiority.

"This is Kelsi." The call connected.

"I just got the report from the FBI. Your team, or should I say 'man'? Failed again. This Trace Conner has taken off with the drives. No clue where he has gone."

"Yes. It turns out that this Mr. Conner is not the simple consultant we were first led to believe. A history search shows that he has spent a great amount of time in the martial arts." Kelsi replied.

"Wait. That's it?" Alicia demanded. "Basically, you've been stopped by Jackie fucking Chan? I thought you had pros, I thought you were a pro?"

"He is not a simple karate teacher. The art he teaches is specifically geared to do what we have been attempting. Obviously, this gives him unique insight and skills to counter our attempts. Also, he is very ...original...in the way, he dealt with our specialist and the team we sent."

"My report said that it was MIGIsoft's security that stopped the team you sent." She said. "Have you been able to talk to the man that was captured?"

"No. Once we knew about him, we arranged for a lawyer to represent him. He died in the holding cell, an innocent victim of a jail gang fight. A terrible shame." Kelsi said with clear sarcasm. "Anyhow, I don't think MIGIsoft's security team could have taken him alive with no injuries at all. I think this consultant was there and it was hidden from the FBI or kept out of the reports."

"How much did he tell the FBI, before he got out?" She asked, her nerves ratcheting up.

"According to the lawyer, nothing. Plus, he didn't know anything." Kelsi calmly said, attempting to allay her fears. "Only the team leader knew that they were there for the program. All the team members were told that they were supposed to grab a guy in a lime green shirt. Since that man was the encryption expert, even if the FBI learned that, they would think it was so he could be forced to remove or bypass the encryption."

"Was that our mole?"

"Really Alicia, that's none of your concern."

"Right, right...of course. Sorry." She stammered out.

"Do you have any information that will help us find the drives?"

"I have a number for the consultant, Conner. It was buried in the reference material with the report. If he's gone off the reservation, maybe you can scare him into giving up the drives." She said.

"This 'consultant' went toe to toe against my best man and lived. I don't think he scares that easily. No....we will have to go a different direction, I think."

"Well, I can't get the NSA to listen to his calls, not without a warrant. If I ask for that, it'll really highlight my interest in the program." Alicia answered.

"No, we don't want that. We need to keep the paperwork and red tape between you and the program." Kelsi thought aloud. "Can you request location on the phone without a warrant?"

"I'll check, but I think so. Especially, if I point out that Conner is not answering the phone and has the drives. It'll look like 'due diligence' on my part." She said. "National security and all that nonsense."

"Good, good, that will help a lot. Please see to that and let me know when you have any information." Without waiting for a reply from Alicia, Kelsi ended the call.

Trace looked at his shaking hands. He couldn't stop them. When he and Larry had gotten back to his house, they grabbed some gear and Conner's 1980 Jeep CJ7, his hands had begun shaking. Small at first, then so hard that Conner had asked Larry to drive. Now Trace sat in the passenger seat making fists and focusing on his breathing.

Larry looked over at the curled fists and said, "it's from the adrenaline dump. Sometimes it seems like it'll never stop. It will."

"Yea, that's what I thought. Just never really experienced it before." Trace said.

"Really? Not the other time you went against Neko or the attack at MIGIsoft?"

"No. I don't know why. Maybe I had too much to do. I thought it happened right away? You know, right after the action stopped?"

"For most guys, yea, but it's different for everybody."

"Did you have it today?" Trace asked.

"Nah. My heart rate went up, but I wasn't in the thick of like you guys. You were blown up and then had to fight for your life, so a huge adrenaline dump is normal."

Breathing deep, Trace responded. "I thought, with all my training, I had more control over my body's responses."

"Hahaha." Larry laughed. "You may have great control, but some things are just beyond anyone's control, like getting blown up. I remember my first mission in the sandbox. When the mine blew up behind me, RPGs started coming in, then AK47 fire like a bee swarm out of hell. I remember the whole thing, like a slow-motion movie, guys screaming...." Larry visibly shook his head. "Anyway, after that I shook for a whole day, I think. At least, it seemed like it."

"Great, that's just what we need. Me shaking like a leaf, while we dodge hired killers."

"No worries. When you get a new adrenaline dump, it all goes away in an instant."

"Not sure I want to hear the story that makes you say that." Trace said.

"Not sure I want to tell it," Larry replied. "So, back to the present. We're gonna head up here then to the other side of the Grand Canyon?"

"Yes. It's very remote and I know it well. That'll give us a tactical advantage. If negotiations with Kelsi go as I think, he'll send somebody after us at first. This is very rugged ground, few innocents. Especially at this time of year. Perfect ground for a Marine sniper." Trace said with a smile.

"You think it'll be Neko again?"

"I hope not. My plan won't work against him. He can sense a shot from you and I don't think he'll let me get close to him again. I just can't see him making that mistake twice." Conner said.

"I still can't believe you had the drives sitting in an old pizza box behind the seats." Larry shook his head. "Aren't they worth something like twenty million dollars?"

"By the aggressiveness of the opposition and the number of dead people, I would guess it's worth three hundred million or more."

Larry whistled. "Holy shit...and you just left them in a pizza box?!"

"I wanted something that Neko would ignore in a quick search but would probably find in a more thorough one. After all, If I was dead, MIGIsoft could claim that they had tried to protect it and the opposition wouldn't have any more reason to go after MIGIsoft. Hopefully, nobody else would have had to die. At least that was my thinking." Trace concluded.

"Damn...for a 'non-soldier', you seem very willing to sacrifice yourself to save others."

"Haha, don't give me that much credit. I was trying to be pragmatic while shitting my pants inside the house." Conner replied.

"You do know that's the very definition of bravery, right?"

"No...this is more like being in the middle of a car-jacking and just doing what needs to be done."

"Sorry, brother, no," Larry responded. "You could have walked away after the first time you tangled with Neko. You're still here, still drawing fire to protect others. That's heroic shit man."

Uncomfortable with the direction of the conversation, Trace tried to steer it away. "What does that make you then?"

"Marine, once a Marine, always a Marine. We have a thing for being in the middle of crazy shit." Larry replied with a big smile. "Although I have to admit, I never thought working for MIGIsoft would get this crazy."

"Yea," Trace chuckled, "Me either. I thought I was just doing a security test. Wrong!"

Larry laughed, then slightly soberer, "so, maybe you should explain the next plan to me? Is this plan D or F?"

"I think it's plan D, we know that plans A, B, and C all failed..." Conner replied. "We're headed into the Kaibab national forest. It sits on the North Rim of the Grand Canyon and heads North from there. Very remote, very rugged. Where we're gonna camp can only be accessed by foot or an extreme four-wheel drive like this baby." Trace patted the Jeep affectionately.

"Oh, so that explains the crappy drive up here."

"Yea, this baby isn't so great for highway driving, but once we get off-road, it'll make up for it. Anyway, the nearest town is Jacob Lake, pretty much only a tiny hotel, gas station, restaurant, and Forest Service office. One cell tower. If they can track my phone, they'll know what area I'm in, but they won't be able to triangulate. Kaibab is huge, over a thousand square miles of some very harsh terrain." Trace said with a wicked smile.

"So, we're gonna set up camp and wait?"

"Yea. The place I usually camp is out on a point, overlooking a small canyon. It'll leave me about a hundred thirty-five degrees to cover. We're gonna build you a hide across the canyon, maybe three hundred yards, so that even if they come with helicopters, drones, or thermal, you'll be shielded from almost every direction." Trace answered. "It'll get cold and we'll be at about eight thousand feet, so I hope you don't get altitude sickness."

"Never had a problem with it. I'm actually from Ruidoso, New Mexico."

"Really? Never been there, but I've heard of it."

"We have a lot of the same wildlife you have around Flagstaff, but some of your bull Elk looked abnormally large. Speaking of which, are we gonna have a bunch of them in the way here?" Larry queried.

"Not so much on the Elk. A lot of Mule deer and whitetail here. The Mulies get huge. Very popular place for the archery deer hunt in the early fall, late summer. Elk are moving down from Utah, but not too much yet. Deer hunting is why I know this place so well. I do archery hunts and bring people sometimes.

"I definitely want to come back and do some hunting. Some of those bulls were massive."

"Yep. I had a friend who shot one so big, even after he skinned, gutted, and quartered it, he still had to make four trips to get it out and he only took the meat. That was on horseback and he had to keep switching out horses. Good eating too."

"Wow," Larry said, impressed. "I would love to take one like that."

"Well, not this trip, my friend. Maybe the next one." Trace said, getting back to business. "Once we establish camp, get some sleep, then tomorrow, I'll check-in and we wait."

"Roger that," Larry said as he crossed the Marble Canyon bridge, trying to see the bottom while driving. "Is that the Colorado river?"

"Yes. We are at the very far Northeast end of the Grand Canyon now. Lake Powell is farther north, on that road we just left. The river down there will go all the way in and through the Grand Canyon. There's a road that leads down there, to a place called Lee's Ferry. About a hundred and twenty years ago, that's how they crossed to get to the Northside of the Canyon."

"Shit, way down there?"

"Yep. Really good fishing there too. Nice campground now."

"Well, it's impressive, the canyon and the mountains around us." As he said this, he let his eyes wander up. The sun was beginning to set now and the sides of the mountains looked to have caught fire. It was beautiful.

"Just wait, it gets even better," Conner said this proudly.

They drove on without speaking or yelling as it was. A true off-road vehicle like Conner's Jeep was not a quiet ride and necessitated almost yelling to be heard. As they continued, the road climbed steeply, with sharp switchbacks, bringing them up to the Kaibab plateau just as the sun finished setting.

Larry pulled the Jeep off the road and onto the shoulder, looking off the edge below. He could see the other sheer mountains on one side, the crack from this distance that marked the Northeast end of the Grand Canyon and the valley below. He whistled, "wow...you weren't kidding. That is amazing."

"Yep. Rough country but yea, wow." Trace replied.

They changed seats, Conner driving into the Kaibab forest because he knew where they were going. Larry was fine with that, driving the big Jeep on the highway was no fun at all. They continued in near silence as the 'golden hour' worked its way to full darkness.

"I'm gonna take us straight to the campsite. We'll set up, get some food, and rack time. In the morning, I'll show you where I want to build your hide, then I'll go into Jacob Lake and let the powers that be know where I am." Trace said.

Larry saw a sign that said '461' and that was the last sign he saw. Conner took a dizzying number of turns, then bounced over boulders that looked big as a VW Bug, between trees packed so densely, he couldn't see the stars. When they finally emerged onto a small plateau, the view of the stars was breathtaking. Stars beyond counting and you could see the entire milky way. The moon had not yet risen and Larry drank in the sight. "Oh my god....this is....wow..."

"Yea. Exactly." Trace said.

They stood there enjoying the stars, the brisk chill, and the stunning silence for five minutes. Finally, Larry rubbed his bare arms.

"Guess we should start a fire and get camp set up." Trace offered. "Don't walk off without a light. We're sitting on the edge of a canyon that drops off about a hundred feet."

"Really, where?"

"About twenty feet in front of you."

"Oh...ok. Good advice." Larry said as he backed a few feet.

Morning brought a pot of black coffee and protein bars. As they sat, silently enjoying the view, the quiet and the rich, dark brew, Trace pointed across the canyon to a slightly higher rise with some large boulders visible from where they sat. Larry just studied it, then nodded. Conner finished his coffee, but Larry refilled his insulated cup and climbed into the Jeep. This turned out to be a mistake. Jeeps from 1980 didn't come with cup holders and even if they did, nothing was staying in place the way Conner drove that beast. Larry tried hard to drink the coffee but wound up wearing most of it.

"Jesus, Trace." He said, trying to hold on to the roll bar and the insulated mug at the same time. "Isn't there an easier way to get there?"

"Sure, you could hike it. It's only a few miles, but I didn't think you wanted to hike that far carrying all this stuff." Trace said, pointing to what gear they had put back in the Jeep.

Finally, they reached the boulders that Conner had pointed to earlier. Stopping just behind the rocks, they began to unload the materials. Making a dome with his hands, Trace said, "I figure we put the pieces of wood between the big rocks down low, then lay the emergency blanket over that, then cover with rocks, dirt, and whatever camouflage you can find. Should make a nice little cave for you to stay in and be invisible from everything except a direct infra-red looking in the front."

Nodding his head, Larry said, "yea, I like it. That looks to be about three hundred yards, so I can cover you easily. I see why you chose that spot for the tent. Gives you real good sightlines and this point is the only one higher."

"Right and any opposition won't know that until they get here. The canyon is too deep to easily cross, and I highly doubt they'll come prepared to do rock crawling. So, they'll have to approach me on foot, making it easy for you."

"Okay, I'll get started."

"Right. I'll go let the locals know, as well as the big wigs." Trace said as he strapped himself back into the Jeep.

"Well hello, Mr. Conner. Kind of late in the year for you to be up here."

"Hi, Bill. I keep telling you to call me Trace."

"No sir. Not unless you drink with me." The old man said with a mischievous wink.

"Sheila might not think too highly of me if I let you drink, just so you'd call me by my first name."

"If he drinks, Trace, it won't be your fault. It'll be because he wants to die." Sheila said as she entered the small store and glared at Bill.

Bill and Sheila had managed the small store and gas station for as far back as he could remember. He knew their names, but that was about all. They were always here when he came hunting and they knew his Jeep. Conner didn't want them to know about Larry, so he had come in alone.

"The reason I'm here so late is that I'm meeting some people for a scouting trip. They are positive that they're gonna get drawn for the hunt next year. Oh well," An exaggerated shrug, "the client gets what they want. If they stop in looking for me, just tell them where I camp. I gave them directions, but they probably tried to Google map it."

Bill laughed, "city people don't get it, that stuff just don't work right out here. The same place as usual? Off 461?"

"Yep. My favorite spot." Trace answered.

"That's a good one," Sheila said. "Will they have a crawling rock car too?"

"Like my beast? Probably not, and it's called a 'rock crawler'."

"A horse is better." The older woman retorted.

"See you guys later." Trace said as he headed out to fuel up the Jeep.

"Later, Mr. Conner," Bill said.

After fueling the Jeep, Trace pulled out and sat at the edge of the road, as if waiting for someone. He pulled out his cellphone, installed the battery, and powered it on. After it finished booting up, he saw that there was a voicemail from Catherine.

"Mr. Conner, this is Alan Wells, at MIGIsoft. Ken Tellu left here a little while ago. He was very convinced that we couldn't recreate the program. We spent a few hours looking for options. I'm also sure that he got your number off of this phone, Ms. Dewal's phone. I left it dialing you quite a few times while he was nearby. I gave him the whole story we agreed on. Hope this works."

"Me too." Thought Conner. *"Me too."*

He turned right to head back to his campsite and see if Larry needed help. As he turned right again, on to road 461, he pulled the battery back out of the phone.

"NSA just messaged me, they got a location ping for that cellphone." DARPA Deputy Director Alicia Parks said quickly.

"I'm ready, give it to me." Oswald Kelsi responded.

"It's in a place called 'Jacob Lake Arizona'."

"Okay....and?" Kelsi asked.

"And what?"

"That's it? No address? No actual coordinates?" Kelsi pressed.

"Apparently not. That was all I received. There is a note attached, saying that there is only one cell tower in the area and no way to triangulate." Alicia answered.

"Great. How am I supposed to find him then?"

"I'm sorry, that's all I got. I'll let you know if anything else comes in."

"You do that," Kelsi said angrily and disconnected the call. Opening a browser, he typed in 'Jacob Lake Arizona' and watched the search returns, getting angrier as he read them and looked at a map of the area. He thought, *"Over a thousand square miles.....shit!"*

As he pondered how to find the consultant, his secretary spoke over the phone intercom. "Sir, there is an urgent call on line two. The caller will not identify himself."

Picking up the handset and punching the appropriate button, he said, "Kelsi here."

"I just left MIGIsoft, I spent a few hours with the lead programmer, trying to recreate the thing you want. No chance at all, we really tried." The caller said.

"That's why -you called me on an open, unencrypted line? To tell me something you had already told me?" Kelsi growled, even angrier now. "Are you calling from your home phone too?"

"No, of course not. I'm in a bar a few miles from the office. Using a good old-fashioned public phone, couldn't believe they had a real, working one." Ken Tellu replied. "I'm calling because I didn't know how long it would be before you checked the encrypted app and saw a message. What I have for you is time-sensitive, I think."

Slightly appeased, Kelsi said, "go on, then."

"While we were trying to recreate the item, the lead guy kept trying to call the consultant. He's not answering his phone and they've left a ton of messages, that he's not returning. They think he's taken off with the item and is going to sell it himself!"

"Why would they think that?" Kelsi asked.

"Something about him almost dying twice but not getting paid commensurate with the danger," Tellu responded. "I got his number off the phone they were using. I was thinking you could call him and try to buy it directly."

"You think he might sell it?"

"The lead guy was really freaked out about it and he had orders from Ms. Dewal to get hold of him or get fired," Tellu said.

"Interesting...very interesting...give me the number." Kelsi prompted.

Ken Tellu gave the number, convinced that this would solve his problem, and allow him to reap a harvest of dirty money.

"Yes!" The FBI tech shouted. "We got him!"

"Tell me exactly what you have." Agent Jares said.

"Tellu went to a bar near Fisherman's Wharf. He found an actual public payphone. The mic on his cell was still live and we've been tracking him, so we have the location of the phone, the number he called and he asked for Mr. Kelsi again. Said it was an emergency. Then he gave the story about the consultant going rogue and selling the 'item', he called it."

"And..." Jares prompted the tech. "Where did the number go to?"

The second tech was furiously typing on his computer. He held up one hand, then a moment later the second. "According to AT&T, the number goes to Terrace Software. It's a landline. That's a solid connection to Terrace and Oswald Kelsi, sir."

"Finally," Jares breathed, "we're getting somewhere. Time to take Tellu off the board and throw him in a hole, while we round up all the other bad apples."

"Should I put in a warrant request for Oswald Kelsi?" The first tech asked.

"No. What we have is very circumstantial, it's a link, but they never said anything concrete. A good lawyer would get it all thrown out. Saying that his client was talking about making bread or something stupid and then we'd have nothing." Agent Jares answered. "We'll grab Tellu and start sweating him. I'm betting we can get him to crack pretty easily. Then, we might have something to take to a judge. After we pick up Tellu, we'll switch all surveillance to Terrace and try to pick up Oswald Kelsi. Maybe, we'll get lucky."

"Yes sir." Said the second tech.

"Laura, get me Jeff McCan on the line, please," Kelsi said to his secretary, through the phone intercom.

"Yes, Mr. Kelsi." Came the quick reply. Moments later, "Mr. Kelsi, I have Mr. McCan on line three."

"Thank you, Laura." Pressing the button for line three, Kelsi spoke quickly. "Jeff, do you have the burner phone here? The one you use for Sara?"

"Sure, I keep it in my desk, with the battery removed. Once a day, I put the battery in, power up, and check messages."

"Good, good. Can you bring it to me? I need to make a call I don't want a record of, but I need to do it right now." Kelsi said. He needed to get hold of that consultant, Trace Conner, as fast as possible. If the program was for sale, Kelsi had to get it first. He knew there was a risk of using the phone for this, but since it wasn't connected to him or anything else, he felt it was a small risk.

166

"Of course, let me run it up to you. Be there in three minutes." Jeff said as he hung up.

"Mr. Conner, I have heard that you are considering selling a certain item, that is in your possession. I can take it off your hands, for a good price and assure your safety." The voicemail said to Trace as he held the phone to his ear. "Please call me back at this number as soon as possible." The voice continued to list a phone number and the time of day.

Trace listened to the message four times. He wrote the number down, then dialed FBI Special Agent Will Jares. "Jares, I have been contacted. No name, but here is the number. I need to call him back soon. How long will it take for you to set up the trace and record it from my phone?"

"Let us track the number and its history first, then we'll set it up for the return call. Stay put, we should be no more than fifteen minutes." Jares answered.

"Okay, good."

Before Trace could disconnect, Jares said, "Conner, you should know that we did get a definitive link between Terrace and Ken Tellu. Not enough for warrants, but they are definitely involved. I wouldn't normally tell someone this. The circumstances make normal procedures a little....off in this case."

"I appreciate that Agent Jares, I really do." Trace said and disconnected the call.

Trace fidgeted in the Jeep, feeling like a satellite was staring straight down at him, imagining a giant bullseye painted on the roof of his rock crawler. Seventeen minutes later, Jares called back. "The phone number was purchased in LA, in the Watts area, by USC. Until you, all the calls have been to and from only one other number. You're gonna love this."

"I'm sure I will." Trace responded.

"All the calls go to or come from a Sara Bellis. She works in MIGIsoft's accounting department. According to the Colonel, she is only an assistant to one of the accountants, but her primary duty is vetting incoming charges from company credit cards or existing charge accounts, like local hotels." The agent finished.

"Of course, geez, I can't believe none of us thought of that. As long as MIGIsoft paid for anything I did, she would have had almost real-time intel on where I was and what I was doing." Trace said, mentally kicking himself. "God...that was stupid... I should have thought of that."

"None of us did. You're right though, stupid that we didn't."

"Picking her up?" Trace asked.

"No. The Colonel is going to have them move her up in the department, so she doesn't get suspicious and fly the coup. Seems she has a good work history and two small kids. Probably just got into something over her head. He's gonna make it harder for her to have direct access to the intel that might affect us but keep her there. In case we need to use that connection."

"I'll leave that up to you pros. Are we ready to make the call?"

"Yes. We have a tap on your line, which you approved in writing, by the way. We also have the tracking software running. It's showing that the number is at a coffee shop about a mile from Terrace software. So, we don't have a distinct link to them...yet." Jares said.

"Alright then, here we go." Trace disconnected and began dialing the number.

"Hello, Mr. Conner. Thank you for returning my call." The man on the other end said.

"Well, I have the T-FAX, you want it, so we need to talk price." Trace responded.

"No, not on an open line. I want you to download an app, called 'Red Phone'. Once you have it loaded, call the number I am texting you now. This is an encrypted app so that we can talk safely." Kelsi said.

"I don't like installing apps that I know nothing about on my phone. Let's talk now."

"I will not deal on an open line."

"Then I guess we won't be dealing."

"Mr. Conner, you can sell it to me or I can come to Jacob Lake and have it taken from you."

"Hahaha.....yea sure. You've tried that...how many times now? I've stopped you every time that I was involved. This time I'm on my home turf and I'm prepared. Nobody short of a platoon will get it from me...and you know it. Just because you have a spy somewhere in MIGIsoft or the FBI or the DOD, doesn't mean you can touch me when I'm alone, in my backyard." Trace bluffed, trying to sound convincing and hoping Kelsi believed that he was alone.

"After I text you the number, this phone will be destroyed. It was never used to contact anyone but you." Kelsi lied. "I will destroy it to protect us both. Get the app, call the number." With that, the call ended abruptly.

Trace was still staring at the phone, wondering what he should do next, when it rang in his hand, making him jump. *"Shit, this spy stuff is not for me!"* He thought.

"Conner", he said as he answered it.

"You're gonna have to do it. Get the app." Agent Jares informed him.

"Can your guys tap it?"

"Not sure, we're looking at it now. If nothing else, we can turn on your microphone and listen to that. That's what we were doing with Tellu. Just get it downloaded and start the install. Who knows how long it'll take." Jares said.

"Fine." Trace brought up the app store and looked for the app. Finding it and accepting the permissions, he began the agonizingly slow download. "Will this app even work out here if the internet service isn't very good?"

"Not sure, I've never used it. It's becoming more popular with the bad guys. They use it and apps like it to encrypt their calls. Protect them from us and the NSA."

"Will..?" Trace heard a voice in the background.

"What is it?" Jares said, talking away from the phone.

"The newest version of the app blocks any other usage of the microphone, when the app is running. We won't be able to listen to even half of Conner's call." The first tech said.

"Alright, special agent...what do I do?" Trace asked.

"I have no idea, Conner. You have to call him back, but we need a mic of some kind."

"Is the phone he was using, still working? Can you turn it on? Can I call him back on that?"

A glance from the second tech told Jares that was not an option. "No, either he pulled the battery or he already destroyed it." The agent replied.

"Wait, I have an idea." Running into the store, Trace said. "Bill, my battery is dying, but I'm trying to direct those guys up here. Can I use your cell for a few minutes?"

"Sure, Mr. Conner. It's not a fancy smartphone, but the internet works better off the landline anyway." Bill answered.

"Great, thank you. This is perfect." Taking the old-fashioned flip phone back outside to the Jeep, he climbed in and grabbed his own cell. "Jares, I'm going to call you on another phone, I'll try to put the call to Kelsi on speaker so that this phone will pick it up."

"Good idea. Not the best solution, but it should work." The agent said as he disconnected the call.

Dialing Jares number on the flip phone, Trace tried to follow the installation instructions on the app. Then he quickly read the directions of how to use it.

"Agent Jares."

"How's the sound on this one?" Trace queried.

"Not great, but I don't see many options. You better hurry up and place the call."

Placing the open flip phone in his breast pocket, Conner started the Red Phone app and dialed the number he had been given by Oswald Kelsi.

"That took quite a long time, Mr. Conner." Kelsi began.

"Hey," Trace said acting irritable, "I teach martial arts, I'm not a computer tech. Besides, you know where I am. Internet service here is spotty at best. It takes time!"

"Fine...I want the drives and I'm willing to pay for them." Kelsi said.

"Now we're talking, what are you offering?" Trace said bluntly.

"Two million dollars."

Trace laughed out loud, then snorted derisively. "Look, Mr. whatever, that's bullshit and you know it."

"I have to find a buyer, overhead, and so on. I'll be lucky to get twenty million for it. That would be ten percent."

"Haha, ah haha." Trace laughed even louder and more dramatically. "Ten percent is a good number....but... with all the effort you have gone to for this program, I'm pretty sure you're gonna get something like two HUNDRED million or more. Probably as much as half a billion. So, my ten percent will be twenty million. That's what I want."

"I can't possibly..." Kelsi began.

"Bullshit!" Trace cut him off. "Anybody that has an interest in the T-FAX and the ability to use it, will be able to pay me twenty million and still get a deal. I have to disappear, probably move out of the U.S., for that, I need money, a lot of it. Besides, I think you owe me for trying to kill me so many times."

"Seems like you owe me. For all the people and money I have spent already."

"You mean like your Chinese assassin? I bet he costs a lot. He's really good." Trace pushed.

"Yes, Neko told me that you had laid a trap for him. Three times. Seems like you failed as well." Kelsi said smugly.

Inwardly, Conner cursed himself for using Neko's name when he had confronted the killer in Flagstaff. At the time, he was trying to use it for a psychological advantage, but now, Kelsi knew that Conner had learned it. Aloud, he answered, "I didn't fail. I stopped him, I still have the drives. I'm just tired of being the target, I want out."

"So, give me the drives and you have my word, you're out," Kelsi said seriously.

"Wow, you must really think I'm stupid. Give you the drives and then you have Neko kill me anyway."

"By the way, how did you learn Neko's name? I am quite curious."

"Somebody with his skills is memorable, especially if the person asking the questions, asks the right questions. I know dojos all over the world. Turns out, a few people remembered him." Trace answered honestly. "Any chance you'll tell me yours?"

"I could, but it would be fake, so why bother?"

"True. So, you are going to put two million dollars into the account number, I am sending you now. It's for a bank on the island of Nevis. When I verify that you have done that, I will go to a big city. You will be able to verify my location by triangulation. You will send another ten million to the account. At that point, we will set a meeting place and time. When we meet, you transfer the last eight million and I'll give you the drives." Trace finished.

"How do I know I can trust you?" Kelsi asked.

"You don't have any choice. I've managed to not get killed so far, but I want more. A lot more. Do it my way or I'm gone. I'm sure the Chinese, Russians, Iranians, or somebody will pay me what I want."

"Fine," Kelsi said suddenly, surprising Conner. "But...if you screw me, I will have Neko chase you down and finish you, slowly."

"I just want the money. I'm tired of fighting your people and your pet psycho." With that, Trace disconnected the call. Checking the phone repeatedly to make sure the call had ended before he spoke to the other phone.

"That was very risky." Agent Jares said. "You should have just taken the two million he offered upfront."

"No, that would have made him suspicious or make him think I was stupid, which would have made him suspicious." Trace answered. "I needed to put a real price on it. Something that was too much to be just pocket change for Terrace, but not so insane as to be ridiculous."

"You think twenty million dollars isn't ridiculous?"

"In May of 2018, the game 'Fortnite' raked in 318 million dollars. So, no, I don't think so. Did I sound legit?"

172

"You sounded good on our end. I was buying it and the guys here all agree." Jares responded.

"Good, good. This really isn't my thing, you know. I'm gonna return this phone now and I'll call you back as soon as I get anything." With that, Trace hung up the flip phone and took it back inside to Bill. "Thank you, Bill. I really appreciate it."

"So, are they on the right road now?" Bill asked.

"No. Looks like they just decided to skip the scouting trip for now. Apparently, finding stuff without GPS is just too hard for some people." Trace winked conspiratorially, then turned and walked back to his Jeep.

"Haha, amen to that," Bill answered and dropped the phone back on the counter.

"Do you think the offer is legitimate?" Cross asked in his nasally voice.

"I do Sir," Kelsi answered.

"What do we know about this consultant?"

"Our DARPA contact gave us the jacket on him. He had some brushes with the law when he was very young. Nothing as an adult, other than a few speeding tickets. Never served in their military or worked for any government agency. He has no family left. His mother died when he was nineteen. He had an older brother, who was killed in Afghanistan, early in the war." Kelsi replied.

"In short, he has nothing to tie him here?"

"Other than his Dojo, no. As far as anybody knows, he doesn't even have a best friend or a long-term girlfriend. The file notes that he can be very abrasive. This probably contributes to the lack of close friends."

"Three Dragons has plenty of soldiers here and we can bring more in from Hong Kong. Why not just go after him and take the drives?" Cross questioned.

"Many reasons, sir. First, the area he is in has virtually no cell service, so triangulating a location will be very hard, even with handheld units. Second, it is very rugged terrain and he is very familiar with it. Our city people would be at a severe disadvantage. Third, he may have backup. There were three other men at his house in Flagstaff, according to Neko, we don't know where they are. These were, no doubt, some of MIGIsoft's elite team. Former combat soldiers. Fourth, the initial amount is relatively small, part of it would have paid for the South African team that failed. Fifth, he told Neko that he had buried the drives in the forest. If he has repeated this tactic, we could have a thousand men there searching for years and never find them. Sixth and most critical, Trace Conner has stopped us at every attempt we have made since he became involved. It's his location, his knowledge, his skills and he has had time to prepare. We would undoubtedly need a force of fifty or more. That cost makes it imprudent." Kelsi said all this as he counted them off on his fingers. "If the initial deposit gets him moving to a more populated area, with more cell towers, we stand a much better chance of taking the drives. If we don't want to pay for them, which might be easier."

"Where will twenty million dollars come from Oswald?" Cross asked angrily.

"I've been thinking about that. If we get rid of all our spies, permanently, that will free up another twelve million. It will also protect us from future testimony."

"I like it. We definitely won't need Tellu anymore, but the DARPA spy may come in handy in the future." Cross pointed out.

"She is actually our biggest threat. She knows the most and is motivated only by money. She doesn't hold a grudge against MIGIsoft. If the FBI gets hold of her, I think she will cave immediately. Her portion is ten million and I feel this would be a better use of those funds. Besides, government employees that are willing to take bribes are easy to find. We can get another one later."

"Hmmm....very well. Go forward with this but keep me in the loop." With that, Cross turned his chair around, dismissing Kelsi.

Chapter 20

"I thought you said we were going to Vegas?" Larry said groggily, as he looked at the mileage sign in front of him. "That says 'Provo and Salt Lake City', that's Utah." He had been dozing in the passenger seat since leaving the Jacob Lake area.

"I want to go far enough into Utah so that when I turn on my phone and make some calls, it'll look like I'm headed to Salt Lake. My hope is that they'll send bad guys there and not to Vegas, waiting for us." Trace responded.

After finishing his call with Kelsi, Conner had gone back to Larry's hide. Together they disassembled the hide, returning the area to its pristine, natural state. Then they headed back to camp. After an hour, Conner drove back to the store and used the better internet signal to check the balance in his Nevis bank account. Seeing the deposit of two million, Trace headed back to camp, and together they broke it down, returning that area to its original condition. Then they headed out, taking state route 89A up through the small town of Fredonia and into Utah. Conner filled Larry in on his plan as they left camp, then Larry had dozed off. After passing through Kanab, Utah, Conner turned on his phone. The first call was to the Colonel, filling him in on the current plan. Next, he called agent Jares and updated him.

"You should know that we found a link, through Homeland security, somebody at DARPA has set a request for location pings on your phone," Jares said.

"Does that tell you who it is?" Trace asked hopefully.

"No. It came from the 'Office of the Director', but she has secretaries, assistants, Deputy Directors, their secretaries, their assistants, and so on. Probably a hundred people, which is a smaller number than we had before, but still..."

"She?" Trace queried.

"The DARPA Director is a woman, has been for a while. Didn't you know? Word is that the next one will be too. Apparently, several of the deputies are women too."

"Oh, no, I didn't know that. Is there anything there that can help you locate the mole?"

"Maybe. We're trying to get the notification list. If we could find out who is getting the emails with your location pings, that'll narrow it down a lot more, but that's an internal thing at DARPA. We can't hack in. Very illegal and as you can imagine, they have very good cybersecurity." Jares sighed. "We'll keep chasing leads, but unless we put the entire Director's office under surveillance, we may not get anything."

"I'm betting you can't do that?" Trace asked.

"Not without an order from the top, and I mean the very top."

"Is there anything Catherine or the Colonel could do to help narrow it down?"

"I doubt it. Maybe if she keeps pushing for them to take the program...." Jares said.

"Okay, I'll leave it to you to coordinate all that. In the meantime, I'll keep ducking and weaving, keep their attention on me." Trace finished.

"Right. Be in touch." Jares signed off.

The call had concluded just as they entered the small town of Orderville, Utah. Taking advantage of the chance for a late lunch and fuel. Larry and Trace ate, then removed the cellphone battery before climbing back in the Jeep. Turning around, they headed back to the Mt. Carmel junction, taking the small UT-9 road west, they connected to Interstate 15 south to Las Vegas.

"The consultant's phone started pinging just outside Kanab, Utah. He's on highway 89, headed north. The last ping was in Orderville. I think he's headed for Salt Lake City." Deputy Director Alicia Parks said.

"Why do you think that?" Kelsi was looking at a map online while he spoke to Alicia, curious about her reasoning.

"Big city, easy to get lost. An international airport, plenty of food and hotels, he'll have access to anything he needs." She replied.

"That makes sense. Yes... you are probably right."

"On a separate note, the Dewal woman has started calling again. Demanding that we pick up the program. Bitching about their employee safety and stuff." Alicia said.

"Interesting....they supposedly don't have the drives right now or contact with the consultant." Kelsi pondered this news, wondering what it meant.

"Should I keep stalling then?"

"No." Kelsi answered, coming to a fast plan for verifying Conner's revelation that he was selling the program and getting out of the country. "Contact her. Find out where she wants to meet. If it's in Salt Lake, let me know immediately."

"Okay..." She said hesitantly. "What are we going to do then?"

"Just pick your team, men you don't like. Let me know where the meet will be, then we'll decide what to do." He answered

"Alright," Alicia concluded, without conviction.

"I just got a call from a Deputy Director Parks." Catherine began. They were pulled over just outside of Las Vegas. Larry's phone was on speaker so they could both hear. "She is sending a team to get them. Where should I tell her to send them?"

"Hmm, if she's the spy, she might be doing it to see if my offer is legit. If we send them to Vegas, they'll wonder why that is and get suspicious. If we send them to Salt Lake, they'll know that I'm still in touch with you." Trace pondered the moves in his mind, attempting to see a few steps ahead. "Ask them to come to San Francisco. Once they get there, stall."

"For how long?" She asked.

"Until we have a better idea of what's going on."

"Why not just have them fly to Vegas and take it? Get rid of this problem once and for all."

"And what happens if she is the spy and sends a fake team? I'll be handing it to them on a silver platter." Trace replied.

"That wouldn't be good...no."

"Get them to SF. Verify their Ids. See if you can grab some pictures of them, then send those to Larry's phone."

"What's that for?" She asked.

"Just in case." Then another thought crossed his mind. "Send them to Jares also. See if he can verify their Ids."

"Meanwhile, are you planning something else incredibly dangerous and stupid?" She asked.

"No, at least I don't think so. I'm not trying to, anyway. I want them looking at me, but not through a gunsight. Right now, we're in a chess match. If I can keep them believing that I'll sell the program, we might be able to get it to DARPA without any more bloodshed."

"Alright," Catherine said dubiously. She thought he was leaving something out, but she didn't know what that was. "Do you need a room in Vegas?"

"Yes, but not through MIGIsoft. We'll use Larry's card, in case they can track mine somehow. Soon as we get one, we'll let you know where. Please fill in Will Jares on all this. Especially the DARPA Deputy." Trace finished. "Talk to you later."

"Goodbye." She said, then disconnected and dialed a new number. "Deputy Director Alicia Parks, please."

"She wants me to send the team to San Francisco," Alicia stated flatly. "What should I do?"

"Send them. This will work..." Kelsi replied.

"How does a DARPA security team taking the program, work for us?" She asked, stressing audibly.

"Relax. Have the team check in to a hotel. Order the plane back to D.C. If she says they have to go to Salt Lake City to get it, we'll know that Conner is screwing us. You'll provide a different plane, one of ours. We'll take out the team and replace them with our people."

"Why not just let the team get the program, then take it from them?" She asked.

178

"Leaving San Francisco, they won't be on guard. Once they have the program they'll be jumpy and far more suspicious of everything. It will be much easier to take them on the way." He answered.

"What if Conner knows they are impostors?"

"How could he know?"

"I'm not sure. Just asking." She said.

"Let me worry about that."

"Okay, I'll get the team rolling to Frisco." Then she disconnected the call.

"I'm in a big city now. Send the next ten million." Trace said into the burner phone he was using.

"How do I know that?" Kelsi queried.

"Because I'm telling you. I'm calling from a burner phone I picked up and loaded the Red Phone app on to. Also, in case you haven't noticed, my internet connection is much better. Virtually no lag, so I'm in a major city."

"A salty one maybe?" Kelsi asked.

"How would you know that?" Trace said guarded, although he suspected that he knew already.

"I have many resources."

"Exactly the reason I'm using a burner now. Gives me a little more protection."

"We can track this phone too. You have no protection."

"Wrong. This one will get trashed, you taught me that. I'll get another one for every call." Trace said, pushing hard. "Send the next ten million or I won't tell you where I am."

"You are in Salt Lake City. I already know this."

Trace smiled, "it's a very big city and I know it well." He was actually referring to Las Vegas, but Kelsi didn't need to know that, yet. "You won't find me unless I allow it. You do understand what I teach, right?"

"Oh, that. The mysterious Ninja and all that hocus pocus, magic malarkey. I am not impressed. I have known Neko for a while, nobody will impress me more than he does."

"Yes, he is impressive. How did you say you met?" Conner was hoping for a slip.

"Valiant effort, Mr. Conner, but you need not know that."

Was that a British accent that slipped out for a second? "Did he tell you that I beat him? He's not as good as you think." Trace lied.

"A fib, Mr., Conner. If you beat him, he would be dead or captured. He is not, therefore you failed to best him."

"Really? Wasn't his job to get the drives? He failed, right? I beat Him!" Trace was gloating, hoping to make Kelsi slip.

"You stopped him, nothing more."

"Stopped" was pronounced with the long O of the British, and Neko had a slight British accent, another possible link to Hong Kong. Trace wondered if he should ask about that, but investigation was not in his training. Would Jares get mad if he let this slip out? Would it matter? Well...nothing ventured, nothing gained, right?

"Hong Kong", Trace said.

"Excuse me?" Kelsi was thrown off by the sudden words from Conner.

"That's how you knew Neko, isn't it?" Trace pressed. "Was he an enforcer or something there? For one of the Triads, maybe?" He knew that Jares would be pissed at him now, but he wasn't sure how many more times he would talk to Kelsi. He needed as much information as he could pry out now.

"Really, Mr. Conner, do you think I'm going to tell you my history or that of my man?"

"Wet work, right? That's what they called it back in the nineties, right?" Trace was trying to get a reaction now. Hoping Kelsi would slip, any slip at all.

"That is none of your concern. Stop asking."

"Fine. Send the money."

"Tell me where you are." Kelsi pushed back.

"Not gonna happen. Send the ten million or we can keep chatting about your history. Either way, you're not learning where I am until I tell you and that's not gonna happen before you send the money." Trace was laughing inwardly. This was getting to be fun.

"It will take time. At least a day to move that much money into one account. If I know where you are, I can have a man in place to take the drives immediately and conclude our business."

"Ha! If you think I'm going to trust you in the least, you're crazy or stupid. Are you stupid?" Trace was really beginning to enjoy this.

"Hardly, Mr. Conner," Kelsi said harshly, his British accent slipping out again. "Watch your account. I expect a call with your location immediately afterward. Failure to do this will make you a marked man. We will hunt you to the ends of the earth."

"Oh, you'll hear from me. That, I promise." Trace said gravely.

Standing in the bar, looking down from the top of the Stratosphere Casino in Las Vegas, Trace pointed south. "Look there, sort of diagonally from the IHOP. See the flat, gray building?"

"Yea. That's a gun range?" Larry asked.

"Not like what we're used to, but yes. They have all kinds of weapons. From simple pistols to full auto SAWs." Trace was referring to a Squad Automatic Weapon, commonly referred to as a SAW. Typically carried by one man in a small unit for suppressing fire.

"Why?"

"Because people visiting here, come from all over the world, where they can't even see some of these weapons. Here, they get to shoot them, like in the movies. Big business for Tommy. Hell, most of his business is from Americans, that live in repressive states like New York or California. They want to know what it's like." Trace answered.

"So, the plan is to hang out there, because he has the firepower to back us up?"

"Yep. Tommy is one of the local Ninjutsu family. Pretty good, but I think he relies on weapons too much. I generally prefer to have my hands free. A weapon, of any kind, forces you to react in a minimized capacity. A

181

pistol, for instance, makes you think you have to shoot the enemy. The bullet only comes out one way, so you have to orient the gun in that direction. That limits you." Trace explained. " That said, firearms are the best choice there is to reach out and touch someone from more than fifteen feet. Tommy isn't his real name, by the way. I don't know what it is, but he took up the moniker 'Tommy Gun' a long time ago. It works well for the club."

"Well, it'll be nice to have some backup in case we need it," Larry said.

"His staff consists of mainly former military. Most of the ones I've met were leathernecks. All seem like really good guys. Solid." A compliment, coming from Conner, Larry knew.

"Should we go get the drives from the room? Take them with us?"

"No. I think they're fine. Kelsi can't possibly have tracked us here, nothing's rented in our name. I think we're good. Of course..... I've been wrong before." Trace smiled.

The room at the Stratosphere had been rented, as well as a new Ford Explorer, four-wheel drive, by Dr. Wells, under one of his personal credit cards. After arriving in Vegas, it occurred to them that Kelsi's people might have been able to get Larry's name off the rental vehicle he had in Flagstaff. They used a burner phone to call and ask the Colonel for options, Dr. Wells just happened to be in the same room and offered his card. The rental Ford allowed them to move faster and less obvious than the rock crawler Jeep. The Jeep was now parked in the garage at Tommy's house for later retrieval, it being too tall to fit in most of the Vegas parking garages. Taking the high-speed elevator to the retail level on the second floor, they split up and wandered the shops. Each man watching for someone following the other. When they were confident they had no tails, they took the escalator to the ground floor and out to Las Vegas Boulevard. A short walk and they were at the range.

As they walked in the door a large man, his skin glistening like oiled, dark chocolate, came towards them. "Trace, I thought you had to use a cane now? You move like an old man!"

"You only say that because you need a pistol to use as a crutch for your taijutsu." Trace replied, referring to the body movement inherent in the Ninjutsu style.

"Ouch, man. I have feelings, you know!"

"No, I'm pretty sure you don't!" Trace shot back.

The big man laughed and wrapped Conner up in a rib popping bear hug. "Ouch, easy there big fella." Trace said.

"You hurt?" More of a statement than a question, but Tommy had concern on his face.

"Took more than a few rounds to the vest from a nine-millimeter Beretta a few days back. Still suffering." Trace answered.

"You'll have to fill me in over beers. Sounds like a good story."

"No, you'll just laugh. It was stupid. Tommy, this is Larry, reformed jarhead. He's been my wingman on this little caper." Trace pointed to Larry, the two men shook hands.

"Trace says your real name isn't Tommy. What is it?"

"Doesn't matter. He died in Fallujah, along with a bunch of friends and the stupid ideas he had growing up in the projects. Tommy Gun is a whole new person, who loves life and people. Well, most of them." The big man said with a wink. "Hard to love someone like Trace, such an arrogant prick."

"Jealous....you're just jealous." Trace laughed at him.

"Do you need some gear?" Tommy asked them seriously.

"Nothing for me." Trace answered, then pointed at Larry, "but he might want something."

"See?" Tommy said looking at Larry, "he doesn't even need a weapon, he's sooo good." Sarcasm dripping from his voice.

"Haha, no. I'm going to have to move around the city a lot. I don't want to get popped in a casino where some random Barney Fife might see it and decide he has to give me a hard time or worse, call the cops."

Tommy looked at the other former Marine, raising an eyebrow.

"Pretty much anything in a .45. A 1911, Sig or S&W would be great." Larry responded.

"Take a Sig. The new P320 Nitron Compact is easier to carry and conceal. Excellent weapon." Tommy said, heading behind a counter to grab one of the new pistols and a small rear carry holster.

"Ooh...very nice," Larry said as he dropped the magazine and pulled the slide back to check for a round in the chamber.

"You'll have to load your own mags." Tommy placed a 50-round box of ammunition and two more magazines on the counter next to the holster. "We never keep any preloaded here, for safety."

"No worries. I think I'm going to make you my new best friend. Trace is out!" Larry quipped.

"Absolutely, you can't trust somebody who never served in the corps, right?" Tommy said as he flashed a big smile at Conner. "So, tell me what this shit is, that you stepped into with both feet and went chest-deep?"

"Well, it started what, about a month ago?" Conner looked at Larry for help, who nodded. "I was teaching a class and in walks this older military type, you know, the ones that look like you two." Trace gestured at the two Marines, then went on to describe all that had happened before then, since then, and what his plan was now.

"Geez..." Tommy breathed, "That's some insane shit Trace! You know you could've easily been killed at your house, by Neko or your team."

"That's what I said!" Larry interjected.

"I wish Luka had taken the headshot. This might be over already."

"No way. I used to be Recon. Even with the best CQB training, his round probably would have gone through Neko and into you. Even a subsonic nine-millimeter, and it sounds like your heads were only inches apart." Tommy said.

"It would have been worth the risk to stop him." Trace retorted. "Too many people have been killed by him, by them."

"Then you'd be dead, just like your big brother, only here, more people would still die. You would've sacrificed yourself to take a bishop off the board. I bet they still have rooks, knights, and a lot of pawns. Sounds like this Kelsi is the Queen." Tommy said, looking at him gravely.

"You had a big brother?" Larry asked Trace.

184

Trace glared briefly at Tommy then turned and said, "Yea, he died early in the war in Afghanistan. He was a hero, not me."

Thirty minutes later, the three men sat in a bar off Paradise Road, near the Las Vegas Convention Center.

"You couldn't take us to the Wynn?" Trace asked Tommy.

"Too much video security. The manager here is a friend, so we won't get hassled for carrying. If they notice at all." The big man answered.

"Tell me about your brother." Larry prompted. He wanted to hear the story but suspected that Trace needed to tell it too.

"Amazing guy..." Trace began slowly, his eyes glazing over. "After 9/11, he was a senior in college, he heard about the early Army guys that had gone in and he was dead set on joining up."

Both Marines nodded, thinking about where they were on that terrible day.

"So, Kyle signed up as soon as he graduated. He was bigger than I am now, taller and wider. Solid muscle. He breezed through basic and on graduation day, they asked if he wanted to go to Airborne school. He did, he loved it. He deployed in 2003 with the 82nd Airborne. He finished that tour, came back, and told me how much he enjoyed it. He signed up for a second tour and went to Ranger school. He didn't just love the action, he actually loved helping the people, he really believed in the whole 'hearts and minds' thing. After he finished Ranger school he went back to Afghanistan in 2004.

Almost to the end of that tour, they got word that their interpreter had been identified. The Taliban was going after his family. Kyle was the LT, he loaded his team without hesitation, and off they went. I heard later it was against orders. Anyhow, they got to the small town at the same time as the Taliban element. The interpreter grabbed his son, while his wife grabbed their infant daughter. They ran for the armored Humvees. Kyle saw it coming in as one of his men screamed 'grenade'. He dropped on top of the wife and baby girl, completely covering them with his much larger body. The grenade went off right behind him, he was shredded and the blast tossed all three of them about ten feet. Kyle looked at the wife, he was covered in blood, he yelled 'Go!' She did, running with the baby. Kyle rolled on his side and fired at the Taliban warriors, protecting her while she ran. His men provided covering

185

fire, pushing the Taliban back, and grabbed him. Their medic tried his best, but Kyle bled out in the Humvee." Tears were running freely down Conner's face now, unashamed of them. "I know all this because a few years later, the wife found me. She told me the story. It's still classified and the Army wouldn't tell me. Her husband had stayed in Afghanistan, even though she and the children had been relocated stateside, he died because he continued helping us. He said he owed us for saving his family. Today, the baby girl is a beautiful, polite, young woman who brings her mother to see me every year on Kyle's birthday. They live over near Santa Fe, New Mexico."

Larry nodded and whispered softly, "Awesome."

"The point is that Kyle died doing more than just killing the Taliban or taking a section of rock and dirt. He died saving two people. I know he's happy with that. That he gave his life so this little girl could grow up to be this amazing woman. It sucks, but I'm okay with it because I know he is. THAT is a hero." Trace stated solemnly.

Tommy nodded soberly, "it is. He was a real hero, a huge set of balls."

"That doesn't make you any less," Larry said, looking at Conner.

"Drop it." Trace commanded. "I'm not in the same class as Kyle, not even close. I didn't even have the guts to go serve."

The two former Marines looked at each other and then back at Trace but held their tongues. For the next ten minutes, all three men sat drinking their beers and looking inward. Thinking about the brothers they had lost, blood relations, and brothers in arms. Finally, Trace reached into his pocket and grabbed the latest burner phone. Powering it on, he logged in to the bank account in Nevis.

"Well, it looks like we have to go on to the next step. Kelsi just put that ten million in my account." Trace said morosely.

Tommy whistled, "ten million? Holy shit, I'm in the wrong business."

"They already gave him two million, did you know that?" Larry said.

"What?! Damn! Imagine the dojo you could build.."

"and a boat! Girls... oorah!"

"Quit you guys! I doubt I'll get to keep any of it. The government will probably seize it all and charge me interest or something." Trace said. "I have to go call the FBI guys now and arrange the next step. In the meantime, can you take Larry to the nearest Fry's Electronics store or something like it? We need to buy some stuff."

"Sure," the big man answered. "Not a problem."

"Wait, I almost forgot." Trace said suddenly.

"What?" Larry asked.

Turning to Tommy, Trace asked "Is there a junkyard around here. One that recycles cars?"

"It's Vegas, baby. We got everything." Tommy answered, then after seeing the look on Conner's face he added. "There's one off of Interstate 15, you probably passed it coming in."

"Pick me up in front of our hotel in ten minutes." With that, Trace headed back to the Stratosphere and his room. Ten minutes later he climbed into Tommy's jacked up Ford Raptor.

They drove to the junkyard, where Conner got out and went over to an operator that was moving cars around, some into the crusher, others were getting stacked. He handed the man something small then walked over behind one of the stacks. Larry saw the big crane swing over towards Conner, descend for a minute, then rise and return to what it was doing before. Conner looked like he was having an attack behind the stack of cars before he ran back to the truck and climbed in.

"To Hoover dam, driver." Trace said lightly.

"The dam?" Tommy asked, "you want to go sightseeing now?"

"I've never gone out on the new pedestrian walkway, next to the road on that super high bridge. I want to see it."

"Really? Larry asked. "You're sure?"

"Yes, I'm sure. I could get killed any day now, I want to see it. Don't worry, you two can stay in the truck. I know how Marines have a problem with heights." Trace jabbed them.

"It's not a Marine thing," Tommy answered back, "it's a smart thing. You're just not that smart." As he turned the Raptor to head back south in the direction of Hoover Dam.

They didn't actually go to the Dam, instead taking the Hoover Dam bypass bridge that crossed the Colorado River, pulling into the parking area for the pedestrian walkway. Conner got out and walked on to the bridge that soared more than eight hundred and eighty feet above the river. Conner got to the middle of the walk, waited until there was nobody near, and opened the bag he was carrying.

"I already waited too long to call him back." Trace said to the conference call.

"Why?" Catherine asked, "he's a piece of shit. What do we care if he gets upset?"

"Because he'll know I was bluffing and we'll lose what little advantage we've gained," Conner replied.

"Mr. Conner is right." Agent Jares said. "We have Tellu in custody and he hasn't told us much yet. If Kelsi reaches out to Tellu and there's no response, and Mr. Conner doesn't call him back, there's no telling what will happen."

"Jares, have you been able to tell if that Deputy Alicia Parks, is the spy?" Trace asked.

"No. The team she sent is legitimate. I even know the leader. He doesn't know that I'm involved, but Ms. Dewal got some good video of them. So, we know Parks didn't send a fake team. If she's involved, I'm not sure why she would do that."

"Maybe because she would know their itinerary, be able to intercept the drives on the way back?" Trace asked.

"Very unlikely. The team lead, Eric Wan, is a former HRT guy with the FBI. I did some training with him way back. Short but tough as hell, he wouldn't let anything go that he's responsible for. I imagine his team is all serious hard asses." Jares answered.

"The ID he showed me, said 'Eric Wan'. So, he even gave me his real name and he is short, maybe five-seven or eight." Catherine put in.

"Don't forget to send me those photos." Trace said, then, "any special suggestions for me, when I call Kelsi back?"

"Try not to give him any more information." Agent Jares said seriously.

"I was trying to fluster him and I think I was successful. I'm pretty sure that he's British and trying to fake an American accent. He was really thrown when I said 'Hong Kong'."

"or he could be a lot better at this than you are. What if he's a former security service or counter intel from some country? You may be thinking exactly what he has carefully given you to think. An identity he crafted for you to believe." Jares responded.

"I hadn't considered that. Shit. This is out of my league. I'm just not trained for this." Trace griped.

"I think you're doing fine Trace," Catherine said soothingly. "You've saved lives, caught our first bad guy, helped us identify Ken Tellu, and made more headway on this by shaking them up. I say keep going the way you are."

"I agree with Catherine." The Colonel put in. "Your instincts have been good, thus far. Stay with them."

"I didn't say you were doing bad," Jares quickly amended. "Just don't tell him anything you don't have to. We need as much information as we can get and we need to keep Kelsi from getting any, if possible."

"We still can't prove that the Kelsi I'm talking to is the same Oswald Kelsi from Terrace? We don't have anything concrete?" Trace asked.

"We're pretty sure, Tellu did call a number at Terrace software and ask for Mr. Kelsi. The voice is very similar to the one you spoke to, but the voice match has been inconclusive due to the bad mic pickup on that call." Jares answered. "If you were here, we could put a mic on you for better audio, even through the phone. But, to answer your question, no, nothing concrete. A good lawyer would have him out in ten minutes."

"Once I give him my location, we'll have very little time to come up with other options. If we tell Director Parks to send the pickup team to Vegas and she's the spy, she'll tell Kelsi, and then who knows what will happen? She might send the team someplace else, while Kelsi sends his people to pick up the drives, then we'll have to run again." Trace pondered aloud.

"Why don't you call Kelsi, give him the location. I'll give you twenty minutes, then I'll call Parks and tell her to send the team to Vegas to meet you. Even if she is the spy, it'll look to Kelsi like you were upfront with him." Catherine said.

"Not great, but I don't see any other options. Anybody else got a better idea?" Trace asked. When there was no response, he said, "okay, then that's the plan."

"Conner," Jares interrupted, "I can have agents from the Vegas office there to help you. Give you some backup. Keep things more legal."

"I appreciate the offer Will, but if things go to hell, I would much rather know who is on my team and who isn't. Having to worry about accidentally killing an FBI agent, is something I would like to remove from the situation." Trace said seriously.

"I don't like it, but okay. I'll give them a heads up, to be ready, but nothing more." Jares said in return.

"Okay, everybody except Agent Jares, please hang up, so I can call Kelsi." Trace said as he powered up his personal phone. There was a "goodbye" and "good luck" from Catherine and the Colonel.

"Mr. Conner. So, kind of you to call me back." Kelsi said mockingly. "Ready to tell me where you are in Salt Lake?"

"Absolutely, like I promised. I'm at the Wynn casino in Las Vegas."

"You said you were in Salt Lake City," Kelsi said darkly.

"No, you said that. I just didn't dissuade you from that belief." Trace countered lightly.

"How do I know you are telling me the truth now?"

"Because I'm on my personal phone and I'm betting you have someone who is going to verify my location very soon. Go ahead and send one man to get the drives. Only, one man. Understand? If you send more, you'll lose the drives and the money you already gave me. I want to make that crystal clear to you." Trace said very slowly as if speaking to a slow-witted dog.

"Don't patronize me, Mr. Conner. I don't take it well." Kelsi seethed.

"Then don't screw it up. One man." Then Trace disconnected the call.

Kelsi was still staring at the phone in his hand, trying to decide if he should hurl it into the wall and shatter it when he saw the icon for an incoming call on the encrypted application. "Yes, Alicia? Is he in Las Vegas?"

"Why, yes. He is, how did you know?" She said questioningly.

"Have you triangulated to the Wynn casino?"

"Yes again, how?"

"Never mind. Please keep me informed of any more.."

The call was interrupted by a voice on Parks end, "Director Parks, Ms. Dewal from MIGIsoft is on line three. She says it's urgent."

"Thank you June, I'll take it in a sec," Alicia answered.

"Go ahead and answer it, while I'm on the line with you. In case there is information I need." Kelsi said.

"Okay," turning and picking up the desk phone handset, she said "This is Deputy Director Alicia Parks. What can I do for you Ms. Dewal?"

"I need your team to head to Las Vegas. We have reason to believe that our consultant is there and we can get him to give your team the program. Finally, get it out of our hands." Catherine said.

"Of course," Alicia said sweetly. "Any place in particular?"

"We don't have all the details yet, we just wanted to get your team closer. Have them land and wait at the North Las Vegas airport."

"I will get them moving immediately. Thank you, Ms. Dewal. Goodbye." Without waiting for a response from Catherine, Alicia dropped the handset in the cradle, ending the call. Turning back to her cell, she said "What do we do?"

"Exactly what the lady asked you to do. Give me fifteen minutes. Then call the team, tell them to go back to the private aviation terminal at San Francisco International. Tell them you had to order a private charter and to look for a Cessna Citation XLS, tail number..." Kelsi trailed off as he looked for the number. Once he found it, he read it aloud to her and she repeated it back. "We'll take it from there."

"Okay, fifteen minutes, starting now," Alicia said and disconnected the call, looking at her wall clock.

Meanwhile, Kelsi had simply dialed a new number and given his pilot and crew very specific directions on how to handle the new passengers that would arrive within the hour for a short trip to Las Vegas. Smiling now, Kelsi set the phone down. One way or the other, he was getting the T-FAX program today.

The DOD security team led by Eric Wan arrived at the airport and found the waiting Citation XLS, a very polite Asian captain and co-pilot. Fifteen minutes later, they were airborne and climbing to thirty-six thousand feet. Forty-five minutes after that, the plane landed again at San Francisco International's private aviation terminal and took on four more, serious-looking men. The first four had not returned. As the eight-person plane taxied for takeoff to Las Vegas, the copilot said to the new men, "Here are their Ids, you had better get to work on them and learn the names. The flight is not very long and we don't know how soon before the consultant will show up with the package."

"How did you dispose of them?" The new team leader asked as he looked around for blood.

"We went to thirty-six thousand feet, we just never pressurized the cabin. Once they all blacked out, I came back and gave each of them a shot of Fentanyl, then we dropped low enough to push them out and came back. Simple." The copilot spoke like he was talking about washing the dishes. No doubt he had been working for the Triad for a long time.

The team leader smiled. "Clever, very clever." Not knowing that it was Kelsi's plan, not the copilot's.

"You had better be clever too. If you fail at this, we may all get fed to the dogs. I was told that this package was of the utmost importance to the head of the Triad." The copilot said gravely.

"It'll be fine. We're all American born, our English is perfect and we barely even look Chinese. That's why we were chosen. We won't fail." The leader said confidently.

"I do not share your confidence. Get to work!" With that, the copilot went into the flight deck and shut the door.

The team leader, who would be called Eric Wan from this point on, headed back to the small table, where one of the team members was already setting up a portable laminating machine. They carefully cut the small photos they had brought of themselves and glued them over the photos of the real agents. Next, they ran the Ids through the laminating machine. The doctored Ids wouldn't pass close inspection, but they would have to do. That done, each Id was carefully placed back in the wallet. Now they could flip open the wallets, just like in the movies. All the men began checking weapons next. Ten minutes after that, the plane began its descent towards the North Las Vegas Airport.

"This is Catherine Dewal." She said as she answered the phone.

"Ms. Dewal, it's Director Parks. My team is at the airport you specified. Where is your man?"

"Um...well...it's a little embarrassing...we know that he's in Las Vegas, but we haven't actually got hold of him yet. Just keep your team there, we're working as fast as we can." Catherine lied, going with the story Special Agent Jares had suggested.

Since they knew about the NSA phone location request, Jares had said that they could claim the same thing, that they were using the phone pings to find Conner. It seemed like a good way to cover their knowledge of his location, just in case Parks was the spy.

"You haven't got hold of him yet? What the hell? Why did I send a team of men if you lost the drives?" Parks asked angrily.

"Hey, if you had sent a team a few weeks ago, you'd already have it. Somebody at DOD was dragging their feet and people here got killed. It's no surprise that a private consultant might get cold feet." Catherine shot back.

Parks tried to reign in her anger. It was her fault, after all, that no team had been sent sooner, but she didn't say that. "I'm sorry. I came into this mess when I found out we hadn't received the program yet and there were multiple murders. It just upsets me." Alicia said apologetically.

"Thank you. I'm glad someone finally decided to step in and come get it. I'll call just as soon as we know. I promise." Catherine lied, ending the call.

"You heard?" Alicia said into her cellphone.

"Yes. Interesting. They must be using the phone pings to find him too. That's good." Kelsi smiled. "When they call to tell us where he is, we'll probably already know, but we'll send the DOD team either way."

"Alright. I'll let you know when she calls back." Alicia said and hung up.

"I'm at the gun club on the strip." Trace said into the phone. "I'll be here for one hour. Remember, one man."

"Why a gun club?" Kelsi asked.

"It's loud and people with weapons are not unusual."

"So, you have a weapon?"

"I'd be an idiot not to." Trace replied coolly.

"Of course. My man is at the North Las Vegas Airport, he will be there soon. His name is Eric." Kelsi said.

"Understood. When he gets here, you send the last eight million. As soon as I verify that, I'll get the drives and hand them off. Are we clear?"

"Crystal clear, Mr. Conner."

"Good. Nice doing business with you. Hope I never hear from you again."

"I hope so as well, goodbye."

"Later." Trace said, turning to the room. "The bad guy is on his way. Keep your eyes open, I seriously doubt they'll honor the deal and send just one man, but we can hope."

All shooting sessions had been canceled for the day, claiming an electrical problem on the range. The 'people' that were shopping were fake, all former military. Larry was acting like a customer with Tommy helping him. Sue was a former Marine corpsman with a combat trauma kit tucked behind the counter. She was pretending to be a blonde bimbo, thanks to a fake blonde wig, who would be loud and annoying, as well as visually distracting. About five foot six, she was pretty and very curvy. Zach was the store employee that would be 'helping' her. He was a former Marine Recon, five-eleven, and all muscle. He was the club instructor for CQB and concealed carry permits. He trained the bodyguards for most of the local big wigs. Occasional customers came in, were quickly helped, and sent on their way. Ten minutes after the call, the first man came in and began to examine the offerings.

"Be right with you, sir," Tommy called out as everybody fell into their assigned roles and began the charade.

The first man was hard looking. Trace got a bad feeling off of him. He was trying too hard not to look at Conner and he quickly declined the offer of help. The next two men came in together, talking and laughing, but there was something off about them as well. Neither of those men looked at Conner and they also declined help. At almost exactly twenty minutes, a fourth man entered the club. He was almost Trace's height, about six feet. A slight Asian cast to his eyes, like the other men that had just entered. He looked around, spotted Trace, and headed directly towards him. Trace finished looking at his phone and put the cell in his pocket.

"Eric Wan", the last man said, holding out his hand to Conner.

Trace didn't move, standing with his hands loose. "You were supposed to come alone." He said coldly.

The man froze, trying to decide what to do. He was blown before he had started. The other men all looked at him to see what he would do.

"Oh, wait. You're the team from the DOD, aren't you?" Trace said suddenly.

'Eric' smiled big and relaxed a little. "Yes, you were expecting us right?"

"Yea, can I see some Id?" Trace asked.

"Sure." Eric pulled the identification wallet out and flipped it open with his left hand. "Here you go."

"Great!" Trace said a little too loud as he reached for the Id to examine it.

That was the word that would trigger everyone to move. As Trace reached for the wallet, his right-hand went past and grabbed the outside of

'Eric's' hand, shoving it hard back into the fake DOD man's face, Trace took satisfaction in hearing the crunch of cartilage behind the nose. Trace's left hand landed on the back of 'Eric's' right-hand as he attempted to pull his pistol from a cross draw holster. Instead of trapping it, as Trace had done to Luka, he allowed the fake Eric to pull the weapon free. As it came free, Trace rolled the man's fingers back towards the inside of his wrist. Hyper-extending the tendons of the fingers and popping the weapon loose. Trace quickly tossed the gun across the room to an empty corner.

At the same time Trace had begun the weapon strip, the two men that had been speaking together drew their weapons and sighted on Larry and Tommy, but too slow. Zack was already in motion. He took both men with headshots. The third man ducked behind the safety of the counter, firing as he went. They would have had a stand-off, but Sue ran at the end of the counter and dove, sliding past the opening, she put four rounds into the man.

Meanwhile, the fake Eric had not stood still. As his gun sailed across the room, his left knee came up, hitting Conner hard in the ribs, once, twice. He heard Conner grunt hard, then he used his left elbow, the one Conner had bent backward, bringing it across the side of the consultant's head. He sent Conner sprawling.

"Muy Thai." Trace thought, *"Damn, he's fast, that really hurt. Same ribs Luka shot."*

Using the energy of the strike, Trace continued the momentum, rolling to create some distance and then standing. "Hold fire." He said looking at all the Marines with their weapons out, pointing at the impostor.

"Kelsi said to be careful with you. He told me not to kill you until I had the drives. I don't see what he was worried about, you're not that tough!" Fake Eric spat blood at the floor and moved forward. Hands up, bouncing slightly, definitely Muy Thai. Fake Eric pushed forward off his left foot, his right knee coming up hard, looking to collapse Conner's left side.

Trace did the last thing fake Eric expected, holding his own hands up to create a shield for his head, he turned to the inside of Eric. Using his own right knee to strike Eric high inside the right leg, almost to the groin. As fake Eric staggered, Trace shot both hands into the would-be killer's neck. Trace dug his thumbs deep into the muscles and nerve bundles running down the sides of Eric's neck. Gasping in pain, unable to command his own muscles, Eric dropped to his knees, hands weakly pulling at Conner's iron grip. The man finally went limp, relaxing. Trace released his grip and moved to reposition. Fake Eric threw himself sideways, in an awkward roll. It was enough, he pulled a dark folding knife that flicked open. Trace saw instantly that it was a karambit style blade, wickedly hooked, it mimicked a tiger's claw. Trace prepared to counter the blade, when fake Eric, became dead fake Eric. His head exploding before Trace's eyes. Looking around Conner yelled, "damn it, Tommy! We needed him alive!"

"Hey, you're the one who taught me to just shoot someone skilled with a knife! That dude was skilled! You're welcome!" Tommy yelled back.

"Aaaaah!" Trace yelled at nobody. "I wanted him alive. Damn it! Damn it! Damn it!" Looking at Sue now, he asked, "Are any of them alive? Any at all?"

Sue shook her head. "We're all pretty good shooters." She said with a shy smile.

Aloud, Trace said, "You need to call the cops. Go with the attempted robbery story like our FBI guy suggested. Larry, we need to go."

Larry stood there with his gun in hand, he hadn't fired a shot. Everything had happened so fast, he was surprised that he hadn't been shot himself. "Sure, Trace." To Zack, he said "thanks, man."

Zack simply smiled and nodded. Like a shop shootout was an everyday occurrence.

"Sorry, brother," Tommy said.

"No, you're right. I probably would have gotten carved up and you would've had to shoot him anyway. Seriously, thank you." Trace replied, a little calmer. "Thank you for everything."

"Anytime, Sensei."

To the rest of the group, "thank you all. I appreciate the help and I'm sorry I have to leave you guys with the cops and the clean up, but you know how it goes 'national security' and all that stuff." He smiled as he dragged Larry out the back door, heading to the Stratosphere for the preloaded vehicle.

Kelsi looked at his cellphone and the incoming call. Wondering why he was getting the call. *"What went wrong?"* He thought.

Sighing, he accepted the call. "Mr. Conner, to what do I owe this call?"

"You screwed up... Mr. Kelsi."

A pause, "I'm sorry?"

"You heard me, Mr. Kelsi. You screwed up. You thought you could take me, you just don't learn." Trace was working off the script he had arranged with Agent Jares, who was listening to the call via Larry's cell. After arriving back at their hotel room in the Stratosphere, they had initiated a conference call with Agent Jares, Catherine, and the Colonel. After filling them in on what happened at the gun club, they had discussed the next step. It was to start with calling Kelsi, putting pressure on him, hoping he'd mess up. "I was very specific. I told you one man.... one man. You sent four. They're dead, I killed them all, but before he died, Eric told me, 'Kelsi said to be careful with you. He told me not to kill you until I had the drives.' Well, he's gone and now I know your name, or at least what they call you."

A long pause. "That... was not their instructions. Eric was supposed to leave the rest of the team at the airport." Kelsi lied. "I am sorry that my man did not follow directions."

"Ha, bullshit Kelsi! Your man wasn't making things up, I wasn't torturing him when he said that. He volunteered it. That makes it true to me." Trace hoped that his fake anger was coming across as he wanted.

"Please, Mr. Conner, believe me. Those were not his directions." Kelsi was almost pleading now. "What can I do to make it right?"

"Put the next eight million in my account right now. Then get ready with another five! This mistake is going to cost you. God! I can't believe you're that stupid! I stopped Neko, took out your shooters at MIGIsoft and you still thought you could take me with only four men." Trace was lying quite a bit, but Kelsi didn't know that. Eventually, the truth would come out about what really happened at the gun club, but for now, Trace wanted all attention focused on himself. He didn't want Tommy or the club to be targeted for retribution. "Why?! Why did you think you could take me? I should call the FBI and give them the information I got from Eric. Yea, I got more than your name."

"Yes, of course. I will move eight right now and have five more ready. Where?" Kelsi was beginning to panic, the British accent coming out more often now.

"I'll call you. My phone's getting shut down again and I'm going offline. I'll move to a new city and let you know when I'm ready." Trace barked.

"You must give me those drives before you go anywhere," Kelsi stated.

"Wrong, Kelsi. I don't have to do shit. In fact, I might bring the drives directly to you in San Francisco, right?" Trace said threateningly. "That's right... I know where you are."

"Please, Mr. Conner, we can take care of this. Threats are not necessary." Kelsi definitely sounded nervous now. Good.

"Move the money now, Kelsi. I'll be in touch and if you try something stupid like that again, I'll come to see you personally." Trace said and ended the call.

Kelsi's emotions were bouncing between anger and apprehension. He had told Jal, fake Eric's real name, to go alone. Not to bring in the other men until he had the drives.

"Jal, what kind of name was that anyway? You idiot." Kelsi thought.

Jal had the authority to transfer the money, then get the drives, then make Conner give the money back and kill him. Simple. Kelsi worried about the veiled threat. Conner had stopped Neko, no simple feat. Jal was sent because he was the best enforcer they had, next to Neko. Although he eschewed the Wing Chun that most of the Triad used, he had beaten everyone else that he had trained against.

Conner knew where he was at, did Jal tell him it was Terrace? Jal worked for the Triad and shouldn't know that, but still... What would he do if Conner did come after him? Could he escape? Doubtful, Conner was on a par with Neko, Kelsi knew that if Neko wanted him dead, he would be. Picking up the phone and activating a new number on the app, he called Alicia Parks.

"I was just going to call you." She said as she answered. "The consultant's phone just went dark."

"Yes. I assumed it would. Just wanted verification."

"Did we get it?" She asked.

"No. Something went wrong. I need you to keep updating me on the location pings when you get them. "Don't be surprised if they pop up somewhere far removed from Las Vegas. Tell me immediately, please."

"Okay, are you going to tell me what happened?"

"No." With that, Kelsi terminated the call. Next, he turned to his desk phone, dialing an in-house extension, that didn't stay in the house at all. "The pickup failed. Jal decided to disobey my orders and took all the men in with him. They are all dead. At least, that's what Conner said. He is quite angry, Mr. Cross. I am to send the next eight million now and be prepared to send another five when he gives us his new location. I have already spoken to our DARPA person. She has confirmed that his phone went offline. We have no idea where he is."

"If it just happened, he must still be in Vegas. We have plenty of muscle there. I can send more to take it." Cross replied.

"With respect sir, he may have called as he was driving out of the city or he may be lost in the city. We will never find him."

"You think I should have let you pay the money and leave him alone? You think I was wrong, don't you Oswald?" Cross asked menacingly.

"Sir, I do believe that you were right to want to take the money back, unfortunately, Jal disobeyed orders and planning, so that option is gone now. I believe we have to give the consultant what he wants. After we have the drives, we can send a wet work asset to find him, retrieve the money, and kill him." Kelsi hated the wet work euphemism, but the Triad and Cross, in particular, liked it, so it stayed. He was walking a fine line here, telling Cross that he had been wrong, without making it appear so.

"Very well, Kelsi, send the money. Did he give us any idea of the timeline?"

"No sir. I imagine he will travel quite far, before checking in again."

"Keep me updated," Cross said as he hung up, not waiting for a reply from Kelsi.

Wet Work

Chapter 21

Larry watched from the bed in their small suite at South Point Hotel off of Interstate 15 in south Las Vegas. Trace had assembled what looked like an experiment from a Frankenstein movie, on the small table. Wires were everywhere, power cords, the new Toshiba laptop he had purchased, and all the other items. "What are you doing with all that?"

"Do you really want to know?" Trace asked.

"Probably not. Do you know what you're doing? Looks pretty technical."

"Not really. I saw it in a movie once." Trace joked as he put a new program CD in the drive. "Can't be that hard."

"Is that why we needed a place with really good internet?"

"Yea makes loading programs much faster since most of them aren't even on the CDs they give you. They're usually just the keys to let you download the full program."

"Like the one from MIGIsoft?" Larry asked.

"Yep. Why don't you come over here and start a conference call with the Colonel and the others? We'll plan our next step."

"You sure? You seemed pretty mad when you called Kelsi."

"Did I?" Trace asked. "Good, that's what I wanted him to think."

"Sounded good to me. Gave me chills when you said you might bring the drives to him personally."

"Hahaha...that's awesome. I hope he took it that way too. It'll give us more breathing room." Trace laughed, he had already used the new Toshiba to log in to the Nevis bank and check the balance. He smiled at the thought of these dirtbags being relieved of twenty million dollars.

"Hello Larry," the Colonel's voice came through the small speaker. "What's up?"

"Trace wants to initiate a conference call with everyone. Can you start that sir?"

"Yes. Hold on." The call went silent as the Colonel worked to connect all the parties on his end.

"Trace," Catherine's voice came on the line, "are you alright? Larry said you squealed when that imposter hit you."

Trace rubbed the swollen spot below and slightly behind his right eye, that was beginning to darken. "I didn't squeal. It was more of a grunt." He gave Larry a dirty look.

Larry held up his hands and whispered, "I said you cried out, not squealed."

"That's not how we heard it." She responded.

"Well, he hit the bruised ribs, then smashed the side of my face. So, I grunted." Trace said, emphasizing the 'grunted'.

"Why do I care what she thinks? If it was one of the guys, I'd have taken it as just teasing." He thought.

"Maybe he squealed when he went flying." Special Agent Jares added, helpfully.

"I," Trace bit his tongue and the response. "What are we going to do? I can stall for another day or two, then I'll have to do something."

"Catherine and I have an idea." The Colonel said. "Tell us what you guys think. Go ahead, Catherine."

"I'm going to come to pick you two up, in Laughlin, in our plane." She began. "You jump in and off we go, to Washington."

"Why?" Jares and Trace both asked at the same time.

"If we take the drives directly to Director Parks, then we have met our obligation. Also, it should allow the FBI to follow her and see what happens. Especially, if she takes the drives with her. Then the FBI will have reason to watch a member of DARPA and if she's dirty, Agent Jares can grab her. Try to get some useful information from her about Terrace."

"That would work." Jares said, "but what if she manages to get the drives out and give them away? Then what?"

"Our thinking is that either way, MIGIsoft is out of it. You and the rest of the Feds can sort it out." The Colonel answered for them. "So, you better not drop the ball."

"Why take us?" Trace asked.

"Because, if she's dirty," Jares answered, "she'll know the drives are legit if you're there with them."

"Bingo," said the Colonel. "Larry will act as extra security for the trip."

"You know what? I like it." Trace said. "I would prefer to keep Catherine out of it, but otherwise I like it."

"Sorry, Trace. Catherine is the only one who will be able to walk in the door at DARPA and request a direct, unscheduled meeting with Parks." The Colonel replied. "That part is very important."

A long pause and then Jares said, "well, then I better get moving. Commercial travel takes longer than private and we need to be there before you."

"What's the schedule then?" Trace asked.

"I'll be landing in Laughlin about nine a.m. tomorrow, be ready," Catherine answered.

"Understood, good luck everybody." Trace ended the call and resumed his work with the computer. To Larry, he said, "takes about an hour to get to Laughlin from here. We'll have to leave no later than seven-thirty."

"Got it." Larry replied, "so no late-night parties?"

"No early night parties either. We can't be any more visible than absolutely necessary. Remember, people, are dying over this."

"Right," Larry said, properly chastised.

"When this is all over, I'll take all you guys out and get blind drunk. My treat. You deserve it and I do have twenty million dollars to work with." Trace said with a big smile.

At 9:10 a.m. The next morning, Larry and Trace climbed aboard the luxurious Gulfstream G650. Both men eyed the interior of the plane hungrily. "What does one of these babies cost?" Trace asked.

"In the neighborhood of sixty million." The Captain answered.

"Oh, so I can't have my own?" Trace quipped.

"If you keep bringing in deposits like you have been the last few days, maybe," Catherine said, smiling. "Captain, please take off as soon as possible for DC."

"Yes, Ms. Dewal." The Captain replied as he headed to the bridge.

"Larry, have a seat anywhere. There's a fully stocked minibar there." She pointed. "Mr. Conner, come with me." She headed to the aft section. As she got there, she paused to let Trace past her, then she pulled a folding screen across the cabin, separating it from the front of the plane. "Take off your clothes."

Trace stood there mutely, not sure what to say or do. This stunning woman had just told him to strip. What was happening? That stuff only happened in the movies, not real life. Right? Frozen, his mind bounced back and forth between fantasy and reality.

Catherine saw the confusion in his blue eyes and realized what he was thinking. She decided to mess with him. "I told you to take your clothes off. Don't you want to?" She purred.

Needing no more urging, Trace began to tear his shirt off. Only stopping when the pulling on it caused him to wince. At which point, Catherine began to laugh.

"Men, you're all alike."

"Huh?" Trace asked dumbly.

"I want you to strip because I know you're hurt and you won't tell anyone how bad. Not because I want to sleep with you."

"Oh.... right... of course." He stammered out. Slightly rejected and hoping that his pants weren't as tight as they felt.

Catherine smiled and felt a little bad for messing with him, then frowned as he finished undressing. He was covered in bruises. She could still see a little of the welt across his torso from their first encounter with Neko.

"When he saved my life." She thought. Then scores of bruises on his face, chest, side, and legs.

Aloud, she asked "Don't these hurt? How are you still moving?" As she gently probed each one, surprised at her own trembling hand and the flutters moving through her.

"Of course, they hurt. I just deal with it. Pain is only a problem if you let it define you." He said, looking into her green eyes with his clear, bright, blue eyes. He continued to look, as she probed more of the injuries.

Pushing harder on the bruise on his right side, he winced, finally. "I'm going out on a limb and say that's broke or at the very least cracked." She definitely had flutters now.

"What's wrong with me?" She thought.

"Thanks, Doc. I couldn't have figured that out on my own." He said with a smirk.

She swung her right hand to slap him playfully, away from the bruised section of his face. He easily grabbed her wrist with his left hand, pulling her even closer. She could feel the heat of his skin now, the smell of his soap, she gasped involuntarily. Big flutters, but she had to be in control, using her left hand, she pushed on the bruise over the cracked ribs. He winced and the spell was broken, he released her wrist. Catherine turned and opened the door to the lavatory, returning a moment later with a dark bottle, covered in Chinese characters.

"I discovered this a long time ago. Very good for bruises." She said as she began to rub the dark liquid into his various bruises. She rubbed harder than she probably should have, but she was trying to hide the shaking in her hands, which she was sure was obvious. He didn't make a sound, when she looked into his blue eyes again, she saw that they were half-closed, almost like he was meditating.

"Didn't it hurt? It always hurts so much to work a bruise." She thought.

As she began to work on the ribs, she made a mental effort to be gentler. He showed no sign of the pain that she knew he must be experiencing. After finishing with the dark liquid, she retrieved bandages and wrapped his damaged ribs.

"Lie down, get some rest." She said.

"Thank you." Trace said gratefully, lying down.

Her hands still shaking, Catherine headed for the minibar. Feeling much hotter than should be possible in the lavish plane. She decided that she needed a dirty martini, very dirty. Then, holding the bottle of Grey Goose vodka, she paused. Catherine knew well her own amorous response to martinis and she was still feeling the effect Conner had on her, deciding that the two combined would make her regret the next few hours.

"Maybe tomorrow, if all goes well today." She thought, putting the unopened bottle back. Settling for a spicy V8 instead.

"What am I going to be doing, ma'am?" Larry asked her.

"You'll drive. We're going to land at Reagan International. It's not too far away from Arlington and then we'll drive in. I'm hoping the crowded airport will hide us, although I doubt anybody will be expecting us to show up there."

"Yes, ma'am. When in doubt, attack. Pretty much the Marine motto."

"and nobody wants an angry redhead running at them, right?" She said with a big smile.

"Definitely," Larry nodded and went back to the window and his open beer.

"Thank you for being so prompt with the next payment. I guess I don't need to go back to Frisco anymore. I never did like it there." Trace said into the burner phone. The call was being run through the wi-fi on the plane, then through a VPN and out, so that it couldn't be traced. Just in case.

"Thank you for contacting me to let me know," Kelsi said politely, though he simmered. It had taken the consultant more than a day to call back. "Where should I send my man?"

"Kansas City."

"Kansas City, Kansas or Missouri?"

"Like I give a shit, Kelsi." Trace barked. "That's the middle of the country. I'm heading east, I can't take the drives on a plane, so I have to drive. I'll let you know where I am, when I get somewhere I feel safe."

"I would prefer a definite location."

"and I would prefer you to follow my directions and stop trying to kill me. I don't think either one of us is getting what we want." Trace said.

"No, I don't believe we will."

"Send your man and I do mean one man, to Kansas City, tell him to wait. I'll be in touch." Trace said and disconnected the call. To Catherine and Larry, he said, "that'll give us at least a day of breathing room."

"Well, it's already afternoon, so we better get going," Catherine said.

With that, they headed out of the plane and down to a rented BMW that had just arrived. Larry climbed behind the wheel, Catherine and Trace got into the backseat, hidden behind the darkened windows. Larry pushed the speed limit, but only a little. They didn't want to get pulled over for speeding, they had no idea how well-connected DARPA was to local law enforcement. The BMW stopped in front of the menacing-looking building in Arlington, Virginia that housed DARPA headquarters, long enough for his two passengers to get out. Larry pulled away from the curb and found a spot a few blocks away, close enough that he could get back there fast, but not so close that local law enforcement would hassle him. Agent Jares had suggested this the local police kept a close eye on the building and the surrounding area. People were even discouraged from taking photographs of the building.

Trace and Catherine entered the lobby, heading straight for the security desk. "I'm Catherine Dewal, this is Mr. Trace Conner. We are here to deliver these drives" She pointed at the briefcase Trace carried, "to Deputy Director Parks."

"Hold for a moment, please." The officer at the desk said and picked up the phone.

"I'm glad you picked up right away." Alicia Parks said quickly. "The Dewal woman is here, with the consultant and the drives. She wants to give them to me. Right now! What do I do?"

Kelsi fumed inwardly, Conner had lied to him. He had no assets in place there. No options. "Can you get them out of the building later?" He asked.

"Uh...I think so. As long as we don't register them, I should be able to."

"Take them, then. Bring them out later, don't change your schedule. I'll get somebody there just as soon as possible to pick them up from you."

"What if DARPA asks me where the drives went and Dewal tells them she gave them to me?"

"You will be long gone, right? Who cares at that point?" Kelsi knew that his idea of 'long gone' was going to be very different from hers.

"Oh, right. Of course. Okay, if you're sure."

"I'm sure Alicia. Can you verify the program?"

"Probably."

"Good, do that, then get the drives out later. I'll have a man there just as fast as possible." Kelsi disconnected and dialed a new number.

Alicia Parks turned back to the phone on her desk, picking up the handset, she took the call off hold. "Vince, go ahead and send them up."

"We've scanned them ma'am, but they won't let me scan the briefcase. They say that they're delicate electronics."

"Yes, very delicate. Please don't."

"Ma'am, I can't let them up there unless I scan it," Vince said.

"Vince, you're the on-duty supervisor, correct?"

"Yes ma'am"

"So, you can okay it, right? For me?" Alicia asked sweetly.

"Bitch" Vince thought, *"any other time, you treat all of the security staff like shit. I'm not doing something against the rules for you."*

Aloud, he said, "no, ma'am. The rules are very clear on this."

"What if they open the case, verify there is not a bomb or something in it, and then let you carry it up here? Would that work?"

"I suppose." Vince didn't like it, but he didn't need a Deputy Director mad at him either. "Okay, I'll do that." Handing the phone to Catherine, he reached for the case.

"Yes, I understand," Catherine said into the phone. Turning to Conner, she said, "open the case for him, he's going to carry it up with us."

Trace did as instructed and followed the officer to the elevator. Arriving on the seventh floor, they got out and turned left. Turning into a large office and a secretary, who stood waiting for them.

"Director Parks is waiting for you. Can I bring you anything to drink? Coffee, tea, water?" She asked sweetly.

"No, thank you," Catherine replied for them both and followed the security officer through the second set of doors, into a spacious office with floor to ceiling windows.

Trace looked at the size of the office and thought once more about how much of his tax money the government wasted on things like this. He turned his full attention to Parks now. Instantly, he knew she was bad. He could feel it, kidzuki telling him what the other five senses couldn't.

"Thank you, Vince. You can go."

"Not yet, ma'am. I need to see you verify them, that they aren't some disguised bomb or something." Vince answered.

Sighing audibly, Deputy Director Parks picked up the phone, dialed an extension, and asked for a few items. Minutes later, a bespectacled young man entered the room carrying a box of ribbon cables, HDMI cables, USB cables, and plugs. "Thank you." She said to the young man in way of dismissal. She immediately began connecting cables to her laptop and the drives.

Trace watched dispassionately as Parks finally began to check the drives for the T-FAX program. Scrolling through the registry values and then the hard drive storage itself, she clicked on the program titled TFAX.exe. A password window popped up. Deputy Parks looked at Catherine, but before she could say anything, Trace spoke up, "t...!..k..(...U...$" Parks typed as he spoke.

Everyone watched as the program displayed the MIGIsoft logo and the usual copyright warnings. Next, the program paused as a window came up and displayed, "looking for thermal camera". After a minute, the program displayed a new window, "No thermal input found, please specify path or location."

"It looks good, Vince. Now you can go." She looked at the security man like a teacher.

"Yes ma'am," Vince said reluctantly and began to leave.

"Well, guess that's our cue as well," Catherine said as she rose. "Please tell the accounting department to send our payment."

"Of course," Alicia said, rising as well, she extended her hand, "thank you for bringing this directly here. It will be much safer with us."

"We're just glad to be rid of it," Catherine said honestly.

"Of course, thank you again Ms. Dewal," Alicia said, smiling sweetly.

Trace smiled back, hoping that his smile didn't look like the snarl that he felt inside. He was positive that she was dirty. They approached the elevator that Vince was holding for them.

"Nice lady there." Trace said sarcastically, "my condolences for you."

Vince snickered but said nothing. Smiling he pushed the button for the ground floor, where he returned their phones. They had been held at the security desk, for safety reasons.

Trace looked at his phone, he had powered it on when he had arrived. Both to show security that it was a real phone and to let everyone watching his location pings know that it was really him there. He hit the speed dial for Agent Jares, "She's got them and there's no doubt she's dirty." He said.

"Do you have proof?" Jares asked pointedly.

"No, but she is. She'll try to leave with the drives."

"We'll keep watching," Jares replied, "if she leaves, we'll follow her."

Trace ended the call and headed towards the parked BMW that he could see a few blocks away.

"Suck it?" Catherine asked.

"Huh?" Trace replied.

"The password you gave her was 'suck it', backward. How did you change the password?"

Trace smiled, "what makes you think I changed it?" Wondering how she was able to reverse it in her head as he spoke it. She was obviously way smarter than he was.

"Because that's not the one I had Dr. Wells put in." She answered wondering if he was smart enough to have gone in and changed the password. She was attracted to him physically, she wondered if he was that brilliant'.

"Could he have hacked the original password and replaced it with his own? No, Wells must have given it to him, that's it." She thought.

"Oh, yea, you're right." Then he opened the rear door to the BMW and climbed in, never answering the question, but that damned smirk was back.

Trace, Catherine, and Larry sat in the lounge of the G650. Trace had turned his phone back on, using the Red Phone app, he called Kelsi.

"Mr. Conner, are you ready to tell me where you are and where my drives are?"

"I'm in DC, I just gave the drives to DARPA. You'll never get them."

"You what?!" Kelsi had to act outraged, he couldn't let the consultant know that Parks was his spy. "I paid you for those! You owe me!"

"I don't owe you anything, I tried to make a deal with you, but you just had to test me. Too bad. Guess you'll have to deal with DARPA now." Trace was getting tired of this game, all the players, who knew what and who didn't. He just wanted to go back to teaching classes.

"So, you think that you're out now? That's it? You can just walk away? We will find you." Kelsi threatened. "No matter where you go."

"You're right," Trace replied, "I should probably get rid of you and your boss first. Good idea, see you soon Kelsi." Trace said darkly and disconnected the call.

"That'll make him sweat, for sure," Larry said.

"Haha...seriously, what are you going to do?" Catherine asked.

"He knows that Parks has the drives, I doubt he'll bother with me, for a while. His focus will be on getting the drives and moving them far from the U.S. Government, I'm betting on China. I'm sure he already has someone on their way here."

"That didn't answer my question, what are you going to do?" She asked again.

"Talk Special Agent Jares into making me a secret agent man for a day." Trace said seriously. "I feel like I have to be there."

"Where?" Larry asked.

"I don't know yet."

"Then we'll all go," Catherine said.

"No, Jares will never let that happen. I think you should head back to California, both of you."

"No way, brother. I'm not leaving you in the middle of a fight." Larry said.

"Me either. We may have to sit on the plane, but I'm not leaving DC till this is over." Catherine finished.

Trace sighed. "Fine, stay here. I'm gonna go chat with Jares." With that, he picked up his cellphone, grabbed a small black duffel bag, and headed down the stairs to the BMW.

"Where are you?" Kelsi said bluntly.

"I am in a small rental outside of Provo, Utah," Neko answered easily.

"Is that anywhere near Salt Lake City?"

"Yes, not far at all."

"Are you able to move?"

"Yes, my injuries are healing and I can cover them. Commercial travel might be an issue.." Neko was saying, but was interrupted,

"Get to the Salt Lake airport. I am sending the Citation to pick you up, it was still in Las Vegas."

"The reason?" Neko queried.

"I'm sending you to Washington, the consultant and the Dewal bitch just dropped the drives with our contact at DARPA. I want you to get the drives, then get rid of her. After that, fly back here, give me the drives, and then take care of a few loose ends here."

"By 'her', do you mean the DARPA contact?" Neko asked.

"Oh, right, yes...contact is a woman. I'll send the pertinent details to your secure email."

"Do you care how she...leaves?" Neko said, picking an obtuse euphemism, just in case someone could hack the secure phone app.

"That will be in the email. The supplies you need will be on the plane. Make sure her fingerprints are on it before you leave."

"I know how to do my job."

213

"Yes, I know that, but you have not done so well on this particular contract." Kelsi reminded him.

Neko gritted his teeth. He couldn't say anything in his defense, he had underestimated the consultant repeatedly. He was angry at the failures, but he was enjoying the challenge. Sadly, he did not think he would get another chance at Conner. This bothered him greatly. Aloud, he asked, "will one of the loose ends be the consultant?"

"Not right now. We have more important things to worry about. After the transfer, maybe we will. I can't see the Dragon Head letting that go. Even for them, that is a great deal of money." Kelsi answered.

"If a contract is drawn up for the consultant, I would like it. I will do it for free. I owe him." Neko said before ending the call and bringing up the secure email.

"Neko is on his way, then?" Cross asked over the line.

"Yes sir."

"Do we have people headed to take Mr. Conner?"

"No sir, not yet. I do not think that would be wise at this time." Kelsi said, hoping to dissuade his superior from pursuing that tactic at all. "The consultant has our money, but we need to focus on getting the program out of the U.S., Parks said she verified it works, so we don't need to bring it back here."

"Yes, we need to get it to China right away then. We can go after the consultant later. Take our time teaching him a lesson." Cross said maliciously.

"Yes sir. Neko has orders to get the drives, eliminate Parks, and get out. He's on the Cessna Citation, en route now. It will have to make a few stops to get there."

"Very well, Oswald. I'm not happy about the twenty million, but getting the program is the most important thing. Beijing will be happy and that is what is most important, for all of us." Cross finished and disconnected the call.

"Asshole.." Kelsi whispered to the dead phone line.

Trace was pleading his case. "Will, just let me ride along. I'll be a good boy."

"No, we have trained pros for this. We don't need a civilian in the mix."

They were standing at a table in a Starbucks, not far from the DARPA headquarters. Agent Jares had a minuscule earpiece that allowed him to monitor what was being said in the surveillance unit.

"If Neko shows up, you don't have anybody that can handle him. I'm here, I could be right there in a second." Trace pleaded.

"We have HRT on standby, they're the best there is." Jares was referring to the Hostage Rescue Team from the FBI.

"We both know that they can't set up here, outside her house or someplace we don't even know about yet. They'll have to stage farther away and take longer."

Jares's hand stopped in mid-air as a voice in his ear said "Director Parks is leaving the parking garage, in her car. The tracking beacon is moving with her. Should we follow?"

Out loud, as if still talking to Trace, Jares said "affirmative. Follow at the maximum safe distance. Don't wait for me, I'll follow in another vehicle." He looked at Conner, "guess you are going after all, but you're driving."

"Yay, I get to go with the grownups." Trace mocked him.

Special Agent Will Jares of the FBI just shook his head. Wondering what he had done wrong in life that had left him working with this weirdo.

"She went inside her house and there hasn't been any movement since she got there." The voice in his ear told Agent Jares. "Nothing on audio, thermal, or video."

"Roger, make sure all the recorders are running. She has the program, so she is technically a spy and a traitor, we need all the evidence we can get." Jares answered from the passenger seat of the BMW.

Trace and Jares had gotten hung up in an accident traffic jam shortly after the surveillance unit pulled out. Because of that, it was nearly an hour later that they arrived at the Deputy Director's house. The update was brief and concise, the way it should be.

They sat there for hours. At one point, they made a run to a local 7-11 to use the bathroom and get fresh coffees. A little past one a.m., the surveillance team came over the radio unit. "We've got an Asian male, sporting some old cuts and bruises on his face, coming down the street. He's not looking around or anything, maybe just a guy on a walk."

"Asian male with cuts and bruises on his face? You're sure?" Jares said aloud.

"Shit, that's Neko." Trace said.

"Everybody stays cool," Jares said, looking at Conner. "Let's see what happens."

"He just turned and is walking up the sidewalk to Parks' house. The door opened and he walked in, he never even knocked or rang the bell."

"She was expecting him," Jares said. "Let me know if there is audio, plug me in."

Jares pulled out his radio and disconnected the earpiece so that Conner could hear what was going on in the house also.

"Good evening." A male voice.

"That's Neko." Trace whispered.

"Good evening, I have the pro.." Parks' voice.

"Shh," The male voice.

"Sir, they're not talking, but thermal shows them moving upstairs to the back of the house." The surveillance team reported.

"Shit." Trace said as he grabbed the duffel from the back seat. Pulling rolls of black fabric out, he began to wrap his hands and wrists with the fabric. "He's moving her to the back of the house, where passive audio won't work. He probably spotted your team."

"You don't know that. Maybe he's just being careful." Jares replied.

"Doesn't matter. We need to know what's going on, we can't afford to wait and see what happens." Trace pulled out a set of shuko, metal bands attached by a short leather strap to another metal band that had metal spikes sticking out and bent like claws. Sliding these over his hands, Trace grabbed the radio and earpiece, then said "get to the surveillance unit. I'll tell you what's happening."

"Now just hold..." Jares started, but Conner was already gone. Grumbling under his breath about undisciplined civilians. He climbed out and headed the two blocks to the surveillance unit.

Running to the house directly behind Parks' home, Trace used the shuko to scale a block wall, digging the sharpened claws into the mortar joints on the tall wall, then dropped silently on the other side. He ran to the block wall dividing the neighbor's yard with Parks and scaled that wall the same way. Once in Parks' backyard, he used the shuko to bite into the trunk of a large oak tree near the one lit, upstairs window.

Jares had just climbed inside when Conner's voice came over the radio.

"I'm in a tree. About twenty feet from the bedroom window and slightly elevated. There are sheers instead of drapes, I can see them talking. He has the drive briefcase, wait he just set it down. He's pulling out something from his coat. He just grabbed her in a sleeper hold. Christ, I think he's gonna kill her." Trace moved closer along a thick limb that ended ten feet from the window, where gardeners had cut it back for safety.

"Conner, don't do anything. We'll get HRT." Jares said over the channel.

"Then get them here, now. Wait, he let her go, he just knocked her out. That's strange."

"See, no reason to panic."

"I suggest you get HRT here anyway." Trace whispered.

"Sure, if it makes you feel..."

Jares was interrupted by Conner, "he set her up in a chair. He's wrapping her arm with a tourniquet, and he's got a needle. Damn it! He's going to kill her right now." Trace didn't hear if Jares said anything, he jumped to his feet and ran the last two steps to the end of the thick branch. Launching himself into a dive, he crossed his arms in front of his head and flew at the bedroom window.

"Please don't be bulletproof glass." He thought, just before he struck it, shattering the window and taking the sheers with him. Slamming into Neko and Parks, they flew, tangled across the large bedroom.

Neko rolled back and into a standing, ready posture. What had just happened? How did someone attack him and he didn't feel it. Where was his sixth sense? Then he realized it was the consultant, Conner.

Trace continued the momentum, into a diagonal front roll and on to his feet. He looked around the room and settled on Neko. "Surprise!"

"That would be an adequate word. How did you defeat my...sense?" Neko asked.

In truth, Trace didn't know, he wished he did. Maybe it had something to do with the fact that he hadn't planned the attack, it was spontaneous. Was that key? He'd have to look into that if he survived the next few minutes.

"Ninja have ways around that. We know all about the mystical, how to use it as well as defeat it." Trace bluffed, hoping it didn't sound as lame to Neko as it sounded to his own ears.

"Luck, then?" Neko asked.

"Call it what you want. I surprised you, I call that skill."

"Indeed... I will kill you, then research how you did that." Neko stated flatly.

"Kill me and you won't get the drives."

"I already have them, Director Parks was kind enough to give them to me," Neko said as he circled Conner. Looking for his opening.

"No, I gave her fakes. The real ones are back in Arizona." Trace said.

"You lie."

"Do I? You may never know, but if you kill me and take fakes back to your boss, I think you'll be in big trouble." Trace answered, really hoping that Neko wouldn't kill him and Parks before HRT could get there.

The radio had flown out of Trace's hand as he landed, but he thought the wireless earpiece was still in place and hoped Jares knew he was stalling for HRT. "The FBI will be here any second. You should take those drives and leave now. Go ahead, I won't try to stop you."

Neko looked at the case and back at Conner, then Parks. Indecision weighed in his eyes. "Again, you lie. The FBI would not let you, a civilian, in on their operation, if they even had one."

"You saw the surveillance unit, right? You know they're here." Trace said, wondering if Neko had missed the team.

"There was no surveillance team. I looked carefully."

"Crap" Trace thought, *"the one time I wish the FBI wasn't so good."*

"You are bluffing, Mr. Conner." With that, Neko launched himself forward. A fist shot at Conner's head, grazed it as he swiveled left. A hand spear came in low, for a crippling blow, Conner was expecting this, he struck down hard, knocking the wrist down and aside. Neko spun, a back kick coming for Conner's head. Dropping to a knee, Conner punched Neko high on the inside of his exposed thigh, causing him to miss his landing and roll away, creating space.

"The first time we crossed, I had no idea, who or what you were. You surprised me." Trace moved in fast, his right hand-spear shooting for Neko's throat, hoping to end it quickly. Neko blocked the strike, Wing Chun style, but failed to block the right stomp kick that was immediately behind it. Trace pushed through with the same kick that had sent Neko flying at his house in Flagstaff. This time, Neko didn't have body armor on, but neither did he. Trace extended his rigid toes at the end of the kick, driving them painfully into and under the pectoral muscle on Neko's right side.

Neko struggled to breathe. He couldn't believe the power and excruciating pain that the kick had dealt him. Nobody had hit him that hard since the early days of training with Sifu in Hong Kong. He flew across the entire room, hitting the bed and flipping wildly out of control. He was immediately back on his feet, but now he had to keep distance to get his breath back.

"I must kill him quickly, too dangerous to toy with." Neko thought, *"but, what if he is telling the truth, what if the drives are fake?"* Then an idea came to him, he could do this. He knew he could.

Trace was happy to keep his distance. He doubted that Neko would make that mistake again, he had made it twice now.

"Come on HRT, come shoot this asshole for me." He thought and desperately wished.

Now, he couldn't even tell if the earpiece was still in place. His ears were ringing from the glancing blow he had taken moments earlier. So, he couldn't hear it, even if it was still there.

Neko kept the distance for nearly a minute, finally getting his breath back, knowing that another blow like that, especially on his previously injured side, could be the end for him. "Why didn't Conner press the advantage? He must be scared." Thinking this, Neko moved forward again, confidence rising. "Yes, he's afraid of me."

Trace was scared, this guy was a killer. A 'wet work' specialist from the nineties. Trace had been a teenager then. *"How old was Neko? Had to be close to fifty, right? How come I can't tell? Shit...here he comes.."* The thoughts ran wildly in his head. Trace settled back into the 'wind' posture, loose, relaxed, accepting.

Neko launched a right kick at the left side of Conner's head. Conner dropped his whole-body low, not bending, just dropping. Neko shot a right-hand forward, Trace faded back at an opposite forty-five-degree angle, only lightly pushing on the incoming missile to ensure that it missed.

Neko stepped back, assessing. Conner had easily deflected or dodged both those blows. *"I will have to speed up the attack, not give him time to move."* He thought. He stepped forward, fast and to the right, his left foot launching with a heel strike.

Trace felt, more than saw the heel strike coming for his right knee. He pulled the at-risk appendage and dropped it forty-five degrees behind and to the left side, causing his whole body to pivot around ninety degrees. As Neko's left arm shot forward, Trace gently guided it away, like the one before, but Neko was ready for it this time, changing the direction of his left arm. The top of Neko's forearm, the radius bone hammered flat against Trace as Neko shifted his weight ninety degrees to the right. Trace just managed to drop his chin and protect the soft cartilage of his throat, but that meant he took the blow on the side of his neck, staggering, Trace launched himself into a dive roll, hoping to gain distance and time.

Neko nodded his head up and down, thinking. *"Yes, I have him now. I've figured out his system and can beat it."*

He swaggered close, his confidence showing. Neko was enjoying this, Conner was a real opponent. Not since Sifu, had he met anyone so skilled.

This was good, "You are a terrific warrior. You should be proud. Your death will be honorable." He said and he meant it.

"I would prefer not to die at all. Can't we go have a beer and talk about how great we are?" Trace grunted out.

Inside his head, he struggled to figure out how old this killer was. *"Doesn't matter. He's faster than an Arizona rattlesnake. Have to change tacks."*

He moved from the 'wind' posture to the 'bear' posture, facing Neko straight on, his feet shoulder-width apart, his hands in front of and to the sides of his head, relaxed. The change meant that Trace was changing from deflecting and dodging the blows to breaking bones. He wouldn't try to parry the speed, it was time to break parts of Neko.

Neko's right hand shot out, Conner pushed it off to the left, dropping his stance just a little, he used the energy of the incoming blow to pivot his own body, driving his right 'immovable' fist into the joint in Neko's right shoulder. Neko gasped, felt the joint pop loose for just an instant, but more importantly, it caused his second blow, with the left hand to strike the consultant with no power at all. Bouncing off Conner's rigid right side, But Conner was still moving in, his right elbow coming up and under Neko's chin knocking him back as his teeth slammed together. Conner was bigger, stronger, and younger, Neko had to overcome these advantages, but he knew he was faster.

As Neko stumbled back slightly, Trace moved back also. The blow to his ribs had hit the fractured area. *"Damn, that hurts."* He thought, *"but I can't show it. He'll keep attacking that spot if he sees a weakness."*

Without a visible cue, Trace settled back into the 'Bear' posture. Waiting, his breath slowing, eyes defocusing, not watching anything in particular, which allowed him to see everything.

"Why didn't he press the advantage? Is he that scared of me? Is he waiting for someone? No...there was nobody else outside. It's understandable

221

I missed Conner, a trained ninja, but I'd never miss a whole team. He must be afraid." Neko thought all this and his confidence grew again as he moved in.

"Come," he said to the motionless consultant, "let's finish this."

"Stop now, Neko. I don't want to kill you."

"You won't, but I do want to kill you. It will be my equivalent to a trophy hunt."

Trace knew that the killer wanted him to be flattered, but he wasn't feeling it. He was genuinely concerned that he wouldn't survive this long enough for HRT to show up. *"If I fail, Parks dies and Neko escapes...again."* He thought.

Neko came with a left heel strike, straight in, going to break the ribs on Conner's right side. Conner dropped his right leg back and behind the left leg, pivoting out of the line of attack, his left fist hammering the ankle bone on the inside. Again, Neko's second blow was robbed of all power because of the sudden pain to his first assault. His right-hand spear struck Conner's left, exposed neck, but was weak and ineffectual. Only then did he remember that Conner had broken the index finger on his right hand a week earlier.

Trace knew the blow to the neck was coming and he was too slow to block it. Mentally relaxing the muscle, he took the blow, weak though it was, it still hurt and rocked him. He struggled not to show it. Instead, he brought his left hand up, opening it and dropping it over Neko's still extended right hand. Trace twisted back, his left hand pulled Neko's arm straighter, while his right fist punched directly into the bottom of the elbow joint, hoping to break it.

Neko felt the blow coming. He tensed his elbow, taking the blow, feeling the strike almost break the joint. Pain flared, but the consultant had unknowingly turned exactly the way Neko wanted. Seizing the opportunity, he stepped behind Conner, hitting the right kidney as his own right arm dropped in and on to Conner's exposed throat. As the consultant arched from the blow to his kidney, Neko brought his left arm up and over Conner's left shoulder. Neko hooked his right hand into his left elbow, his left hand hooked behind the consultant's head. Fully locking the 'sleeper hold', Neko pushed his left knee forward, preventing Conner from throwing him over the top. Smiling, Neko squeezed hard.

"Thirty seconds, no more," he thought, *"Then I'll tie him up and interrogate him about the drives."*

"He just messed up," Trace thought.

He knew that he had very little time before he would black out, knew it from experience. He twisted enough to bring some energy to strike Neko's ribs with his right elbow, he knew it wouldn't be enough, but that wasn't the point.

Neko felt the blows coming, they were expected. He tensed his right side, even so, the blows were tremendous. He was grateful that it wasn't on the side with his cracked ribs. The consultant was able to get the actual point of the elbow to make contact, maximizing the blows.

"One, two, three, move on the fourth." Trace thought. Neko had made the mistake so many people did.

"No hold is inescapable, there is always a way out." Trace told his advanced classes. Many a big, male student had questioned this, so Trace demonstrated multiple escapes, including the famous 'sleeper hold' that most instructors preached there was no escape.

As the fourth elbow strike came in, Neko had tensed, arching just a little to take the blows, creating space. Trace let his elbow continue past his opponent's chest, then behind Neko's back. Trace's right leg also came back, stepping over and back. He was now standing perpendicular to the killer, and he dropped straight down.

Neko smiled as Conner made this move, he maintained the sleeper hold, knowing that he only needed a few more seconds. It was an ungainly position, but Conner would not escape it. He prepared for the blows that would probably come for his kidneys, then Conner dropped his weight, pulling Neko down as he struggled to keep the hold.

Now, Trace smiled. His weight drop had the effect of locking Neko's feet in place. Next, he reached under Neko's forward, left leg. His right hand behind the killer's back and his left hand coming up under the leg. Trace stood straight up, lifting the slightly smaller man completely off the ground and up, making him level with Trace's head.

Neko struggled to maintain the hold, it lessened now, simply because of the angles and the physics.

Trace dropped again. All the way to the ground, his right kneeing hitting the ground, but his left knee stayed up, pointed, his foot locked in place. Their combined body weight driving them both down, hard.

Neko realized what was about to happen but was too late. He twisted, preventing his spine from being snapped, but not the ribs on his already damaged left side. He struck the pointed knee, taking the combined weight of both men on his ribcage. They broke. At least two, he knew, probably more. Broken badly, he instantly had trouble breathing.

"Punctured a lung," he thought. He had lost the hold when he twisted, so now he rolled away, getting back to his feet.

"Stay down!" Trace yelled. He was dizzy, the move taking too long with his already overtaxed body. "I don't want to kill you."

Neko stood, shakily, breathing was an effort. He smiled. "It would be a good death. Honorable."

Trace rushed forward, still dizzy, but wanting to end it quickly. A mistake. He struck with extended knuckles of his right hand, aiming to split open the scab under Neko's left eye. His left-hand shooting for the killer's throat.

Neko didn't even try to block the first blow, taking it on his injured orbital bone. It split open again and he felt it crack too, that was fine, he would heal. The second blow was exactly what he was hoping for. Blocking the hand spear with his right hand, then grabbing the wrist. He pivoted a full one hundred eighty degrees, pulling the arm forward and down, he broke the elbow joint. Continuing the motion, he leaned hard in on the damaged joint.

Trace understood too late what had happened. He felt the joint go. Throwing himself over Neko, as the killer tried to throw him, Trace flew over and through the air. He had added his energy to Neko's throw, creating considerable distance. Twisting in midair, he took the landing on his good, right shoulder. He rolled forward, and after the first full roll, made a quarter turn, continuing the energy and into a back roll. Trace finished, now standing, his right, uninjured hand pointing at Neko, his right foot forward. Trace's now useless left arm hung limp.

Neko gasped for air. The throw had been a mistake, he had taken the consultant over his left shoulder, further compressing and aggravating the broken ribs. He sucked air, feeling the gurgling. This couldn't go on too much longer. He would lose just from the accumulation of damage.

Trace roared. A primal roar, full of fury and pain, then he took a deep breath, pushing the pain away. He took a straight line and when he looked up at Neko, he was calm.

Looking at the consultant, he marveled at how calm Conner looked. Not angry, just determined. His hard, gray eyes looking back.

"Wait, hadn't his eyes been blue?" He thought, *"must be a trick of some kind."*

Neko moved forward, intent on the kill, no matter what it cost him. His right hand shot out, then his left, right hand, then a right foot, attempting to drive the ball of the foot inside the exposed front leg. Each blow was deflected, almost nonchalantly, Conner moving steadily backward.

"No matter, he'll run out of room soon." Neko thought.

Trace was glad that the injuries were slowing the killer down. He was able to block all the blows now, or in the case of the kick, simply slide that leg back and out of the way, before pushing it back out, resuming the straight-line posture. He could see aggravation in Neko's eyes, Trace waited, looking for that opening.

Neko looked at Conner. The consultant was calm, barely breathing, no movement.

"Finish him!" His brain screamed. Moving in, a right kick, a left kick, pulling the left leg back he staggered a little as he set the weight back on that injured side. Then he shot out his right fist then his left.

Trace saw the slight stagger as Neko landed on his left foot. The right punch came in, Trace pushed it aside, then the opening he was expecting arrived. The left fist came fast, but weak. Trace pushed it a hair offline with his right forearm, leaning deeply forward on his right knee, he used a Ninjutsu variation of what Bruce Lee had called the 'one-inch punch'. His right fist rolled over, allowing the large knuckles to strike the front of Neko's collar bone, breaking it cleanly. Trace didn't stop, he took a small jump forward, keeping the straight line, his right elbow going up, like a piston, bending the arm, he drove the point of the elbow straight down, into the broken bone, driving it down and into the top of the already damaged left lung.

Neko gasped..and gagged. So much pain, incredible pain. He understood what had just happened, he knew he was dead if he didn't get to a hospital quickly. He tried to turn, to flee, but it was no use, the consultant was on top of him, pounding him.

Trace continued the battle, in close and brutal. This was nothing like a movie fight. This was close, violent, deadly. Neko wouldn't suddenly get up and win the fight, he was already as good as dead, but Trace kept pounding. He drove his right knee into the broken ribs on Neko's left. Now Trace was holding on to the killer's head, keeping him up high enough for Trace to use knee strikes. He felt Neko's body finally go limp. Trace released him and let the killer slump to the floor. Trace knew that the left lung was probably shredded from all the blows, he would die soon. Suffocating on his own blood, probably had a severe pneumothorax too.

Neko knew he shouldn't roll on to his right side, the blood would flow over and into the good lung, suffocating him, but it just hurt too much to stay on his left. Besides, he was okay with this death. His private fear had been that he would waste away like so many others. Now he would die in battle, like his father.

Trace dropped down, rolling Neko on to his back and slightly on the right, lifting the head and sliding his legs beneath. "Stay still, there is an FBI team here. They'll be here any second." Trace could hear the FBI banging on the front door, *"why didn't they just break it in?"* He wondered. Aloud, he said, "we can still save you."

"To live in a cage? No. I die here." Neko gasped out, his polished English slipping away. "It is good death. To die warrior, in battle, a good death." Blood frothed at his lips.

"You can live, just hold on."

"No..... Thank you."

"What?" Trace asked, confused. Was Neko thanking him?

"Thank you," Neko said again as he struggled to pull his phone out of his pocket.

Trace tensed, fearing a knife, but then he saw the phone.

"Please, hold it up for me, I will unlock it." Neko struggled to rasp out.

Trace did as asked, holding the phone up, Neko typed a code in unlocking the screen. He next tapped on a banking icon, opening it. Aloud Neko said, "all password codes are 'vietchin', no capitals. Please take the money. I ask you return my ashes Vietnam."

"You're Vietnamese?"

Neko nodded weakly, "and Chinese. Nung father fought with U.S. in war."

Trace felt tears threaten. He had essentially just killed this man and Neko was asking him to take care of his body. "*What the hell?*" Trace thought, confused beyond belief.

"Thank you", Neko said again, then in Chinese and then in what Trace assumed, was Vietnamese. The killer closed his eyes as Conner looked at the phone, the account balance was well over five million dollars.

Trace could still hear the banging on the door, finally, the sound of an explosion and it crashed open, moments after Neko had stopped breathing. Seconds later the HRT came flying through the bedroom door. Trace tried weakly, to raise his hands, but failed. He couldn't move, he had managed to drop the phone in his shirt before the front door crashed open, but he was spent, his left arm screaming in agony. He realized that Director Parks' eyes were open and staring at him and the dead body. "He was going to kill you. Make it look like an overdose. Guess they thought you knew too much." Trace said, nodding at the syringe laying on the floor near her.

One of the HRT assaulters ran over, holding a weapon trained on Conner. Another one reached down to check Neko's pulse, while a third one went to cover Director Parks. Moments later, "Clear" echoed from different parts of the house. Seconds after that, FBI Special Agent Will Jares entered the room, he pointed at Conner. "That's my man." The assaulter covering Conner moved his weapon down and away. "That him?" Jares asked, looking at Neko, who appeared to be smiling.

"Yea, he's gone." Trace answered

"Is he smiling?" Jares asked.

"Maybe...he actually thanked me....damn strange...he thanked me for killing him. Said it was a good way to die, a warrior."

"Did he say anything else?"

"Other than how he was going to kill me, no." Trace lied. "What took you guys so long?"

"All the doors and windows on the first floor are bulletproof. Somebody had to run back and get breaching charges. Nobody expected that." Jares answered.

Trace sighed, remembering how he had hoped the glass in the bedroom wasn't bulletproof. *"Thank god she decided to save money on the second-floor windows,"* He thought, *"or I'd be piled up at the foot of that tree, and Parks would be dead."*

Agent Jares turned to Parks. "Deputy Director Alicia Parks, you are under arrest for treason, murder, attempted murder.." Jares went on but Trace faded out. "and theft of government property. Treason is a capital offense, so are a few of those other charges." Jares finished as he cuffed her hands behind her back, then a female agent came in to search her.

Parks looked at Conner, the dead man in his lap, the syringe, her destroyed bedroom, and life. Crying, she said, "I want to make a deal."

"Take her to the car. Keep two guards on her at all times." Jares said, then turned back to Conner. "Why are you still sitting there?"

"Too trashed to move and I only have one good arm."

Looking at his left arm, Jares winced. "Does it hurt?"

"Not at all.....of course, it fucking hurts! Are you stupid?!"

"Right, of course, sorry." Grabbing Neko's lifeless body, Jares drug it off Trace and yelled, "I need a medic in here!"

Chapter 22

Kelsi was getting mad. Very mad. Neko had not returned yet, not to San Francisco, not even to the plane, still waiting for him. He wasn't answering repeated calls or emails.

"Either he took off with the drives or somebody got him," Kelsi thought.

He wasn't worried if the FBI or some other agency had captured Neko. The man was a machine, he would never reveal anything the government could use. Parks was another matter entirely, Kelsi couldn't reach her either, but in her case, that was good. Her office didn't know where she was or when she would be back in. Kelsi was headed back to Terrace, after lunch, to update Mr. Cross with the bad news. Knowing that it would be very bad for both of them.

"Mr. Oswald Kelsi..."

Kelsi looked up to see several men in suits... *"FBI"*... he instinctively knew it.

"I am Special Agent Will Jares. You are under arrest for espionage, murder, attempted murder, conspiracy to commit murder....." The list went on.

After making sure that Oswald Kelsi was safely locked away, Jares turned his team loose on Terrace. They rolled up to the front door and dozens of agents ran in all different directions, holding copies of the warrants in their hands. All the employees were told to back away from their computers.

The intercom on Dr. Sung Cross's desk fairly shouted, "Mr. Cross, the FBI just came through the front door. They've got warrants and they're seizing everything!" The security officer at the front desk said.

Cross quickly pulled a compact 10mm pistol from a drawer, setting it on the desk, he began to compose a fast email. He was about to convert the email to Mandarin, when the door to his office burst open, men rushing towards him. Cross grabbed the pistol and shoved it under his chin, pulling the trigger and ending his reign as President of Terrace software.

Jares walked over, careful not to move anything. President Cross was dead, no reason to kick the pistol away. Looking at the open laptop, he quickly read over it. The email was addressed to an innocuous Gmail account, but the content was all about Conner. His name, address, description, everything someone would need to put a contract on him. Jares knew that he should preserve everything, even an in-process email, but at that moment, he could not see how any of this was necessary. Leaning past the dead man, he used the knuckle of his index finger to hold down the backspace button, until everything but the address was deleted.

Two days later, Trace was back in the G650, heading to Arizona. The local hospital had stabilized him, administering pain killers and securing his damaged left arm. His ribs were examined and re-wrapped. He had declined surgery in the nation's capital, preferring to use an orthopedic surgeon who worked on the Arizona Diamondback pitchers. Close to home and excellent.

Larry had been sent back to Las Vegas on a commercial flight, with instructions from Catherine to get Conner's Jeep and drive it back to Flagstaff. Larry had grumbled but had gone off to take care of it.

Catherine handed Conner a cut crystal glass, filled nearly full of Dalwhinnie, single malt, scotch whiskey, fifteen-year-old. Trace looked at the glass, wondered if he should drink it with the painkillers, then decided, *"What the hell? If Neko didn't kill me, this won't."*

"With Neko dead, Director Parks is cooperating with the FBI and the government has the program, we should be able to go back to our lives," Catherine said.

"No." Trace replied flatly.

"No...what?"

"The government doesn't have the program." He stated.

"But, I saw the drives. I watched her test the program." Catherine said.

"You saw, what I wanted her to see. I degaussed the drives after got to Vegas. I didn't want to risk losing them. Fortunately, MIGIsoft hadn't updated those servers to solid-state drives. Then I smashed them and tossed them off the bridge, eight hundred eighty-six feet to the Colorado River. Nobody is getting them for a very long time."

Catherine looked at him, "you know what degaussing is?" Referring to the process of using magnetism, usually an electromagnet to wipe out a magnetic drive.

"Yes....I just look stupid. Anyway, how much do you know about MIGIsoft's construction software?"

"Not much", she admitted.

"Your company makes an energy modeling software that is used to look for leaks, be they water or air in houses. To make houses more efficient. It uses infrared cameras." He paused and looked at her, waiting to see if she got it.

"So, when it said it was looking for the thermal camera...that was actually for the modeling software?" She asked.

"Yep. I bet that your brother probably started from that existing software in creating the T-FAX. Anyhow, I had Larry pick up identical drives, or as close as he could find, ribbon cables and a new Toshiba laptop." Trace pointed at the laptop sitting on the table. "After I partitioned the drives, I just drug the entire C drive over from the laptop. That way, there were all kinds of details in the registry, that didn't really exist, but looked like they did."

"What if she had continued farther?"

"You mean if she went and got a thermal camera to hook up?" Trace asked.

"Yes. What would have happened then?"

"I set up a loop. After it asks for the camera or a data location, it then asks for the house drawing plan. I put in a default location that would cause the program to reboot every time it gets there." He smiled.

"DARPA will figure that out. What then?" She asked.

"I don't know what you're talking about." He said innocently. "We gave the drives to Director Parks, she must have done something to them." Then he batted his lashes.

Catherine laughed. "That's funny, but we could get in trouble. A lot of trouble."

"I don't see how. We tried, and in fact, did give the drives to a representative of DARPA. It's not MIGIsoft's fault that the representative was a spy. Look, the more I thought about it as we drove to Vegas, the more convinced I became that you were right."

"I was?"

"Yes. Your brother meant well, but the T-FAX was only good for a country that is willing to assassinate leaders. We already have SEALs, DELTA, CIA Special Activities, predators, and so on. They're all capable of that. Do we really need something that in our hands, probably won't get used, but in the wrong hands, probably will? I think not." Trace concluded.

"So, you just decided? Without asking me?" She was struggling between admiring him and being angry at him.

"Yes. I couldn't tell anyone, if Terrace thought, for even a second, that the real program was completely gone, who knows what they'd have done. I had to keep everyone chasing me, but it was too much of a risk that I might get killed and lose the program."

Admiration won out. He had put himself in the enemy's sights to protect her, the company, and everyone else. She couldn't be mad at him. He had saved her life. She leaned over and kissed him suddenly, surprised at her own bold move.

"Um...what was that for?" He started.

She stood, headed to the lavatory, and got the bottle of dark, brown liquid. She began to carefully remove his shirt, taking care not to injure anything else. She worked the liquid into his multiple bruises, feeling the heat of his body.

"Maybe lose just a little control." She thought as she kissed him again.

Two weeks later, Trace answered the front door, with his good arm.

"Thought I'd come by and fill you in on what has happened since you had your little deathmatch in D.C.," Agent Jares said, lightheartedly.

Trace still wasn't laughing about it, although he knew that Jares, Larry, and a few of the special operators had taken to calling it 'the deathmatch in D.C.", even though it had happened outside Arlington, Virginia. Aloud, he said, "I appreciate you thinking of me, Will."

"If it wasn't for you, my friend, I doubt any of this would've been possible. Parks started singing right away, she had a drug problem, by the way. That's how they initially got her, then it was for the money." Jares began.

"I thought DARPA screened for drug habits?"

"Yea, me too. Somehow they missed it, maybe she got into it after the initial tests. Anyway, she identified Oswald Kelsi at Terrace as her contact and handler. Ken Tellu said the same thing. We got a warrant but waited until he came out. Tellu was with us, pointed him out and we grabbed him off the street. Then we went to Terrace and executed the search warrant. By the time we got to the top floor, the President, a man by the name of Dr. Sung Cross, had a pistol in hand and blew his own brains out." Jares shook his head at the memory, purposely not saying anything about the partial email.

"Was he Chinese?" Trace asked.

"Yes, he was. Most of the people at Terrace headquarters were. Except for Kelsi. You were right about that too. He's British or was. Apparently, the Brits have been quietly searching for him for more than twenty-five years. He's wanted for treason with them. We have him for spying, receiving classified documents, and so on. He won't be getting out for a very long time, but I doubt we'll ever get him to tell us anything. He hasn't said a word since we grabbed him, not one."

"Did the Chinese link go anywhere?"

"Just let me tell the story, okay?" Jares said peevishly. "After digging through the records at Terrace, as well as the plane that killed the DOD pickup team, we found multiple links to the Three Dragons Triad, out of Hong Kong. Mind you, Terrace has been making software for the military for years. So, everything has been frozen, our people need to remove all of it. We've seized everything that the Triad has touched inside the U.S. Our state department has asked Beijing to crack down on them, but that's unlikely. Three Dragons were probably doing Beijing's bidding. We believe that the program was headed there."

Trace just looked at him, keeping silent.

233

"Well, aren't you happy?" Jares asked.

"I was just making sure you're done."

"Yes. I'm done. Also, since Parks is cooperating and most of the killers are dead, you shouldn't have to testify anywhere. I know how you hate leaving this...cave." Jares paused, then "I do have something for you though." Jares walked back to his car, grabbed an item from the backseat, and came back. He held a small metal box out for Conner to take. "Neko's ashes, like you asked."

"Oh, right. Thank you." Trace said, curiously touched by the act.

"No, Conner, thank you. Seriously, I doubted you at first, but you're really okay."

"Really okay? Wow, don't let that go to my head!" Trace mocked him.

"Gotta run Conner. Talk to you later."

"Thank you, Will, for everything."

Epilogue

Trace knelt on the tatami floor, the tops of his feet flat on the floor. His knees under him. His back straight, head up, eyes partially closed. Calm, slow breathing, slow heartbeat. He was at the 'home' dojo for the International Ninjutsu Budo in Japan. His mind went over why he was here...

Two days ago... it had been nearly a month since the 'deathmatch in D.C.' Trace was sitting alone, after a class. He had already had one surgery to repair the damage to his elbow. The prognosis was good. He might have pain for the rest of his life, but everything should work, once it finished healing. As he struggled to put on a shirt, one-handed, over the cast, his cellphone vibrated. Looking at the screen, he saw it was a Japanese phone number.

"Moshi, Moshi." Trace said as he answered it, knowing this was the common phone greeting in Japan.

"Sensei Trace Conner?" A native English speaker.

"This is Trace."

"The Grandmaster would like to see you as soon as possible." Must be one of the English speakers that live in Japan and translate for the Grandmaster.

"Hai, yes, of course." Trace responded, not sure what this was about. He didn't even think about refusing, when the Grandmaster said, "show up", that's what you did.

"Thank you." the caller hung up, not waiting for another reply.

Trace stared at the phone, apprehension beginning to fill him. *"Why would the Grandmaster want to see me? Does he know what happened? How could he?"* Thoughts swirled in his head.

The Grandmaster had a strict rule about using Ninjutsu, *especially* killing with it. Sure, some members were active military but past members who had gotten into fights with Yakuza, Japanese mobsters, had been summarily kicked out of the Dojo. Declared 'Persona non grata'. Even though they had been fighting known criminals. When this happened, you were cut off from the Dojo around the world and everyone in it. Nobody was allowed to teach or even be seen with you.

Trace began to work on travel arrangements, bringing up his favorite travel app. He was about to pull his airline miles and see if he could get a free ticket when he remembered the ashes and Neko's last request...and of course, the money. Not the money from Terrace, the government had already seized that. Amazing how fast they moved when money was involved... The money in Neko's account was more than enough for a first-class ticket to Japan, then on to Vietnam and back to Phoenix. He'd never flown first class, *"might as well splurge,"* he thought, *"it might be my last trip to Japan."* He didn't plan to keep the money, he just hadn't formed a plan for it yet.

"Two days in Japan, then a week in Vietnam?" He thought, looking at prices. He had enough money in the account, but he was still naturally cheap. It takes nearly a day to get to Tokyo, then, who knows how long before he would actually meet with the Grandmaster. It might take another day for that.

"So three days in Japan and nine in Vietnam." that would allow him to leave on Wednesday and return on a Wednesday, normally the cheapest airfares. *"If I get kicked out, I have to shut the dojo down or create my own school...no...I won't do that,"* he thought.

Trace was in the old Ford pickup, headed to Phoenix and Sky Harbor International, two hours later. A hop to Seattle and he settled into the First-Class accommodations on the JAL flight for Tokyo. He enjoyed the large seat, reveling in the feel. Coach seats were just not made for people over five foot nine anymore, this was so much better. Not as nice as having the G650, but he wasn't ever going to own one of those, and Catherine, like the women before, had already decided he was an ass and left.

"I have to get back to San Francisco, I have a major software company to run." She said as she left angrily.

Trace knew that wasn't the true reason she left, he knew that he had a real problem with sarcasm...

After landing at Narita International Airport, he caught a bus to one of the smaller train stations. There, he boarded a local train and got off after eight stops, on to another bus, and finally two blocks to the Dojo. Entering the Dojo, he removed his shoes, then changed into his worn Gi. No longer black, more of a dark, gray. *"Well, I probably won't need to buy a new one."* He thought sourly. Headed to the edge of the tatami and knelt, waiting.

First came the Dojo secretary, he handled all business and correspondence from around the world. Next to enter was the translator, an amiable fellow from England. He had lived there for more than thirty years. The Grandmaster was fluent in English, but it was his Dojo, why should he have to speak anything besides his native language? After a half-hour, the Grandmaster entered. Nobody was sure exactly how old he was, some said seventy-five and others said ninety. He shuffled when he walked, but that was pure deception. When you tried to strike him, it was like trying to hit smoke.

The Grandmaster stopped directly in front of Conner and looked down at him. Trace immediately bowed in respect and said. "Sensei."

As the Grandmaster began speaking, Trace translated some of it as he spoke, but for other parts, he had to wait for the translation. "I had my translator here, because of the importance of this meeting and I want to make sure there are no misunderstandings."

"Crap," thought Trace, *"here it comes, I'm gonna get excommunicated. That sucks."*

He thought about how the Ninjutsu family was the only family he had left. People he had trained, bled, and drank with, some of his best friends. With his parents gone and his brother dead nearly two decades, he struggled to cope with the idea of having no family, again. That was why he was suddenly confused by what he thought the Grandmaster had just said. Trace looked quickly at the translator, who was smiling.

"You are being promoted to the level of Master." He said in his English accent.

Trace blinked, looking at the Grandmaster, "Sensei, this is several levels above my current rank. I do not deserve this."

The older man looked at him benevolently, "I have received word of what happened in America. What you did. You risked your life, used our art, to stop a killer, and save others. What rank you deserve, is my decision, nobody else's. I am proud of you, your brother would be proud of you."

"How did he know what had happened? Who could have told him?" The thoughts raced through his mind. *"There aren't even that many people who know."*

Reading his mind, the Grandmaster said, "I have many sources of information." He smiled and continued in English, "Neko came here a long time ago. He had made a reputation before he arrived. He asked to train with us, I turned him away. It was obvious that he would use our art for evil, so I would not teach him."

"You knew he existed?" Trace was shocked.

"Again, I have many sources."

"Of course, Sensei."

"I feared that one of our people would have to face him at some point. I am pleased that it was you." The Grandmaster spoke softly, warmly.

"He nearly killed me, twice. I should not have beaten him. If he hadn't made a major mistake, I would probably be dead now." Trace was very confused, but not angry.

The Grandmaster turned to the other two people and waved them out, once they were alone he said "I cannot say this in front of others, but of all the Ninjutsu practitioners I have taught, around the world, you are one of the best."

Now Trace was really confused. He had his ass beaten by so many others in this very Dojo, that he couldn't even count it, some were the last time he was here, a year ago. He was approaching twenty years in this art, but some of the others were well past that mark, some over forty years, how could he be better?

"I didn't say you were better, I said you were one of the best." The Grandmaster said, reading his thoughts again.

"Damn, that's creepy." Trace thought.

"Come, the other Masters are waiting to welcome you to their ranks. We have much celebrating to do. I want you to tell me of these confrontations, what you did, what you thought. It will be very interesting. Do you have any idea why Neko tried to put you in a chokehold?"

Trace did a double-take, "how could he possibly know that?" Aloud, he said "Sensei, may I ask a question first? Before we join the Masters?"

"Of course, Conner-san." The Grandmaster never called anyone by their first name.

"Our 'awareness', what we call 'kidzuki'. Neko was very proficient in it."

"That only makes sense, he fought many battles."

"Sensei, is there a way to defeat it? To overcome one who has the ability?" Trace asked carefully.

The Grandmaster stopped, turned, and looked at Conner for a long moment, then nodded his head. "Hai, but this is a very long lesson. It gets into Maho, do you know this?"

It sounded familiar but Trace couldn't place it. He shook his head.

"It means 'magic'. In order to study this, you must immerse yourself in the magic of Ninjutsu. Something I have never taught a foreigner. We will talk about this on your next trip, you will have to come more often now...Master Conner." With that, the Grandmaster opened the adjoining door and entered a room full of his friends, his family.

Made in the USA
Middletown, DE
24 March 2023

27476676R00144